A SHIFT
IN THE
WATER

PATRICIA D. EDDY

If you love sexy romantic suspense, I'd love to send you a short story set in Dublin, Ireland. Castles & Kings isn't available anywhere except for readers who sign up for my mailing list! Sign up for my newsletter on my website and tell me where to send your free book!
http://patriciadeddy.com.

1

Cade

THE FINE GRAIN of the maple was smooth under his calloused fingertips. One of his favorite scents—freshly milled wood—filled his shop. Cade rolled the little train engine over the workbench. A wobble in a back wheel needed tending. He picked up the small rotary sander and flicked the switch.

A high-pitched whir accompanied his minor adjustment, and when he was done, the wheel rolled perfectly.

As much satisfaction as the project had given him, the new moon was only hours away, and Cade was on edge. His wolf ached for release.

"Boss-man?" Livie, Cade's head of security and shop assistant, glanced back at him from her perch at the front counter.

Cade growled in response.

"Why don't you get out of here?" she asked. "I can hold down the fort until closing. We don't have any more appointments today."

Setting down the sander, Cade took a moment to study the female wolf. She was as much on edge as he was. If not more.

"Maybe. But you can bolt too. Go home to Shawn."

"He's being an ass," Livie said.

"He wasn't born a wolf. The new moon is harder on him," Cade replied.

With a sigh, Livie hopped off her stool. "I know, but I'm still his mate. The stupid jerk needs to remember that."

"He does. But everyone's an ass today," Cade muttered. "It's worse than usual this month, isn't it?" He ran his hand over the stubble along his jaw. Work could wait. He needed to go hide in his basement for the next thirty-six hours. At least no one would give him shit about closing his shop early. One of the perks of being the owner.

And the head of his pack. He'd taken over as alpha five years ago following a freak car accident that had killed Mike, who'd run the pack for a decade.

"Christine said there was some sort of eclipse today. She thought we'd all have it bad this month." Her blue eyes lit up. "If we're closing early, I can run over to Beans and Steam for a coffee. Want one?"

In addition to the woodworking shop, his beta wolf's construction company, and an herbal remedy store down the street, the pack also owned controlling interest in a local coffee shop. A decision Cade hadn't been sure of at the time, but now... he spent as much time there as Livie.

"Nah. Any more caffeine in me today and I'll start vibrating. I'm going—"

The bell over the shop door stopped both of them in their tracks.

"We're closed," Livie said as she headed for the tall, older man wearing an Oakland Raiders cap pulled low over his eyes.

"I need Cade Bowman. This is his shop, isn't it?"

The voice was so familiar, and as the man side-stepped Livie, all the blood drained from Cade's face.

"Bill?" He strode forward and embraced the old werewolf,

practically lifting the man off his feet. "What are you doing here? How did you even find me?"

The wolf withdrew a folded piece of paper from his pocket and passed it to Cade. The news article showed Cade standing in profile next to a large art installation he'd done for the Gates Foundation months ago.

He'd loved that piece. Nearly two stories tall and twenty feet wide, it had taken him a year to design and sculpt and almost a full month to assemble. It had also put almost three hundred grand in the pack's coffers.

"Dammit. I didn't know they'd taken that picture. I told them not to." He hated the publicity. But large projects like that paid the bills.

"I've been looking for you, son. For a long time. We need to talk. If you've got more wolves around besides that one," Bill said, gesturing to Livie, "get 'em here." Shoving his hands into his pockets, he hunched his shoulders and angled a quick look out the door.

"Got a pack of them," Cade said. "But I don't like to bother them on the new moon." He laid a hand on Livie's shoulder. "This is Livie. Pack security. Liv, this is Bill Fixton. He was my father's beta."

The two shook hands, and Livie shot Cade a side-long glance full of confusion.

"So you finally did it. Took over your own pack. Never thought I'd see the day. Always wanted to."

"I had to find my own way. Y'know?" The words tumbled out full of regret. Caldwell, his father, would have loved seeing Cade as alpha. But years ago, Cade had run out on the man, and by the time he'd realized his mistake, his father was dead and gone.

"Is there somewhere we can go?" Bill asked. "Preferably underground?" The old wolf checked over his shoulder again, clearly scared of something.

"Sure. But this is Bellingham. Nothing ever happens here.

Worst we get is some graffiti and petty theft. Calm down." Cade ran a hand through his shaggy hair—he needed to find time to get it cut soon—and met Bill's gaze.

"I can't. Don't make me explain here. We gotta get somewhere safe first."

Livie shrugged and pulled out her phone. "We can meet at our place. It's the biggest. It's not underground, but if we try to cram the whole pack into your tiny living room this time of the month, someone's going to end up with a black eye."

Cade stifled his laugh when he looked back at Bill. Panic radiated off of him in waves, and his eyes flashed with gold as his wolf asserted control.

"Fine. But I need a damn good reason to call 'em all in on the new moon. You've got to give me something, Bill."

"I'm scared." Admitting the truth took something out of his father's beta, and Bill sank against the counter. "There's a fire elemental after you, Cade. After both of us. And if she finds us, we're dead."

LESS THAN AN HOUR LATER, eight werewolves sat in Livie and Shawn's living room. The pack's apartment building was only a couple of blocks from Cade's shop. Out of the eight units, six were occupied. The other two functioned as storage or office space when needed, since Cade and Liam, his beta, didn't want any non-pack neighbors.

"What's going on?" Ollie, the burly Bellingham sheriff said from his perch on a chair by the door. His graying hair was starting to thin on top, and his eyes crinkled with concern.

Cade hadn't told them anything yet, and after he introduced Bill, he gestured for the older wolf to start talking.

"A fire elemental named Katerina killed Cade's father," Bill said.

"Dad crashed his car into a telephone pole after a night at the bar," Cade replied with a harsh edge to his voice.

"No. He didn't. Son, your father never drove drunk in his life. Hell, he hardly drank at all the last few years, but if he did, he'd always call me. I talked to the bartender. Caldwell left with a woman that night. No one'd ever seen her before."

"Then how'd you find out her name?" Livie asked.

"It's a long story."

Cade arched a brow. "Then keep talking."

Bill started to pace. "Katerina killed every member of Caldwell's pack. Nine of us. I'm the last one, and I've been hiding for a year, trying to find you. Pure dumb luck I came across that news article. But if I saw it, she could have found it too."

Liam cleared his throat and straightened from his position leaning against the far wall. "Why is she after Cade? Elementals are usually peaceful. Even fire." A hint of sadness mixed with his Irish brogue, and Cade shot him a look. Years ago, Liam had been close to mating with an air elemental, but the woman had run from him, dying not long after. Cade didn't know the whole story —only that Liam blamed himself for the elemental's death.

"That's Cade's story to tell."

Peter, the youngest wolf in Cade's pack, looked up at his alpha. "Well? Tell us, boss."

With a sigh, Cade ran a hand through his hair again, and Bill looked at him like he was seeing a ghost. He knew he looked a lot like his dad. Steel and flax hair he wore too long, a lean, but well-muscled frame, and arctic blue eyes. Caldwell had been shorter and more bulky, but otherwise, the resemblance was uncanny.

Cade hadn't thought about Katerina—he'd only known her as "the fire elemental"—in years, and he never actually thought she'd act on her desire for revenge.

Before he could recount the story, the apartment building shuddered violently. The strength of it threw Bill to the ground, and Peter toppled off his chair. Glass shattered in the next room.

"Earthquake!" Christine shouted and scrambled up from the couch. "Everyone in a doorway. Now!"

The first wisps of smoke curled under the front door, and the crackle of flames reached Cade's ears. "Fire. Everyone out. Now!" He jerked his head towards the window and the fire escape outside.

By the time Bill got to his feet, the front door was already smoldering, and Cade could feel the heat pulsing, ready to break through at any minute.

"It's Katerina!" Bill growled and gripped Cade's arms tightly. "She's found us! We can't go out there!"

"If we stay in here, we're going to burn." Cade shoved Bill towards the window and helped him over the sill. The rest of the pack followed with Cade staying until the last of them had started their climb down. He'd just thrown his legs over the window frame when a blast of white hot flame arced across the metal grating. Peter screamed, collapsing as his flannel shirt caught fire.

Bill lost his footing on the stairs and fell thirty feet onto the pavement. His neck broke with a sickening crack, and Cade froze, the flames roaring behind him.

Three figures stood not far from Bill's body, illuminated by the orange glow coming from the lower floors of the building.

Anger consumed him, rippling over his skin, calling forth his wolf.

Ollie hefted Peter onto his shoulder and started bounding down the stairs three at a time, while Liam and Livie dropped onto all fours, letting their wolves take control.

Cade was faster, though. His bones snapped and popped, his rib cage expanding, shoulders narrowing, and his hands transforming into massive paws. Fur sprouted from his skin, and he shook himself free from his clothes with a snarl.

Leaping an entire flight of stairs at once, he beelined for the elementals below. But with a wave of her hand, a petite brunette sent a powerful blast of air slamming into Cade's side.

He tumbled and rolled, landing against the curb with a thud.

Struggling to his feet, he lunged at the other woman—taller than the first with long, black hair and glowing red eyes. But she side-stepped him, and her arm shot out, her fingers wrapping around his throat.

A few whispered words, and Cade's body went limp in her grasp. His blood started to boil, and a ball of fire settled in his belly. With a howl, he called for the rest of his pack, but a third figure—a man—leveled a pistol at his flank and fired.

Cade could only watch helplessly as the dart sank into his muscle.

All around him, screams and howls filled his ears. His pack. Liam. Christine. Livie. Shawn. Ollie. Peter.

Behind him—not that he could even turn his head to see—the apartment building collapsed, shaking Cade's rapidly shrinking reality.

He couldn't breathe. Couldn't see more than small pinpricks of light. Couldn't even breathe.

The entire world went soft, then quiet, then black.

2

Cade

His body felt leaden, and whatever he was lying on was so cold, it sent tremors all through him. Yet, at the same time, he was burning from the inside out.

A ball of flame lodged deep in his belly, trying to force its way through his hyper-chilled skin.

Every breath was a struggle, and his head throbbed. A sour taste filled his mouth, and he forced his eyes open a crack, but they felt like sandpaper.

He tried to stretch, but lacked the strength to move. Where was he? All around him, the world was dark gray.

What the hell happened?

A low whimper escaped his jaws. He hadn't shifted back. Usually, when a werewolf lost consciousness, they shifted back into human form—it took less energy to maintain. Why was he still a wolf?

Man and animal existed as one, each half of the whole. They fought for control sometimes—especially when the moon was new—but this...this was something different.

Cade forced another breath and tried to assess his physical condition.

Paws. Burned and blistered. The memory of flames all around him sent Cade into a panic, but still, he could only pant weakly, prone on what he thought might be a slab of concrete.

The coppery scent of blood filled his nose, and he moved his head just enough to see the edges of the slab. Dirt stretched in every direction beyond this hard patch of gray for fifteen or twenty feet, and a high, chain-link fence surrounded the enclosure.

In the distance, up a short slope, lights blazed inside a two-story farmhouse.

He was somewhere isolated. No traffic. Only the chirps and twitters of birds and other small animals scurrying about.

A weak glow to the east provided his only means of orienting himself. Dawn. He could smell the sea underneath the strong stench of scorched earth and the smoke from a fire—probably from inside the house.

Cade gathered what little strength he could and staggered to his feet. But the world tilted on its axis, and he fell over again after only two steps.

Drugs. A dart to his flank. He had to shift back. If he could, his body's natural regeneration process would cleanse the toxins from his system.

Closing his eyes, Cade reached for his humanity. All he had to do was calm his body and send his beast deep inside.

The wolf started to retreat, but then a painful spasm overtook him, and he howled. The man trapped inside slipped from Cade's grasp.

What the hell is happening to me?

Shifting was instinctual, especially since he'd been born a werewolf. Two or three calm breaths, a single thought, and the shift would happen easily. It had never failed before.

He took a deep breath, trying again, but this time, the ball of fire in his belly flared so hot, complete agony consumed him.

Writhing helplessly on the concrete, he whimpered in pain. He tried again and again, but as soon as the first twinge of his shift ran along his spine, the fire took over.

His head cleared from the last of the drugs, and though his body was spent from the pain, he managed to stand on all fours again.

If he couldn't shift, he'd just have to get out of here as his wolf. Get somewhere safe and figure out what the fuck to do next.

But when his front paws touched the dirt, he howled and leapt back. The dirt was as hot as hard-packed lava. Cade licked the thick pads on the bottom of his left front foot. They were blistered and raw, and he'd barely touched the dirt.

Carefully, he tested the dirt all around the concrete. Every single step brought nothing but pain.

He moved to the back edge of the pad, then took off at a run, jumping as far as he could. Landing a full eight feet from the concrete, he yelped. If anything, the dirt here was even hotter.

Cade's whines turned hoarse and weak as he stumbled back to the safety of the concrete. Blood oozed from his burned paws, and the scent of charred flesh soured his stomach.

His pack. Where was his pack?

Oh, shit. The fire.

He'd seen Livie fall. Peter's clothing catch fire. Bill dying. Had his entire pack died? Were they somewhere as unforgiving and alone as he was?

Cade howled loud and long, a cry only his pack would recognize. If any of them were within earshot, they'd return the call.

Only silence greeted him.

His pack was his entire life. Cade shook with anger and fear, their screams and the sickening snap of Bill's neck pummeling his memories.

His family. Gone.

The fire elemental had killed them all.

MORE THAN A DAY PASSED. The sun rose high overhead, and though it was a cool day—wherever the hell he was—the rays beating down on his battered and burned body made the fire inside him rage even hotter.

Night came, bringing the barest hint of relief, but his belly was empty and his tongue was dry and too big for his mouth. He needed water. Desperately.

When the sun rose again, he curled up in the center of the concrete pad and prayed for some sort of relief. They were in the Pacific Northwest for fuck's sake. Where was the damn rain?

Had he been left here to die? Katerina could have killed him instantly back at his apartment complex. Why bring him here—wherever here was—and leave him to rot?

He drifted off to sleep again in the heat of the afternoon, only to be woken by an icy blast of water square to his muzzle. Snarling and leaping to his blistered and bloodied feet, he strained to see through the deluge.

The water chilled his fur, and it was so strong, he backed away until he hit the edge of the pad. But as soon as one of his paws hit the scorching earth, he stopped, forced to suffer the endless, watery assault.

Blind, barely able to breathe through the spray, he prayed to whatever God or Goddess existed, asking to be spared. He wasn't an overly religious man, but he desperately wanted to live.

The blast stopped as quickly as it had begun, and a high-pitched voice rang out. "Drink up, *dog*. I hope you like your cage."

Cade shook his entire body, dispelling as much of the water as he could, and growled at the woman standing just outside the fence. She wore jeans and a red sweater, and a tight ponytail held her black hair high on her head.

A smile curved her lips, but there was no warmth in it, and Cade growled again as he slumped to the ground. He had to conserve his strength in case he found a way to attack her.

"No?" She hefted an industrial fire hose that was hooked up to a pipe next to the house. "I didn't think so. You can't talk or ask any questions, so let me explain a few things to you."

She took a few steps closer, handing the hose off to a man standing next to her.

"Do you know my name?" she asked, and Cade nodded his head. "Good. This will go a lot faster if I don't have to explain everything. My spell—which is a mix of my fire elemental powers and magic—will keep your core temperature well over one hundred and twenty degrees. The runes binding you, combined with the heat expanding your blood volume, hardening your bones, and thickening your pelt will keep you from shifting. Permanently."

Walking along the fence, Katerina gestured to the ground. "I have charmed the soil as well. Nearly three hundred degrees. Now that was a fascinating piece of work. Jeremy, my beloved, helped me with that one. His power is of the earth."

The man next to her puffed out his chest.

Cade whined, hoping she could understand he needed to know why.

"Your father killed my mother without a second thought. She only wanted to practice her charms in the desert—away from anyone who might be harmed. A woman should be able to wield fire in the middle of the Mojave without worrying about any repercussions. And because some old, senile wolf got caught in one of her traps, your father ended her."

Cade growled. That wasn't the whole story. Katerina's mother had lured the wolf into her casting circle and burned him alive. An old werewolf who'd chosen to give up his humanity and live the last few years of his life as an animal. Caldwell had seen the fire from his motorcycle and had investigated. When he found the dead werewolf, he'd tried to arrest the fire elemental, but she'd run, and when he'd gone after her, she'd tripped and fallen over the edge of a cliff, breaking her neck.

Baring his teeth, he tried to convey his hatred of Katerina, but she merely snorted a laugh and shook her head. "I ended up in a foster home, *dog*. And my baby sister? They wouldn't let us stay together."

Another growl, this one louder, and Katerina gestured to Jeremy. He hefted the hose again and Cade fell silent. "I've worked my entire life to perfect my charms, my control, to grow my power so *no one* would ever be able to best me like your father did to my mother. You're mongrels. All of you. The very worst of the *other*. My sister and I didn't even have a father to take us in because a werewolf bit him two months before our mother died. He ran off to Sacramento to be with them."

Katerina swallowed hard and swiped at a single tear that traced a path down her cheek.

"So now, I will have my revenge. For everything. The death of my mother. Losing my baby sister to the foster care system. My father deserting us. You're going to suffer as long as I did."

After the fire elemental nodded at Jeremy, another blast of water hit Cade in the face, but this one didn't last long, and when he shook it off, her eyes glowed even brighter. "Your father had the gall to pretend he was sorry. Hell, he even set aside some money for me and my sister. Mine was stolen by my first foster parents. So as soon as I turned eighteen, I got myself the hell out of the system and found someone who taught me all about harnessing my fire and using magic to make myself even stronger. Hunting down your father and the rest of his pathetic pack was satisfying, but not as satisfying as killing *you* is going to be."

Cade bared his teeth, wishing he could rip her limb from limb. But with twenty feet of red-hot dirt between him and the bitch, there was no way he'd be able to.

He limped to the edge of the concrete, narrowing his blue-gray eyes and growling low in his throat.

I will kill you if it's the last thing I do.

Katerina laughed. "I take it that's a threat? It's a pitiful one. I don't know how long I'll keep you like this. Maybe as long as I spent in my first foster home. A year? That place was a hell hole. Never enough food, no heat, beaten if I talked back. Your father ripped me and my sister from our mother's warm embrace and threw me into hell. My precious *sister* got adopted by a rich family. She's had a charmed life, apparently. Wants nothing to do with me. Again...all *your* doing. You and your fucking kind.

"I want you dead, but not until you've suffered." Katerina turned around and picked up a piece of steak the size of a dinner plate. Cade raised his head and sniffed the air. He was so very hungry.

Katerina unlocked the chain-link door, then threw the steak. The meat landed a few feet away from the concrete pad and immediately started to sizzle.

"Well, go fetch, *dog.* It's all you get for a few days. Wouldn't want it to turn to charcoal." Katerina slammed and locked the door, then stalked back into the house with Jeremy at her heels.

Cade sprinted onto the dirt, letting out a high-pitched wail as the blisters on his paw pads broke open again, but soon, he had the steak in his mouth and was speeding back to the concrete.

Once he collapsed on the pad, he dropped the meat and sniffed at it.

Half-rancid. Gray. Mottled. Disgusting.

No. I can't.

But his stomach growled and twisted in on itself. He had to. If he didn't, he'd die. Gingerly, he trapped the steak in his jaws and laid it on the dirt beyond the pad.

After it had sizzled for another minute, he snatched it back and gulped it down in three bites. Water gathered in pools on the concrete, and Cade lapped up as much as he could. He had to stay alive so his pack—if they lived—could find him.

When the sun finally set, Cade curled up in the center of the pad. His mind was starting to wander. He'd never suppressed the man in favor of his wolf for so long. What would happen to him now? Or his pack? His woodworking shop?

His paws itched as he remembered running his hands over the intricate whorls and cuts in the cedar for the installation at the Gates Foundation.

Who would look after his elderly neighbor, Maggie? She was close to eighty, and she'd taken to bringing Cade casseroles a few times a month.

He didn't know why he was so fixated on Maggie's well-being, but he had to hold onto something. Anything. Just so he could remember the man he'd been only two days ago.

It rained that night—a summer storm that whipped pine needles and leaves against Cade's pelt. The wind howled through the trees, keeping him awake. So he paced. Each step was agony on his blistered paws, but the pain helped him focus. He had to find a way out.

3

Mara

THE THIN BLUE hospital gown didn't do a thing to keep her warm with the air conditioner blowing on full blast. Mara rubbed her hands up and down her arms, trying not to shiver.

The paper spread out on the hard exam table rustled beneath her as she shifted to relieve some of the pressure on her tailbone.

Her fingers and toes were pale, the nail beds almost blue. It was nothing. It had to be. The flu. Mono. It couldn't be anything else.

But doctors and nurses made terrible patients, and Mara knew deep down inside that something was very, *very* wrong.

After a brisk knock, the door clicked and Mara flinched, making the paper crinkle again.

"It's been a while, Miss Taylor," Dr. Pendergast said with a frown. He peered at her chart through a pair of half-height spectacles balanced on his sharp nose. "Headaches, blurry vision, dizziness, weakness, loss of appetite? These are serious symptoms."

"Are you going to chastise me or examine me?" She leveled a

gaze at her doctor, hoping he'd understand she didn't need all this small talk.

"Both. How long has this been going on?" The doctor palpated her lymph nodes. "Slightly swollen," he mused. "Breathe in?" The stethoscope was cold against her back, and she kept quiet as he listened to her lungs.

"Well?" he asked when he paused.

"I've had this my whole life," she replied. "Off and on. I've been to at least a dozen doctors over the years, and no one's ever been able to give me a diagnosis. But the symptoms never lasted this long before."

The doctor arched a brow. "How long are the episodes, usually?"

"A few days." She bit her lip as the doctor's pale blue eyes pierced hers. "A week at most."

"And this time?"

"Six weeks," Mara said as she dropped her gaze. "We've been down two nurses in neonatal—"

"Breathe in and out again," the doctor said sharply as he moved the stethoscope to her chest.

Her job often required ten or twelve hour shifts, and between that and her daily swims, she rarely had any free time. She'd only come in today because she'd passed out at the nurses' station after her last shift, and her supervisor insisted she get checked out before she came back to work.

"It used to only happen when it was hot out," she said. "I lived in Sacramento, and the summers were...difficult. I think I spent every minute I could in the pool." Mara fought the urge to laugh, to babble, until the doctor shone a light down her throat and then into her eyes.

"We'll run some tests. A full blood panel. Maybe a CT scan. What's your diet like? Do you take any vitamins?"

Mara nodded. "Vitamin C, D, and B12. I don't smoke, never have more than a couple of drinks a week. I know I should cut down on the coffee, but caffeine never really affected me. No illegal drugs. Plenty of vegetables. Lean protein, and I swim two miles every day."

She did everything right. Had ever since her adoptive mother died of a heart attack right in front of her when Mara was sixteen.

"Family history?" Dr. Pendergast asked.

"I don't know." With a shrug, Mara sighed. "I'm adopted. My biological mother died when I was a baby. I have a sister, but she's twelve years older than I am, and we do *not* get along."

The doctor leaned back against the counter as he scribbled in her chart. "Try not to worry too much, Miss Taylor. Your last routine physical showed nothing out of the ordinary, and you appear to be in good health. Likely this is exhaustion or some sort of hormone imbalance."

He continued the exam, palpating her stomach, under her arms, and then back to her neck. "I just don't like how these nodes feel. Take a few days off in case this is the flu." He tore a sheet of paper off a pad and passed it to her. "Go down to the lab in the basement for the blood draw. We'll know more in a few days."

With a final nod, Dr. Pendergast breezed out of the room, and Mara shivered again. This wasn't the flu. She'd bet her life on that.

She'd turned thirty only a few months ago, and not long after that, everything had gone to hell.

Hopping off the table, she winced as the cold floor froze her toes. After dressing, she took the sky bridge over to the hospital and up to the neonatal ward. She knew she wasn't contagious, but a few days off sounded like heaven, and little rest was what the doctor had ordered.

After a short talk with her supervisor and the six vials of blood she left in the lab, Mara slid behind the wheel of her Prius. The drive home took her less than twenty minutes, but by the time she got there, everything hurt.

A nap. She could really do with a nap.

FIRST THING IN THE MORNING, Mara filled her thermos with coffee, packed a few clothes, her swimming gear, and her Kindle before heading for the ferry.

If she were lucky, she'd be swimming by noon. Off of Orcas Island, the waters of Puget Sound were cleaner, and the beaches on the north side were always deserted. Or nearly so.

An early spring heatwave had broken the day before, and with the clouds rolling in, bringing spitting rain with them, the ferry line was almost empty.

Huddled in her oversized sweatshirt against a window, she spent the hour-long ride with her face pressed to the glass so she could watch the waves.

Her exhaustion faded the moment she drove off the ferry, and her hands steadied. Pausing in her hotel room only long enough to change into her wetsuit and check out the view from her balcony, Mara hurried down to the beach just outside the hotel's front door.

Her long, red braid shoved into her swim cap, she breathed in the clean, salty scent of the sea and stepped gingerly into the water.

Everything about this day was exactly as she'd hoped. The feel of the frigid water around her toes, the gentle patter of rain against the rubber cap, and the lack of people.

Everything but the threat of a serious illness hanging over her head. But she could put that out of her mind for at least an hour. For now, she was alive, and in moments, she'd be gliding through the water, free and happy.

The tiny waves that lapped against the shore seemed to carry a faint tune. Was there someone around with a radio? She closed her eyes, concentrating on the sound, picking out the individual notes that gradually coalesced into a comforting song as she stood ankle deep in the water.

After a few minutes, she gave up trying to find the source of the music and pulled her goggles down over her eyes. Whatever the music was, it felt like home.

———

LONG SWIMS, room service, and plenty of sleep should have restored Mara's energy. But after three days, she felt only marginally better.

Sitting out on her patio wrapped in a blanket, she hummed the tune that hadn't left her head the entire time she'd been on the island. She felt lighter now, at least, if not still exhausted. Until the ring of her cell phone disrupted the quiet of the evening.

"Hello?"

"Mara Taylor?" Dr. Pendergast's voice sent her heart crashing against her chest, and she sat up a little straighter. "I have your blood work, and I'd like you to come in to talk to me. Does tomorrow work?"

Her stomach flipped. Tomorrow meant the results were...serious. "I can't make it until late afternoon tomorrow. But, um...can you tell me anything now?"

"I'd rather you come in. We need to run some additional tests. Can you be here at two?"

With a hard swallow, she turned her gaze out over the water. "Yes. But Dr. Pendergast, you know I'm a nurse. I won't sleep, eat, or be able to think straight unless you can give me *something*. I know how this goes. If it were the flu, you'd just tell me. So it has to be serious." She fiddled with the blanket over her shoulders and held her breath.

Papers rustled, and the doctor sighed. "Both your red and white blood cell counts are low. And your white blood cells are mildly denatured. I'd like to give you a transfusion. The good news is that you're not contagious. Not a danger to friends, family, or patients. But honestly...I have no idea what this is. You don't have the markers for leukemia, lymphoma, or myeloma, but that's all I can tell you."

"Okay." Mara rubbed the back of her neck, unsure how to feel —other than terrified. "I'll see you tomorrow at two."

THE NEXT AFTERNOON, Mara sat across from Dr. Pendergast, flipping through her test results. "None of my other doctors reported this sort of thing. Usually I get the standard spiel. 'Take a good multi-vitamin, see a sleep specialist, and eat more kale.'"

"You're older now." The doctor chuckled when Mara narrowed her eyes at him. "I didn't say you were old. *I'm* old. My sixty-second birthday is next week. But perhaps something else has changed. It could be anything. But we'll figure it out."

The doc stood and gestured for Mara to precede him through the door to his outer office. "Let's get you across the street to the hospital. I want to admit you for a few hours so we can run more tests and give you a transfusion. It won't fix anything, but it'll make you feel better while we figure this out."

TWO DAYS LATER, Mara was back in the doctor's private office, digging her nails into her palms as she waited for the next round of results.

Dr. Pendergast looked tired when he sank into the chair across from her. "I wish I had better news. Your body is basically attacking itself. Something's destroying your red blood cells. That's why you're so tired. Red blood cells carry oxygen throughout the body. You have approximately twenty percent fewer healthy red blood cells than you should. The blue nail beds, the dizziness..."

"What can we do?" Mara's voice cracked as she fought against the tears burning the corners of her eyes.

"We can keep up regular transfusions for a while, but I've never seen anything like this. Neither have my colleagues. The second round of testing showed an even more dramatic decrease in your red blood cells."

Her brain shut down. She was getting worse.

It wasn't until Dr. Pendergast touched her arm that she flinched and looked up at him standing next to her chair. "Sorry. What?"

"We're not going to give up, okay?"

She nodded, but inside, she was numb. If they couldn't figure out why her body was attacking itself, she didn't have much time left.

4

———

Cade

AFTER A WEEK, he had trouble with complicated thoughts. He'd stopped trying to find weaknesses in the chain-link fence and had started simply throwing himself against it whenever he could stand to touch the searing dirt.

But all he got for his efforts were bruises, blisters, and burnt fur. He had to keep trying. His pack needed him. If they were still alive.

Bill. Katerina had killed him. He remembered that, but not how he'd gotten here. He heard Christine screaming in his nightmares, saw Liam's wolf dodging the flames on the fire escape. But everything after that was a blur.

His body weakened more every day. The little water trapped on the concrete pad from the rain or the hose was barely enough to drink, but he lapped up every bit.

She'd only fed him twice that he could remember, and both times, the meat was half-spoiled, slimy, and disgusting. The man trapped inside hated it. The wolf in control now didn't care.

"Looking a little thin, *dog,*" Katerina taunted.

Cade lifted his head and scanned his body. His fur had burned off in large patches, and what remained was matted and dirty.

A blast of fire hit Cade's spine, and he yelped as he leapt up and skittered to the back of the concrete.

"Jeremy!" Katerina called. The man—an earth elemental— hurried out of the house, and Cade caught his scent. Under different circumstances, it might have been pleasant. Rich, grassy, and loamy.

A growl rumbled in Cade's throat. He couldn't remember why he hated the man so much. His flank ached with the memory of... something. But trapped as his wolf, everything that came before was fading by the day.

Katerina wrapped an arm around Jeremy's waist and kissed his cheek. "Do you want to be the one to tell him about his pack?"

Cade charged to the edge of the concrete with a growl. *Tell me what you did to them, bitch!*

Sauntering close to the fence, Jeremy grinned. "The old one died in the street. Pretty sure his neck was broken. Katerina burned his body to a crisp before we left. The rest...they were trapped in the building when I brought it down. The first signifi- cant earthquake recorded in Bellingham in thirty years."

Cade's entire world crumbled and burned. He didn't care how much it hurt, he would *kill* the earth elemental. Kill both of them if it was the last thing he did.

Bounding across the scorched earth, he threw his body against the fence. Had to reach the boy. Had to tear him limb from limb.

His pack. Dead.

Cade hit the ground with another howl as the blisters on his paws broke open. But he refused to give up. He kept trying, desperate.

After his fifth or sixth attempt, his body gave out. Katerina turned the hose on him, driving him back to the concrete. When he collapsed—burned, bruised, and spent—he whimpered until he passed out.

———

A MONTH. He knew it by the moon. And now, he couldn't remember his own name. He had one. He was a man—a werewolf—but he couldn't shift.

Why not?

He couldn't remember.

Days blurred together. Weeks. Another month. Two. Three. The man would have gone insane trapped as he was, but the wolf was a creature of instinct.

Survive. Escape. Kill.

Those thoughts kept him going. The bad woman—he hated her—came out every few days and threw him a piece of rotten steak. His human mind tried to refuse the disgusting offering, needing the release of death, but the wolf wanted to live. So he ate the meat every time.

He grew weaker. Spent solitary days pacing the pad of concrete that protected him from the burning earth. His body wasted away, but still he paced. It was all he could do.

———

Mara

Stretched out in the transfusion center's hard reclining chair, she gazed at the few leaves still on the trees. Four and a half months after her first transfusion, Mara knew the routine well.

The fat needle pierced her vein, and she grimaced. For an hour, she'd sit there, try to smile, and wait for the blood to replenish her weakened body.

Before each transfusion, she donated a pint of her own blood for study. The University of Washington Medical Center staff were studying it, trying to find a cure—or at least a cause. But so far, nothing.

The first month, she'd needed a single transfusion. The third month, two. Now she found herself here every ten or twelve days.

Her best friend, Jen, sat next to her. They'd been as close as sisters since their first year at college, bonding over all-nighters and a shared love of red vines and cappuccino.

Life had dampened their bond in the intervening years as they'd both been too busy to keep in touch. But once Mara started to worry she wouldn't be around much longer, she'd reached out, needing to reconnect.

Jen had been the one Mara called the first time she'd been too weak to get out of bed. Who'd driven her to most of her transfusion appointments, and who was on her DNR order.

"What do you say we go out to Zig Zag tonight?" Mara asked as Jen fiddled with her phone. The eclectic bar on the Pike Street Hill Climb had a massive selection of premium liquors, fun tapas, and a great staff. "Maybe ride the Wheel first?"

"Adam bought all the fixings for lasagna," Jen replied without looking up. "He's bringing over a movie."

"No," Mara said sharply. She loved her friends. Adam and his wife Lisa—along with their two girls—were like family. But sometimes, they took the whole overprotectiveness thing too far.

Jen's brown eyes widened and her head snapped up.

"You're all treating me like I'm made of glass. I'm fucking sick of it!"

"Crap. Calm down." Jen glanced around the room, catching a few eyes of the other patients and nurses.

Lowering her voice, Mara tried to soften her gaze. "I'm going to feel good tonight. Great even. I always feel great after a transfusion. I want to *live*, Jen. I'm tired of being coddled all the time."

"Mara—"

"Don't get me wrong." With her free hand, she reached for

her friend's fingers. "I can't tell you how much I appreciate the meals and the help with errands and housework and all the crap I don't always have the strength to do, but I'm thirty-one years old and single. I haven't had a date in a year or even stayed out past 8:00 p.m. since May. One night. Drinks. Dinner. Dancing. A bit of fun. Please?"

Neither of them spoke for several minutes.

"I need this," she said quietly.

"Okay, you're right. You're not dead—" Jen slapped her hand over her mouth.

"No, I'm not." Flashing a smile at her best friend, Mara chuckled. "For the time being, I'm very much alive and I want to feel that way. Now, can you go get me some form of caffeinated beverage? If we're going out tonight, I'm going to front-load some coffee."

———

LATER THAT AFTERNOON, Mara almost floated into Dr. Pendergast's office. Her cheeks glowed with color, and the dark circles that had taken up near-permanent residence under her eyes were gone.

Flopping down into the chair across from the doctor, she combed her fingers through her red locks. "All right. Whatever you have to say, let's get this over with. I have two hours left on my shift and then I'm going out tonight."

"Feeling better then?" Though the doctor's pale blue eyes crinkled at the edges as he smiled, sadness lingered in their depths.

"Great. I always feel great after a transfusion. I get at least three or four days of feeling *normal*. And I'm going to take full advantage of them."

The doctor passed her a folder. "We got the results back on this morning's blood panel. They're...not good. We'll transfuse you as long as we can, but pretty soon..."

Mara's breath hitched. "They won't be able to keep up." Every bit of elation she'd felt earlier evaporated in a heartbeat. The world slowed, then ground to a complete halt.

A hum started in her ears, quickly swelling into a clear series of tones that drowned out everything else around her. Dr. Pendergast's face floated in and out of her view. He was talking to her. His lips were moving, but Mara couldn't hear anything but that song. It was both familiar and comforting, begging her to surrender to the melody.

Tears trailed down her cheeks, and the air turned humid.

Stop! Focus!

Mara held up her hand and swallowed hard. With a quick shake of her head, she cleared the fog and focused on the doctor. "How long?"

"Four months. Maybe five if we're lucky. Mara, you should... make arrangements. If you've ever wanted to see the Eiffel Tower, try skydiving, or go on a cruise, now would be a good time." Sorrow tinged his voice, and he closed the file with her test results. "I'm so sorry."

Blinking back her tears, she straightened. Deep down, she'd known. She saw death all too often at her job. The babies that couldn't win their battles all had a way about them—as if their tiny souls knew they weren't long for the world.

Though she hadn't voiced it to anyone, late at night when she was alone, her soul *hurt*. Death hovered outside her door, waiting for her to succumb to the inevitable.

"Will the transfusions keep me functional for most of that time?" she asked.

"Yes. At least through Christmas, I think. After that...the end will be quick. When we can't keep up, it'll be a few days at the most. And...painless. You'll be too tired to get out of bed, then too tired to stay awake. Then..."

"It'll be over."

Dr. Pendergast skirted his desk and took the chair next to her. "I'll promise you one other thing."

"What?"

"You won't die in the hospital. We're either going to solve this or we're not. There's no in-between. I won't prolong your life unnecessarily unless you want me to." He patted her hand, and forced a smile.

Mara nodded. "Thank you. I'll update my living will. Make it easy on everyone. But right now, I need to go." Pushing to her feet, she made a beeline for the door, leaving Dr. Pendergast staring after her.

Katerina

Pacing the living room of the Orcas Island farmhouse, Katerina muttered to herself and played with the pendant hanging between her breasts.

It had been her mother's—the only memento she had from Kylie. They'd been so happy for the first dozen years of Katerina's life. They hadn't been rich, but they'd had a nice apartment, food on the table every night, and love. Her father had played guitar in the evenings, her mother would sing her to sleep when she was frightened, and her baby sister, Mara, was Katerina's whole world.

Until the night Caldwell Bowman had killed Kylie. It was supposed to be Katerina's introduction to her element. She remembered the thrill of the elemental song filling her ears. It was a low, haunting melody, and had become a part of her ever since.

After her mother had died, she'd spent years trying to hone her skills. Now, she was one of the most powerful elementals in the southwest—perhaps anywhere. She led a coven of twelve.

Eight fire, three earth, and one air. Bella, who'd helped her and Jeremy capture Cade, had returned to Phoenix to keep Katerina's occult shop running while she and Jeremy stayed here, and she missed the quiet air elemental every day.

As if Bella missed her too, the phone rang, followed quickly by Jeremy's footsteps thudding up the stairs. "It's Bella."

"What is it, sister?" Katerina asked.

"The IRS is here." Bella's voice was shaky and uncertain. The timid air elemental had been close to death when Katerina had found her in Mexico eleven years ago. She'd needed to hide, to truly *become* someone else, and Katerina had helped her, taken her in, and protected her.

"What?" Shock stilled Katerina's restless movements.

"Two agents. They have warrants. I had to give them all of our books. They," a quiet sob escaped over the line, "want to shut us down. I don't know what to do. Please come back. Just for a day or two. Talk to them. There has to be some mistake."

"Dammit. I don't have time for this right now." Katerina peered out the window at the wolf. Months ago, when she'd seen his death in a vision, the mongrel looked much like he did now—emaciated, feral, and barely able to get up. In two weeks, the moon would be new again, and that's when she wanted to end him. He'd feel the most pain if she set his heart ablaze on the night he was the weakest.

Bella covered the phone and yelled at the agents, and Katerina took a deep breath. "I've been away too long," she said when Bella came back on the line. "I wanted the wolf to suffer for a year, but I can't do it. I have to end this soon. The new moon is—"

"We can't wait two weeks. Please. Come back now. They're going to confiscate everything if you can't show evidence of good faith. Let Jeremy take care of your...business there. We need you. I...need you. It's too hard for me to be alone. I'm scared."

Bella rarely admitted any weakness, but she jumped at every loud noise. Katerina couldn't abandon her.

"I'll be there tomorrow. Don't worry, sister. I'll fix things. I promise. Stay out of the agents' way and let the coven know I'll be at Friday's meeting in person."

"Oh, goddess. Thank you." Bella's voice carried so much relief, Katerina's heart squeezed. These past few months had brought her so much satisfaction watching the wolf suffer, but she'd hated leaving Bella alone in Phoenix.

When Katerina ended the call, Jeremy was at her side in an instant, eyes bright. "We're going home?"

"No. *I'm* going home. You need to stay here and watch the wolf. I can't kill him until I get back." Striding over to the closet, she pulled out her small suitcase.

"He's half-dead already. Just leave him here. Let him starve to death. I hate all this rain. Every time I need to feel the earth, I have to sink into ankle-deep mud. It's disgusting." His voice turned whiny, and Katerina's nerves frayed even more. She loved the boy, but even at twenty-seven, he was definitely still a *boy* and, by the Goddess, she needed a man.

Drawing strength from the fire in the hearth behind her, she called the low, deep notes of her element and wove them into a song in her mind. As her hands started to glow, she stalked towards Jeremy.

Trails of light extended from her fingers when she drew runes in the air in front of him, using the spells she'd learned over the years to compel him to do her bidding. "You will feed him every three days. Turn the hose on him whenever you want. But you will not let him die on your watch. Keep the charms active. Do you understand?"

Jeremy nodded, his eyes dull. "Yes, Katerina."

She let her voice soften as the magic settled over him. "I'm sorry I can't bring you with me, baby. It's just because you're the only one I can trust. You believe me, right?"

Perking up slightly, Jeremy offered her a weak smile. "I know. I won't let you down."

5

Cade

THE RAIN PELTED HIS FUR, soaking him to his skin. A constant assault of pebbles and leaves, driven by the endless wind, swirled around him, but the wolf had stopped caring.

Every breath was more painful than the last. The evil woman who fed him rotten meat hadn't come to taunt him in days, and pain stabbed his stomach.

He no longer paced, spending most of his days curled on the concrete pad. Summer had come and gone, and winter was close.

On the outside, his body was freezing all the time, but his blood still boiled, and though he tried to shift whenever he remembered he was a man, he always failed.

At least here, on the edge of the concrete so close to the super-heated ground, a hint of warmth infused his limbs. His dreams were all of his life as a man. Of a bed. A proper meal. Walking on two legs. And his pack.

But his pack was gone.

The wolf couldn't think any longer—not in words. Only

images. He was a man. He knew he was a man. But he couldn't escape his wolf. He'd die like this. Soon.

The door to the house opened, and the wolf raised his head. Maybe the bad woman would feed him. He hated her, but he was so weak. He needed food.

A weak growl rumbled in his throat at the sight of the boy carrying a half-rotten steak in his hand.

"Katerina might want you alive, but I don't give a fuck. Growl at me again, and you won't eat until she comes back." The earth beneath the wolf trembled, and he remembered. Earth elemental.

Tucking his head between his paws, he whined softly.

Please.

The boy rolled his eyes and threw the steak over the fence. It landed on the dirt ten feet from the pad, and once it hit the ground, he turned and headed back into the house.

So hungry.

Struggling to his feet, the wolf limped for the steak, but stopped halfway there. The ground didn't burn his paws. It was hot, but bearable.

He sniffed at the dirt. For months, as long as he could remember, he'd been able to smell the bad woman's magic all around him. Not today. Today, it was weak.

Food first. The wolf snagged the steak and brought it back to the concrete. The taste was wretched, but it helped him think.

"*Until she gets back...*"

Those words meant something. Was she gone? If her charms were fading, he could dig. A pile of leaves had collected in a corner of the enclosure. He could use those. Hide his attempts to burrow under the fence.

Once the sun went down, he padded over to the leafy corner, pawed the detritus away, and started to dig.

For two nights, he worked tirelessly, nosing the leaves back over the hole each morning to cover his progress. The ground was hard, even with all the rain, and the wolf's paws bled. Several of his nails tore out or wore down to the quick.

He was so tired. But also so close. He could fit his nose under the fence now. Just another few inches.

No one had come. The boy hadn't fed him again. He needed one more night. When the sky turned black and the stars emerged, he dragged his emaciated body towards the fence. Towards freedom.

Mara

She trudged into the hotel room and dropped her bag on the bed. Her favorite view waited for her outside the patio doors, but it held little joy for her now.

After this trip, she doubted she'd be strong enough to swim in the ocean again. Her transfusions were only lasting four days now before the exhaustion set in.

She'd spent the month of October traveling. Her Aunt Lillian had joined her as she'd crossed item after item off her bucket list.

Skydiving, whitewater rafting, paddle boarding. Trips to the Vatican, London for a showing of *Hamilton*, and two glorious weeks on the beach in Hawaii. But now, she was home and had to make preparations for the end.

Aunt Lillian had moved to Seattle and rented an apartment a couple of miles away. It was nice to have her aunt close by, and every few days, Lillian showed up with a casserole or takeout so Mara didn't have to exert what little energy she had left cooking.

She'd make it until Christmas. Beyond that…there were no guarantees. Brushing away a tear welling at the corner of her eye, she opened the patio doors. As soon as the sea air swirled through the room, she felt marginally better.

One last swim. Maybe two. If she hurried, she could take a dip before dinner, fall asleep with a book, and then swim for an hour or two in the morning. After that, she'd say goodbye to this place and close the penultimate chapter of her life.

The weather had turned cold and dismal, and the beach was deserted. At least she had an insulated swim cap and water booties.

Her tears mixed with the salt water as she stepped into the sea. Shivering, she waited for the water to fill her suit and warm with her body temperature. Once she didn't feel like she was about to turn into a popsicle, she dove beneath the murky waves.

The sea played a haunting melody that welcomed her home and comforted her. Stroke after stroke, she sped away from the shore, all the way to the edge of the protected cove. Treading water, she gazed back at the land.

The hotel bobbed, and dark clouds gathered behind the cliffs. The rain would arrive soon, then the wind. As long as it wasn't a freak lightning storm, she didn't care.

I could keep swimming. Until I'm too far away to make it back to shore. Just...let myself sink.

Images of Adam and Lisa and their two kids, of Jen, of Aunt Lillian flashed through her mind. They'd never forgive her. And Mara needed them with her at the end. So much that she'd made them promise. No hospitals. She'd die at home with her aunt and her friends around her.

With a sigh, Mara swam back to shore. Out and back, out and back, until she was both spent and energized at the same time. The water always did that to her.

The whole time, that same faint melody played. The background to her life. Or...at least the end of it.

AFTER HER ROOM service dinner of steak and a bottle of expensive wine, she wrapped herself in a blanket and watched the stars. The wine fuzzed her thoughts, and sadness seeped in.

Everything she was doing now, she was doing for the last time. Thanksgiving was only a few days away. It was all happening too fast. Would there be anything left of her in this world once she was gone?

Or would she fade from everyone's memories?

A gust of wind brought the fresh scent of rain to her nose, comforting her. "Is anyone out there?" she asked the darkness. "Up there? God? Goddess? I don't know if you're real. Aunt Lil believes. I *want* to believe." With a shake of her head, Mara sighed. "I want to have mattered. When I'm gone, please let someone, somewhere, say that I mattered."

6

Cade

THE SUN ROSE, painting the desolate yard in a pale, sickly light. The wolf had heard a car hours ago and thought the boy might have left.

He was so close. All night long, he'd dug frantically, and he could almost wriggle his battered body under the fence.

The ground was hot against his pelt, but he didn't care. Freedom was within his reach. His back feet scrambled for purchase as he tried again.

Twisting, he inched forward, little by little. A sharp piece of metal dug into his shoulder, and he whined. The coppery scent of blood made him retch, but he pressed on. The fence caught on each of his ribs, but his head was free now. Then his chest. Then his hips.

Struggling to his feet, he waited for the world to stop spinning. He could barely stand, but he had to run.

Ten feet separated the cage from the stone wall around the yard. The wolf examined every inch, searching for an exit. It was too high for him to jump over, even if he'd been at full strength, but there had to be a way out somewhere.

He found the front of the house, but the gate was made of metal bars that were too narrow for his body to squeeze through, even as thin as he was. A deep, frustrated growl rumbled through his chest. Maybe he could dig again?

In the southwest corner of the backyard, he found a large blackberry bush with some rotting berries on it. He chomped down as much of the fruit as he could, grimacing when the thorns tore at his lips.

So hungry.

The dirt under the bushes was soft, uncharmed, and muddy from the rains that had soaked this horrible place for days on end, making it easy for him to push it aside.

Deeper and deeper he went. More blood oozed from his paws. He panted, dizzy and exhausted, but he couldn't stop. He was almost through when a car door slammed and his heart started to pound even harder.

Hurry!

"Get back here, you fucking mongrel!" the evil woman screamed. Flames pelted the wolf's back, and he yelped, shoving his body under the stone.

Another blast of the fire elemental's magic hit him, and the scents of burnt fur, skin, and blood overloaded his senses. His eyes teared, but instinct took over.

Faster. Away from fire.

Heavy footsteps pounded towards him, but he pushed his body until he popped out from under the fence. Without a single thought, he took off at a run. The earth shook, a blood-curdling scream pierced the silence of the afternoon, but he didn't care about any of that. He was finally free.

Blackberry brambles sliced at him, and rocks cut his paw pads as he jumped and scrambled over the landscape. He couldn't stop. Not now. If she caught him again, he'd die.

Every day, the blood running through his veins grew hotter and hotter. He had hours. Days at most before his body gave out. Nausea flooded his belly, but he kept going.

The wolf stumbled over endless hills, finding a path here, a copse there. He jumped over a low fence and ran through a small field nestled alongside the forest. Cows, then goats watched him, and his mouth watered. At full strength, he could take down a goat easily, and he was so hungry, but he'd die if he stopped.

An old logging road provided an easier path for a few minutes, but it was too exposed.

Veering back into the underbrush, he thought he might have lost them until a fireball landed a few feet away.

Water. Ahead, he saw water. He could swim. The bad woman couldn't follow him into the water. But in order to reach it, he'd have to get himself down a steep cliff.

More words from the woman he didn't understand, then another blast of fire slammed into his shoulder. The wolf hit the ground, and as hard as he tried, he couldn't get to his feet again. So he crawled.

The earth rumbled, and a gaping maw opened under him. A section of the cliffside broke away and started to slide towards the sea, taking the wolf with it.

He tumbled over and over, his body slamming into the rocks. Blood spurted from a large gash in his side, and when he hit the sea, the salt to his wounds made him howl.

Water rushed into his lungs. His mind went blank. *Up. Swim up.*

When his muzzle broke through, he coughed and choked until he could breathe again, then started to paddle. Within minutes, he'd reached the shore and crawled into the brambles, listening carefully.

Nothing. No voices. He couldn't hear the bad woman or the boy at all. But he had to keep moving.

He wriggled and slunk within sight of the shore as the sun

stained the sky with reds, oranges, and purples. There was nothing but the endless blue-gray of the sea in every direction. *Island.* He knew islands. He knew there weren't easy ways to escape them.

With no idea where he was going, he kept to the underbrush, walking when he could, but mostly crawling as deep in the brambles as he could.

By the time the sun reached its apex, he'd found a beach, and exhaustion made every inch a battle. At least his final sight would be the sea. Not that terrible cage.

Out in the water, a dark speck bobbed, moving slowly closer. A piece of wood? No. A person.

From the wolf's prone position behind a pile of rocks, he caught sight of a squat, two-story building not far away.

A single car was parked at the edge of the beach. Cars meant freedom. Something tugged at him, urging him to move. Belly scraping over the asphalt, he crawled towards the car, finding a place to hide behind some bushes that bordered the building.

The figure emerged from the water. Long red hair spilled out of her swim cap as she tugged it off. Water trailed down her cheeks to the gentle swells hiding beneath her rubber suit.

Clad in black, she moved slowly with uneven steps. Curved hips gave way to lean legs, and the wolf couldn't stop staring at her as she reached under the bumper.

The hatchback opened, and she sat on the edge of the trunk and stripped off the black rubber to reveal a green bikini covering a body that was too thin. Her skin held a bluish tinge that the wolf neither understood nor liked.

She moved carefully, as if a sudden step would shatter her.

Beautiful.

The word came to the wolf, though he wasn't sure what it meant. Not anymore. He only knew he wanted to get closer to her. Needed it.

A storm of emotions washed over him. Thunder rolled in his

ears and lightning sparked against his skin, giving him the energy to stumble closer to her. Spring rain. Coconut. Almonds. Scents he recognized. Along with a bitter, bloody tang that he realized wasn't coming from him.

Dark smudges shadowed her eyes and her lips were pale.

Sick.

She dressed quickly, then wrapped a towel around her red hair, hurried over to the building, and disappeared inside, leaving the trunk open.

Instinct drove him forward, a pull he couldn't ignore.

Mine.

It took the wolf two tries to launch himself into her trunk.

Home. Safe. Mine.

Thoughts he didn't understand raced through his battered mind. He burrowed under a blanket and let himself sleep.

Mara

Cup of coffee in her hand, she trudged back to her car and tried not to cry. She'd never do this again.

At least the swim had refreshed her. In another couple of days, she'd be too tired to do more than get herself out of bed in the morning and maybe shower. But for the moment, she felt okay.

Dr. Pendergast and his team wouldn't be pleased that she'd spent the past two days swimming, but Mara didn't care.

One of the few benefits of dying is that you can do whatever you want at the end.

It wasn't as if the swimming was going to dramatically shorten her life.

A strange scent, almost a presence, filled the car as she headed for the ferry dock. Thin and metallic. But also burnt.

The odd, high-pitched sound of a faraway harmonica or flute distracted her from the scent. Tinnitus now?

"Whatever," she muttered. One more weird symptom wasn't going to make much difference.

Two hours later, her little silver Prius sped down the interstate. Mount Rainier, illuminated by the winter sun, shone against the clouds, and Mara smiled. She filed the image away, locking it in her mind so when she couldn't muster the strength to go outside, she'd still have it with her.

She'd filled the past few months with moments such as these. The Eiffel Tower at night. The brilliant aquamarine waters off of Capri. Seeing *The Book of Mormon* in London. Mara didn't bother with photos or mementos. Not anymore. She kept everything in her head and her heart. She'd had a good life. She'd keep having a good life for as long as she was able.

The strange scent returned. It smelled almost like wet dog. Maybe some sort of algae bloom on her wetsuit? Turning up the heat, she cracked the window to clear the air.

When she pulled into her garage, she tossed her wetsuit bag into the utility sink. Reaching for the blanket she kept in the trunk, she caught movement out of the corner of her eye. There was something under there. Or...shit...*someone*?

Taking two quiet steps back, she eased a hammer from the pegboard on the wall. Holding it high in one hand, she snatched the blanket away with the other.

"Oh my God!" Mara yelped. Curled in a ball was a wet, bloodied...wolf?

The animal jerked and raised its head. A weak whine shot directly to Mara's heart as luminous blue eyes watched her.

This animal was in pain. Terrible pain. How had he ended up in her car?

For a full minute, Mara held her breath. Desperation, fear, and hope churned in the wolf's eyes, and when he shuddered, Mara lowered the hammer and took a step forward.

He seemed to trust her, or at least wasn't in any condition to attack her.

Another whine seemed to be *please*, and she set the hammer down and eased her hip onto the edge of the bumper.

"I won't hurt you," Mara said softly, dropping her gaze so he wouldn't think she was challenging him.

Offering the wolf her hand, she waited for him to sniff her, then nudge her fingers with his nose. It was dry, almost hot. Pushing harder, he slid his whole muzzle under her hand. She risked a quick peek into the wolf's eyes, and he wriggled closer and whined again.

He's magnificent. Or would be if there were anything to him.

"Good boy. Will you let me see your paw?" Mara wrapped her fingers around his leg, stroking the burned and bloody pads under his toes. Only one nail remained, worn down to the quick. When she tightened her grip, he yelped in pain and pulled back, shaking.

He curled his body inward, shrinking away from her touch. Mara stroked a tentative hand down his side, and it came away slicked with blood. "You need a vet."

Adam. He worked down at the equestrian center. He'd know what to do. The wolf trembled, his breath coming in short pants as his eyes closed.

"It's okay," Mara crooned. "Hold on for me."

Adam picked up on the second ring. "Hey, Mara. What's going on?" His voice never failed to cheer her up when she was at her lowest.

"Um, I have a problem." How was she possibly going to explain this?

"Are you okay? Where are you? Do you need an ambulance?" Adam always assumed the worst, and he'd tried for months to get Mara to move in with him and Lisa, but they had two young children, and Mara liked her quiet, solitary house. She wouldn't give up her independence until she had no choice.

"No! It's not me. I'm fine. Well, fine enough. Look, um...when I was on Orcas Island, I picked up a stowaway in my car. I didn't even realize it until I got home. It's a...a wolf and he's badly injured. Can you bring over some antibiotics and a surgical needle and thread? He needs stitches."

"Not a fucking chance, Mara. Call Fish and Wildlife or Animal Control before he kills you!"

"He's not going to hurt me." The wolf watched her, head cocked, breathing ragged. "He's in terrible pain, Adam. I don't even think he can get up, let alone attack me. Please. I wouldn't ask if it weren't important. He needs help, and I need to be the one to help him."

Adam groaned. "Way to bring the guilt."

"I'm sorry." Mara stroked the wolf's massive head. His tongue lolled out from between slack jaws. Every few seconds, he shuddered. "I can't let him just lie here in pain."

"Fine. I'm on my way."

Mara slid closer to the injured animal, and he groaned. "Shh. It's going to be all right, buddy." Angling her body, she let him rest his head on her thigh. The contact seemed to calm him.

Something inside Mara warmed when she stroked his fur. She felt better—stronger. This animal needed her, and she wasn't going to let him down. She hummed to herself, picking out the notes that seemed to form the backdrop of her life these days.

It took Adam less than half an hour, but when his key scraped in the lock, the wolf growled.

"Mara?"

"In the garage." Mara stroked the wolf's gray and brown fur. His pelt was caked in blood and dirt, but his head was surprisingly clean, soft, and sleek.

Adam's dark brown hair stuck out in all directions, and he ran a nervous hand through the thick locks as he eyed them.

Faster than she expected, he was at her side and dragging her away by her arm while the wolf growled.

"Adam, let me go." She shook him off and rushed back to the animal. He calmed at her touch and licked her fingers. "Shh. Good boy. You're okay."

"Shit. He *likes* you." Adam dropped his bag and withdrew a stethoscope. He listened to the wolf's heart and lungs, then palpated his legs. The wolf whimpered and looked up at Mara, pleading.

"I can wrap his paws and you can stitch up his side. But," Adam sighed, "he's dying. That's long term malnourishment, Mara. You can see it in his eyes. If he lasts another day, it'll be a miracle." The wolf panted weakly, whining and licking Mara's hand again. "We need to call Fish and Wildlife."

Every one of the wolf's ribs stuck out. His fur was matted, wet, and bloody, and his pelt practically hung off his body. But he held her gaze, and Mara recognized that look. He knew he was dying.

Mara saw herself in those bright blue depths. Wasting away in a hospital bed, tubes sticking out of her arms, her nose, her throat.

"No. Go to the grocery store and get me two pounds of stew meat."

"What?" Adam looked up from his phone. "You can't be serious. The longer we wait, the more he's going to suffer."

"If he's going to die, he's going to have one good meal first. And he's going to be warm with someone sitting next to him. He's not going in a cage to be put down by strangers who don't care about him." She couldn't stop stroking his soft fur, and the wolf made a weak, desperate sound.

Adam didn't move, and Mara grabbed his arm. "We've talked about this. When it's my time, you promised me. I won't be stuck in a hospital bed hooked up to a bunch of machines. I'll be at home. You, Lisa, Lillian, and Jen will be with me. You know how important this is to me. He's me in a month. Can't you see I need to do this for him?"

"He's a wolf!" Adam backed away, still clutching his phone.

"So? He's an animal. He has a soul. Adam, he found *me*. The one person who could possibly know what he was going through. I don't know how or why, but maybe the Universe knew I'd take care of him."

The wolf inched forward and laid his head on Mara's thigh. A deep, questioning sound rumbled in his throat and he nudged her hand again.

"Please. Go to the store for me. There's money in my purse. If he lives long enough to eat, I'll call Fish and Wildlife myself."

When Adam rubbed his hand over his chin, Mara smiled. She'd won this round. He'd do this for her. Rummaging through his bag, he pulled out two syringes, handed one to Mara, and slid the other needle into the skin at the nape of the wolf's neck.

"What's that?"

"A sedative. I won't take the chance that he'll hurt you."

"He rode all the way back from Anacortes and didn't make a sound. He's not going to hurt me. Are you?" Mara knelt down and met the wolf's gaze. His pupils had turned into saucers already. "No. You won't. I know you won't."

Adam dropped the second syringe next to Mara. "If he looks like he's in distress, use this. It'll stop his heart."

The idea of her wolf dying crushed her, but Mara nodded. "I will."

7

Mara

FIFTEEN MINUTES LATER, Adam had wrapped the wolf's paws, carried him inside, and laid him on a blanket next to the fireplace.

"Let's get you warm," she said, keeping her voice calm as she flipped the switch to light the logs.

Nausea hit the back of her throat, and the wolf whined and struggled to get away from the flames. Swallowing hard, she lunged for the switch, and the hearth darkened again. "You don't like fire?"

It was almost like the wolf nodded. Shit. She was really tired if she thought he was trying to talk to her.

"I don't like this," Adam said as he shrugged back into his coat. "At least don't sit so close to him."

"Store. Meat. Now." Pointing to her front door, she dismissed the man's concerns, then added, "Please? Besides, I have to stitch up his shoulder. He can't even walk, Adam. I'll be fine."

With a scowl, Adam headed for the door. Once they were

alone, the wolf looked up at her with a quick, darting gaze, his eyes brighter now.

"You're pretty smart, you know that? You managed to find the only person on the planet who knew exactly what you were going through. I'm dying too."

The wolf made a desperate sound—something between a yip and a growl. He tried to get closer to her, but didn't make it more than an inch before he collapsed again with his head on her thigh.

Mara stroked his back. "No one knows what's wrong with me. But I'm down to my last couple of months. Adam's right. I should call Fish and Wildlife. But they'll put you in a cage and give you what's in that syringe and you'll be cold and alone. So you're going to have a meal and you're going to be warm, and if you look like you're suffering too much, I'll inject you myself."

Tears trailed down her cheeks as she stitched up his shoulder. It must have hurt, but the wolf never moved, and when she'd finished, he nosed her hand until it was resting on top of his head.

They stayed like that until the door opened again, and when Adam set a bag down next to them, the wolf let out a low growl. "Shh. He brought you food. Trust me."

Not only food. Adam had also snagged a bottle of wine and a chocolate bar in addition to three packages of stew meat, and Mara smiled up at him. "You read my mind."

"I still don't think this is a good idea, but I can't blame you for wanting to make his last few hours better than the past few months have obviously been for him." Adam knelt next to them. "I'm going to stay for a while. Make sure he doesn't hurt you."

"Go home." She draped her hand over Adam's wrist. "Lisa and the girls need you. It's almost eleven. I'll be fine."

He sighed, then headed for her kitchen. Returning with a corkscrew, wine glass, and a couple of towels, he stared down at her. "If you need *anything*, you call, okay? I'll check on you tomorrow."

Mara nodded, too preoccupied stroking the wolf's fur and worrying about his breathing. Still labored, but he'd calmed thanks to the sedative, and he looked like he was close to falling asleep.

After pouring herself a healthy glass of merlot, she tucked the blanket around the wolf's emaciated body and tore into the first package of meat. The scent had him lifting his head, and he whined, trying to get to his feet, but the blanket foiled his movements. "You stay put, buddy. I'll help you," Mara said, taking one of the pieces of cold meat and offering it to him.

The wolf gently plucked it from her palm, his rough lips tickling her before he nudged her hand again.

"You can have as much as you want. But take it slow. Otherwise, you could get sick."

Piece by piece, Mara fed the animal next to her. He licked her palm clean after each bite, making her laugh, and more than once she wondered if he was only doing it because she seemed to like it. Two whole pounds disappeared before he stopped asking for more.

Picking up the syringe, Mara frowned. "What do you think?"

The wolf lifted his head, his eyes clear. The plea in their ice blue depths was so clear, he might as well have spelled it out for her. *I want to live.*

"So do I," she murmured. "It's late. Let me get you some water."

Mara trudged into the kitchen and filled a bowl. Her eyes watered, and a halo of light framed her vision. She needed a shower. She always felt better after a shower. The wolf whined, tried to stand, and fell over, then seemed to panic when he couldn't get up again. His back legs scrambled, and his breathing quickened, turning almost ragged.

Water splashed onto the hardwood floor as Mara hurried

back to him, dropped to her knees, and stroked his side, carefully avoiding the fresh stitches. "It's okay. You're okay."

It took a few minutes, but he calmed and finally made a quiet, almost happy sound. "I feel better too," she whispered. She started to get to her feet, but he tensed again, like he wanted to follow.

"You're not going to stay here while I sleep, are you?"

His back legs flailed, useless, but he straightened his front legs to support his torso and stared at her, expectantly.

"Well, either my condition is deteriorating rapidly or you're really good at communicating. You don't want to be alone, do you?"

The wolf shook his head so hard he fell over.

"Careful there. You're way too drunk on meat to do that." Mara folded the blanket in half next to him and pointed. "Get on."

He inched forward, groaning as he curled up on the thick fleece. Mara grabbed the corners and dragged him into her bedroom, hitting her shoulder more than once on the wall as she staggered and fought not to give in to the dizziness. Dammit. She should have been asleep hours ago.

By the time she had him next to her bed, her eyes were dry and scratchy, and her depth perception had skewed. "Stay."

Stumbling into the bathroom, she stripped, then turned on the shower. After she'd gulped down an entire bottle of water and let the warm spray relax her muscles, she dried off, pulled on her favorite pair of pajamas, and opened the door.

"Shit!" The wolf had clearly been lying with his body pressed to the door, and he looked up at her, relief chasing away the fear in his eyes. "Stubborn thing, aren't you? Come on. Back to the blanket with you."

He crawled after her and flopped down on his side as she got into bed. Mara stared down at the animal who seemed so much like her. Weak, frightened, and alone.

"Don't die on me tonight." She didn't expect him to answer, but after a single vocalization she thought might have been an agreement, he closed his eyes, and she did the same.

Cade

He jerked awake in the middle of the night, unsure where he was. Dark. But...not cold. Or wet. Panic sent his heart slamming against his chest, making it hard to breathe.

Where was the fire woman? Where was *he?* He couldn't remember.

Scents washed over him: water, coconut, and something he could only identify as *home.*

Mara. Man say Mara.

An inquisitive sound escaped his throat. He hadn't thought in words in so very long, though he knew he used to. He was a man. He remembered walking on two legs. Speaking. But those were the only words he could tease from his battered mind.

Mara had saved him. Fed him. His paws throbbed, and he gave one a lick, the gauze around them confusing him. But he remembered how she'd warned him to leave them alone, and he stopped.

Movement from somewhere above him set him on full alert. He shrank back into the corner of the room, trying to make himself as small as possible.

A quiet sigh and a hum a few feet away calmed him. *Mara.* She was here. Asleep. He remembered her getting into bed. He crept forward on his bruised, blistered, and bloodied paws, stifling his whimpers. Mara was sick, and she needed to rest.

He laid his head on the mattress to watch her.

Mine.

It was a risk, but he nosed her hand and licked her fingers, and in her sleep, Mara smiled. Her touch relieved some of his pain, cooled some of the fire that burned him from the inside out.

The wolf tried to get his paws on the bed, but he lost his balance and fell back on the blanket, panting and whimpering.

"Hey. You okay there?" Gentle fingers stroked his head as she leaned over him, and she smiled again, something he wanted to see her do every day. The only light came from a dull glow in the hallway, but it was enough to see his Mara's face. Whining, he tried to get up again, but Mara shook her head. "You're in no condition to jump. Relax, buddy. I promise, I won't go anywhere."

The wolf didn't understand her words, but the tone reassured him. He could sleep here. Close to his Mara.

She slipped out of bed, sat with her back to the mattress, and patted her knee. "Come here."

He wriggled closer, pressing his whole body against her legs. He felt better with her touching him, and closed his eyes, he sank into a dreamless sleep.

8

Cade

SUNLIGHT STREAMED into the room from the hall, and the wolf sat up, his body still weak, but steadier than the night before. Mara had moved back to the bed while he'd slept, and he watched her, memorizing her face, how relaxed she looked, even if she still had those dark circles under her eyes.

She yawned and stretched, her lids fluttering open. "Oh! You look better!" Swinging her legs over the side of the bed, she reached down and scratched behind his ears, a sensation the wolf decided he very much liked.

When she stood, he limped out to her living room, sat by her patio door and yipped. He needed to relieve himself, and he couldn't do that in her house. She'd be mad.

"I didn't think wolves were house trained," Mara said, a hint of laughter in her tone. "But I'll take it. If you come back in when you're done, I'll give you the rest of the meat."

The wolf only understood one word. *Meat.* His stomach growled, hollow again.

Outside, he checked the entire yard. Wherever he was, it

didn't smell like where he'd been before. No burning dirt. No sea air. Only a few small animals, herbs, mud, and decaying leaves. No threats.

A tall, wooden fence offered privacy, and lush trees protected two sides of the yard. No one would see him here. The dull hum of traffic off to one side, but not close by.

City.

He knew that word too. A city meant people. He used to live in a city. But not this one.

After leaving his mark several places around the yard, warning other animals away, he returned to the door and sat patiently until Mara noticed him and let him back inside.

Delicious scents surrounded him, all coming from the semi-enclosed room where Mara moved around for several minutes before picking up two bowls. "Are you hungry?"

The wolf yipped. He'd give anything to have her feed him again. She set two bowls down on the hard floor—one with raw meat and the other with water.

Fresh. Tasty. Not spoiled. Not burnt. He cleaned the bowl, only dimly aware of Mara sitting close by eating something else that smelled good. After slurping up half of the water, he sat up, his tongue hanging out of his mouth, panting and watching her.

"So," she said as she picked up the syringe and showed it to him.

Bad. He growled and backed up, but then Mara laughed.

"Nope. You don't need this." She dropped it back on the counter and knelt in front of him. "You need a bath. And some time with a brush. But you're definitely getting better. I just don't know what to do with you. You're a wild animal, yet you're sitting here like a puppy."

The wolf didn't understand most of her words. Only the tone. Bemused. A little confused. Happy. He wanted to stay with Mara. She was nice and she smelled so good. He leaned into her, needing her touch, and she wrapped her arms around him.

The motion stretched his wounded shoulder, and pain lanced through him. Before he could stop himself, a high-pitched bark escaped, and Mara jerked away.

"I should call Adam. He needs to look at that shoulder again in the daylight."

No.

Adam was bad. Adam wanted someone to take him away from Mara. The wolf growled, shook his head, and nudged Mara's chin. Despite the pain, he forced a happy, contented sound from his weakened body. He had to make her understand. He wanted to stay with her. No one else.

She sighed and scratched behind his ears again. "Where'd you come from, anyway? Someone did all this to you. Were they hurting other animals too?"

He didn't understand her questions, so he just nudged her again, this time close to her ear.

"You make me feel better," she said quietly as she rested her head against his. He licked her neck, and she laughed and pulled away with a little shriek. "Gross."

Pushing to her feet, she groaned, then swayed for a moment before steadying herself against the counter. The wolf leapt to his feet and pressed his whole body to hers, worried. Something was wrong with Mara and he didn't like not being able to fix it.

After a couple deep breaths, she seemed to strengthen. "C'mere. I need to sit down."

He followed her to the couch where she curled up under a blanket and picked up a book. He knew books—even tried to angle his head to see what was on the page, but the black and white squiggles didn't make any sense to him.

Still, the longer he spent with Mara, the more words came to him. *Man. Mara. Help. Mine. Book. Meat.* Others seemed just out of reach, trapped where the wolf couldn't find them.

He needed her help. He just had to figure out how to ask for it.

Mara

The wolf slept at her feet all day. Every few hours, he succumbed to nightmares. Mournful whines, angry growls, and spasms that wracked his whole body. But if she stroked his side or talked to him, he'd calm.

A little after noon, Mara forced herself to make a grilled cheese sandwich. Her appetite was practically non-existent, but Aunt Lillian read her the riot act if she didn't eat regularly. After the butter started to sizzle, her stomach rumbled lightly.

The wolf hadn't moved, and Mara watched him as the sandwich cooked. Nothing about him made sense. How had so powerful an animal been reduced to a mangy, haunted shell? And with whatever time she had left, how could she help him?

After she polished off the sandwich, she felt a little stronger, and then realized he'd finished all the meat Adam had bought. With how she'd felt this morning, she wouldn't have risked getting in the car. But now? She felt good. Normal, even.

Her wolf needed food, and that was one thing she could definitely give him.

IT WASN'T until she got to Whole Foods that she realized it was the day before Thanksgiving. The aisles were packed full of shoppers, and Mara maneuvered her cart through the crowds as she scanned her phone to find out what gray wolves ate.

Meat, berries, even fresh vegetables would work. Piling the cart full of beef and bison, she added bags of baby carrots, blueberries, and blackberries. For herself, she grabbed a chocolate bar, eggnog, chips, and a box of Christmas cookies.

The checker was as frazzled as the rest of the shoppers, but after the fifth package of beef, he paused and stared at Mara. "That's...a lot of meat."

"My family doesn't do turkey," Mara said, forcing a smile. "And we eat a lot."

"You? You're skin and bones."

Her smile fell away. "Yeah, well. Lucky, I guess."

And dying. With a wolf waiting for me at home.

HE WASN'T JUST WAITING, he was excited to see her. Or scared. She couldn't tell. He pressed against her legs, shaking as he nuzzled her hand.

"Whoa there. What's wrong?" She wasn't sure how she expected him to answer her, but the short yip he made in response was full of fear. "I just went to the store, buddy. Nothing to worry about."

Unpacking the shopping bags, she hummed the tune that never seemed to be far from her mind these days. If only she could figure out what the hell it was and where she'd heard it. The wolf followed her, tracking all of her movements.

"I got you some food," she said, holding up the package of bison. "Are you hungry?"

His mouth watered, and he started to drool.

"Ugh. I guess so."

She dumped the chunks of meat into a bowl with a handful of blueberries and carrots. Seconds after she set the dish on the floor, her phone rang and Adam's name flashed across the screen.

"Hey," she said hesitantly.

"Well, what happened?" The blare of a car horn made her wince.

"Are you driving? You better have me on speaker."

"Of course I do. What happened with Fish and Wildlife?"

"I didn't call them." She braced herself against the counter and watched her wolf attack the food with such enthusiasm, she smiled.

"Did you bury him in the yard? Shit, Mara. That's illegal."

Rolling her eyes, Mara shook her head. "First of all, do you really think I care about being thrown in jail right now? I'm going to be dead in six weeks."

The wolf's head snapped up, and he watched her. Fear, longing, and shock churned in his ice blue eyes. Mara tore her gaze from the animal and unwrapped the chocolate bar. "Second of all, he's not dead. He's devouring two pounds of bison as we speak."

"He's going to devour *you* soon. That's not a dog you have there. He's a wild animal. I'm on my way over. Don't go near him."

"Oh for fuck's sake, Adam. He's sitting right next to me, and he's as docile as can be. I can't really explain it, but he needs me right now."

"I'm five minutes away."

The call disconnected, and Mara trudged back into the kitchen to put the rest of the groceries away, then headed for the couch. All of her energy from earlier had faded, and she needed to sit down.

The wolf followed her, lowered his body down onto the blanket, and rested his head on her feet.

"Yeah, me too. But I don't get naptime yet." Closing her eyes, she let herself drift until Adam unlocked the door.

"Mar?"

The wolf's possessive grumble surprised her, and when Adam withdrew a syringe from his bag, it turned into a full-blown growl.

Mara tightened her hand on the wolf's scruff. "What the hell is that?"

"Another sedative. Move away from him."

"No." Slipping off the couch, Mara wrapped her arms around her wolf. "He doesn't need it. He's fine, and so am I."

As if the animal could understand her, he nudged her ear with his nose, then made a contented sound and leaned closer. The headache holding her temples in a vise lessened, and a sheen of moisture made her palms slippery.

The melody in her head grew louder, and she cursed her traitorous body. Why couldn't it just decide what the heck it wanted to do?

The wolf questioned her, nuzzling her neck with an inquisitive sound. Could he sense whatever was going on with her?

"Mara? You're being reckless."

"And you're not my mother. Look at him," Mara snapped. "And me. Does it look like he wants to hurt me?"

Adam crouched next to them with the syringe still in his hand. The wolf watched warily, but didn't otherwise move.

"Maybe he's still drugged from last night?" He pulled back the wolf's eyelid, but the animal jerked his head away and bared his teeth until Mara stroked his fur and whispered reassurances to him.

"He's eaten two pounds of meat today. He *asked* to go outside this morning and came back in ten minutes later. Wherever he came from, he's house-trained. Maybe someone on the island kept him as a pet or in some sort of zoo. He's not going to hurt me, and—" Mara stared down at the majestic animal in her arms, then back up at Adam. "I feel better around him."

"What?"

"I don't feel as sick when I'm next to him. He makes me feel...normal." Absently, she scratched the wolf's ears, and his tongue tumbled out of his mouth.

Adam's brows drew together. "Well, therapy dogs are often used with cancer patients. We talked about getting you one—Lil and I. But the kids are allergic and the condo won't let Lillian have dogs, so we didn't know what we'd do with it when you..."

"Die," Mara said.

"Yeah."

Neither of them spoke for several moments. Finally, Adam went into the kitchen for a glass, then dumped the syringe—along with three others—into it. "There's enough sedative to put him flat on his back for at least a day. If he starts acting *at all* aggressive, you use one and call me. Or just get the hell out of the house. Will you promise me that?"

Mara tightened her hold on the wolf as a smile curved her lips. "Yes. I promise."

"I need to get home. Lisa has a to-do list as long as my arm. Dinner's at three tomorrow, but come over any time, okay?"

Thanksgiving. My last Thanksgiving.

Despite the finality of the day—of almost every day now—the idea of spending the day with family, of Lisa's turkey, Aunt Lil's pumpkin pie, and Jen's stupidly delicious green bean casserole topped with Funyuns made her smile. "Yeah. Sounds good."

Standing, Mara's world tilted, and she reached for Adam's arm to steady herself. He pulled her close. "I wish you'd move in with us," he whispered in her ear. "I don't like the idea of you here all alone. Not when..."

When I'll be dead soon.

The wolf growled and forced his body between them, reminding her she wasn't alone. Not anymore.

"I know," Mara said as she pulled away. "But this is my home, and I'm not ready to leave it. Not yet."

9

Katerina

FOR TWO DAYS, she'd searched. Screamed and berated and ordered and searched.

Every time Jeremy came back empty handed, she sent him out again, marking off quadrants on her map where she was certain the wolf couldn't be. He couldn't have escaped the island. Despite Jeremy letting the charm on the earth lapse, the one keeping the werewolf trapped as his animal would never fade. She'd made sure of that.

Katerina sank down in front of the hearth, praying, begging for help finding him, but her pleas went unanswered. Even talking to the local sheriff didn't get her anywhere.

"Can't we go home?" Jeremy asked as he trudged back into the house covered with mud and scratches from the blackberry brambles. He'd even tried—with her help—to use the earth. To communicate with the land, but his powers were too wild and untamed.

Pouring each of them a glass of wine, he offered one to her, then retreated across the room, clearly afraid of her. Shit. How could she have let things go this far?

"No. And stop asking." Katerina drained the wine in two sips, then threw the glass into the flames, regrets, guilt, and shame eating away at her. "If you'd kept the charm on the dirt active, he never would have been able to dig under the fence."

"I'm sorry, babe. I...I just hate it here," Jeremy said. "I didn't mean to..."

"I know." All she wanted to do was rage, but she forced herself to take a deep breath, cross to him, and caress his cheek. "I shouldn't have left you alone. That was my mistake. But Jer, you have to fix this. The werewolf must die. And unless we find him, I won't ever be able to rest."

The overwhelming guilt in his eyes almost dampened her anger, but she'd been after the wolf for so long, nothing could take away the intense hatred boiling inside her. Before she said something she'd regret, Katerina stormed up the stairs to her bedroom.

After three days of dealing with the IRS, to return to Orcas and find that Jer had destroyed all of her plans for revenge... She'd almost killed him.

Restless, she paced the room. As angry as she'd been—and still was—Jeremy felt suitably guilty. She knew he hadn't done it on purpose.

He wasn't the brightest of elementals, but he was loyal and devoted. He'd do anything for her—and had. If only she hadn't been called back to Phoenix. The wolf would be dead, and they'd be on their way home.

Picking up the phone, she called Bella.

"I lost him," she said as she sank down onto the mattress. "Jeremy let the charms lapse, and he got away."

"Did ya' search everywhere?" Bella asked. When she was relaxed, Bella's voice sometimes held a bit of an accent. It was the same one she'd had when Katerina had found her in Mexico. Scottish maybe? Irish? English?

"Everywhere. Jeremy hasn't slept since I got back. The last time I saw the wolf, he was headed for the shore. We found a patch of blood on the sand by an old hotel, but that's it. I need you to come and try to scent him."

Bella sighed. "I'll never get a flight tomorrow. It's Thanksgiving."

Stifling her grumble, Katerina flopped down on the bed and stared up at the ceiling. She couldn't be angry with Bella. The woman lived to please her. Managing Flaming Objects was a full time job, and Bella had not only done that without complaint, she'd helped to lead Katerina's coven.

"I know, Bella. See if you can get here by Friday or Saturday? If he's not dead, he's still on the island somewhere. They wouldn't let a wolf on the ferry." She toyed with the crimson pendant at her throat, drawing comfort from the power contained within.

"I'll be there as soon as I can."

"Why do you put up with me?" Katerina asked. Exhaustion pressed down on her. The loss of the wolf, her failure to exact the revenge she so desperately needed, her fights with Jeremy.

"Because ya' saved my life. There's nothing I wouldn't do for you," Bella said softly. "I don't know where I came from or what happened to me...before. But I think if anyone else had found me, I wouldn't have survived. I love you, my sister. If you want, I'll get in the car right now and start driving."

A tear balanced on the corner of Katerina's eye. "No. Find a flight. It'll enhance your power. Then we'll find that wolf, kill him, and life will return to normal."

Cade

The house was eerily quiet. Only his ragged breathing cut through the oppressive silence. In his nightmares, he burned. The evil woman stood over him, blasting him with fire, watching him yelp, glee in her eyes.

He whined, needing comfort from Mara, but her bed was empty. Panic drove him to the ground, his weak and aching muscles protesting the sudden movement.

Scrambling to his feet, he explored the whole house, desperate. No Mara.

"Where? Mara!"

He couldn't form words, but his desperate vocalizations echoed in the empty space.

A heavy *thunk* came from the garage, and he ran towards the sound. *Mara.*

She slipped through the door with a bag slung over her shoulder. "Hey there, buddy."

The wolf whined. He wasn't buddy. He didn't know who he was —what his name had been—but it wasn't buddy. Still, Mara could call him whatever she wanted as long as she stayed with him.

Her bag landed on the floor, and the wolf sniffed it. Chlorine, sweat, coconut. He knew those scents. But how?

"You didn't even flinch when I touched you this morning." Mara smiled at him and stroked his head before filling a bowl with meat, fruits, and vegetables for him.

He ate it all while she cooked something for herself. After two days of regular meals, he had moments where he forgot what it had been like to be cold, hungry, and in constant pain.

After she'd eaten, she headed for the living room, sank down onto the couch, and patted the cushion next to her. The wolf jumped up, then arranged himself with his head in her lap.

Cool, comforting fingers scratched behind his ears, and the

fire burning inside him calmed. Not enough for him to shift. Never enough for that. He snuggled closer to her, content with his full belly, comfortable bed, and her sweet voice in his ear.

"I don't think I can keep swimming much longer," she said, a deep sadness lacing her tone. "I won't even be able to drive in a few weeks. I can't..." A tear landed on the wolf's nose, and he ached to be able to comfort her. "I don't know why I'm telling you this. It's not like you can understand me."

They sat in silence for a few minutes, Mara's tears and tiny sobs the only sounds passing between them.

"I have to go out soon," she said when she'd sniffled loudly and swiped at her cheeks. "It's Thanksgiving. Do you think you'll be okay in the house for six hours or so?"

The wolf yipped. *Stay.* He didn't want to be without her.

Mara leaned down and pressed a kiss to the top of his head. "I feel better when I'm with you. It's almost like I'm not sick at all. It won't last, I'm sure. But even if you give me an extra day or two, I'll take it."

With a whine, the wolf nudged her hand. He didn't understand why she was so sad, but he knew sick. Sick was bad.

"You can't stay here forever, you know," she whispered. "I'm going to die soon. I have to figure out what to do with you before that."

Die. That word was worse. He couldn't let Mara die. She smelled good. She was nice to him. She was *his*.

MARA LET him run around the backyard, and he chased birds. The action was instinctual, but he knew it wasn't *him*. Every hour, every day that passed brought him closer to the truth. He wasn't a wolf. He was a man. He'd walked on two legs, spoken in words, worn clothing. He remembered being around other people.

People he cared about. Their faces were only blurs in his memories, but every day, they got just a little clearer.

"Come on inside," Mara called a bit later, and he followed her into her bathroom. She ran a brush through his matted fur and then unhooked the shower head from the wall and let warm water wash over him.

Every time she touched him, he felt better. Like the fire inside was cooling, little by little.

When he shook the water from his body, she laughed and wiped droplets from her cheeks. "You look practically handsome now," she said. After she dried him off, he ran back to the living room and jumped up on the couch where they'd sat earlier.

She shook her head at his expectant look. "I have to go, Bud. But I'll be back. I promise. Please don't destroy my house."

He watched her leave with tears in his eyes, and when her car pulled out of the garage, the wolf jumped off the couch and padded into her bedroom. He curled up on her bed, needing to be as close to her as possible, and fell asleep.

Mara

A pint-sized tornado of activity flew out the bright red door of the house in Queen Anne and wrapped tiny arms around Mara's legs. "Aunt 'Ara!"

Sarabeth, Adam and Lisa's oldest, refused to let go, and Mara was forced to waddle into the house with a forty-pound weight strapped to her thigh.

"I brought you something," Mara said as incentive to get the little girl off of her. Reaching into her purse, she pulled out a chocolate Santa. "Don't tell your mom. And no eating this until *after* dinner, okay?"

Sarabeth grabbed the chocolate, gave Mara her biggest smile, and ran inside. "Mom! Aunt 'Ara brought me candy!"

"Traitor," she said with a laugh. She was going to be so sad to leave these kids. *No. Do not go there today.* But she couldn't help it. This was her last Thanksgiving, and dammit. That wasn't fair.

"Hi, hon." Aunt Lillian glanced up from where she was chopping rosemary and frowned. Setting down her knife, she embraced her niece and whispered in Mara's ear, "Not doing well today, are you?"

"No." Mara kept her voice low. "Kind of hard to smile when you know what's coming. But I swam this morning. It helped."

Lillian guided Mara to one of the stools and urged her to sit down. "I wish you'd let me bring you to my friend Eleanor down in Cannon Beach. She swears you're a water soul and thinks she could help you."

"I don't believe in that stuff, Aunt Lil. Whatever God or Goddess is up there, she's given me a good life. I don't want it to end, but I'm not about to pin false hopes on one of your crystal-wielding friends."

"Mara!" Lil pursed her lips and returned to her rosemary. "Eleanor is *not* some kook. She's an elemental—an expert on the four primary elements and she has some good ideas. I don't understand why you won't give it a try."

"Because she's a nurse who believes in *science*," Jen said as she wrapped Mara in a gentle hug. "I love you, Lil, but stop trying to push Mara into trying some backwoods miracle cure."

"Not all crystal-wielding *backwoods* healers eschew science, you know," Lillian retorted. "I know you teach biology, Jennifer, but you also grew up in northern Canada. You should really be more open minded."

"Stop!" Mara reached for the glass of wine Lisa slid towards her and glared at her best friend and her aunt. "This is a day to relax and stuff our faces with food. No more arguing, and no more talking about my health. Understood?"

"I'm not letting you go without a fight," Lillian muttered as she went back to aggressively mincing the rosemary.

Mara and Jen retreated to the living room and curled up on the sofa. "What's on your mind?" Jen asked.

Flexing her fingers, Mara tried to figure out how much she was ready to admit. She missed the wolf. After his bath, he'd smelled strong and powerful and woodsy with a soft, sleek pelt. Well, except for the burns.

Some of them had looked old, and some very fresh. How could anyone purposely injure such a majestic animal?

"I sort of did something stupid," Mara said. The wolf had looked so sad when she'd left. If only she'd been able to bring him with her.

"The wolf?" At Mara's raised eyebrows, Jen chuckled. "Adam told us. It's really a wolf?"

"Yes. I did some research online. He's a gray wolf. Most don't get as large as he is, but all the other signs are there. His eyes, his markings..."

The kids raced around the room, ducking between Adam's legs, pulling their father into a game of hide and seek.

"Why are you keeping him?"

"I... How did you—?"

"I know that look in your eyes. Spill." Jen settled back against the cushions, waiting.

"Because he makes me feel better."

Jen nearly spit out her sip of wine. "So you won't go to Lil's hippie witch chick, but you'll adopt a wild animal for his healing abilities?" She snorted. "I'm not saying you should go to Oregon, but you can't put any faith in a wolf either."

"I'm not." Mara set her own glass down with a little more force than necessary and met Jen's gaze. "I don't think he's healing me. I said he makes me *feel* better. I was hoping you'd understand."

Jen scooted forward and wrapped Mara in a hug, threatening

to shatter the tenuous control Mara held over her emotions. She ached for comfort, today more than ever.

"I don't have to understand, Mar. If you say the wolf makes you feel better, then he does. But I have to try to protect you at least a little."

BY THE TIME the pumpkin pie was served, Mara's belly was full, but her body felt as empty and drained as the wine bottles she tossed into the recycling bin. But she forced a smile as Lisa set a cup of coffee in front of her. Sipping silently, she took in the scene around her. This was her family. She wasn't biologically related to any of them, not even Aunt Lillian, but they were her family all the same. She loved them so much it hurt.

No one told you about *this* part of dying. About knowing those you cared for would go on without you.

"What's troublin' you, Mara?" Lillian asked. "I know that look. That's your serious face. The one you put on when you're stewing. So spill it. What's got my favorite niece looking like the world's ending?"

"Lil!" Jen snapped as Mara burst into tears.

"Kids, bedtime. Now," Lisa said, reaching for Sarabeth and Annie's hands. She had them out of the room in less than a minute, and Mara swiped at her cheeks.

"My world *is* ending," she whispered. "And it's not fair."

"No, child. Definitely not." Lilian pulled Mara close and rocked her gently. "I've been filling in for your mama for fifteen years, and no mother wants to bury their kids. It ain't right. But you're not dead yet, so don't go giving up on any of us."

"I don't have a choice." The words escaped on a sob, and she mopped a tissue over her cheeks with a shaking hand. "It doesn't matter what I do. In a few weeks, I'll be gone, and there's nothing anyone can do about it."

"Hush now," Lillian cooed. "You're alive today and you'll be alive tomorrow. Every day with you is a gift, hon. One we all cherish. Now, have another slice of pie and let's see if we can get a smile on that pretty face of yours."

Mara sniffled quietly as Adam slid a plate closer to her. She didn't want more pie. She wanted to curl up with her wolf and sob until she didn't have anything left in her. He wouldn't try to cheer her up or give her false hope or force her to pretend everything was going to be okay. He understood her.

10

Cade

HE HATED BEING ALONE in the house. Every noise woke him, and more than once, he hid under Mara's bed, convinced the bad woman had found him.

When the door from the garage finally opened, the wolf wriggled out from under the bed and headed straight for Mara.

The burned, coppery scent of illness clung to her, and she stumbled on her way to the couch. "C'mere, Bud," she said, her voice slurred. He jumped right up on the cushions and wrapped himself around her as best he could.

Mara. Sick.

"They mean well. But they just don't understand." With a sob, she buried her face against his neck and held him. He didn't move for a long time. Not until Mara's tears stopped. Then, he lay down with his head in her lap while she watched television, sniffling from time to time.

The low hum of the TV stirred his memories, an occasional word bleeding through. He tried to focus on the pictures, but they didn't make any sense, so eventually, he closed his eyes and let Mara soothe his pain.

THE NEXT MORNING, Mara was worse. Every time she got up, her gait was uneven. Her voice trembled, she cried often, and though he couldn't understand much of what she said, he caught phrases.

Going to die...

Not fair...

Scared...

The wolf was scared too. He couldn't be without Mara. Didn't want to be.

They spent the day on the couch, and though Mara made sure to fix him two large bowls of food, she didn't eat anything.

Once Mara returned to her bedroom to sleep, the wolf settled next to her. He didn't know how long he lay there, eyes open, scanning the darkness, protecting the woman who'd protected him.

A strange scraping sound from the other room had him lifting his head. The fur on the back of his neck prickled, and he growled quietly. Something was wrong.

Mara didn't stir. Not when a floorboard creaked. Not when the scraping turned into footsteps. Getting to his feet, he stood over her on the bed, his gaze locked on the door.

A shadowed form filled the space, and the wolf growled and sprang. His front paws landed square on the man's chest, sending him stumbling back and onto his ass.

The wolf yelped, and Mara sat up. "Bud?" Her voice was weak, and it distracted him for too long. The intruder shoved him, hard, and he hit the wall, disoriented.

Mara screamed, grabbed the lamp on her bedside table, and hurled it at the man. Her aim was off, and he dodged it, then lunged for her, pinning her to the bed with his hands around her neck.

"Stop fighting me, bitch, and you'll live through this."

Mara rammed her knee into his groin. The wolf clamped down on the man's calf with his powerful jaws until he tasted blood, then wrestled the intruder to the ground.

"Get out...of my house!" Mara wheezed.

The man pulled something from his pocket. A quiet snap was followed by the glint of a knife, and he aimed for the wolf, barely missing his shoulder.

Mara had a bat in her hand now, and she swung it wildly, connecting with the intruder's hip, then his arm.

"Get! Out!"

The man stumbled from the room, and the wolf gave chase. This bastard had tried to hurt Mara, and he'd pay. It had been a long time since the wolf had tasted fresh blood.

Mara

Alone, rooted to the ground by fear and indecision, she only moved when her knees gave out. Dialing 911, she tried not to lose her shit entirely.

"911, what's your emergency?" The man's voice, calm and collected, helped her focus.

"Someone...broke in. To my house." Her clammy palms squeaked against the bat, and the strange melody that haunted her so often these days almost drowned out the operator's words. "What did you say?"

"Is he still in the house?"

"No. He ran. I heard the door..."

"Okay, ma'am. I've sent the call to the dispatcher and help will be there as soon as possible. I'll stay on the phone with you until they arrive. Can you answer some questions for me?"

"Y-yes."

TWO HOURS LATER, Mara had been checked out by a pair of EMTs, recounted all she remembered—which wasn't much—to the police officers who'd checked all around her house and found the busted door lock on her back door.

"Ma'am? Is there someone you can call to come stay with you?" The young officer stared down at her, concern in his eyes. "The crime scene techs are going to be here another hour at least, and you don't look well."

"I'm not." Her head throbbed, and her mouth was dry. "Can... can you get me a glass of water? I have this weird...blood disorder. I get dehydrated easily."

When the officer pressed a glass into her hand, she downed it all in under a minute.

The crime scene tech, a young woman named Daisy, paused as she packed up her kit. "What kind of dog did you say you had?" she asked.

"Um, a Husky. Why?"

She held up a plastic bag. "This doesn't look like any dog hair I've ever seen."

Mara sputtered, "He's sort of a half-breed. A mutt."

The sound that came out of Daisy's mouth was something akin to a *harrumph*, but she didn't say another word as she dropped the bag into her kit and headed out to her van.

"There have been a string of home invasions in North Seattle this month," Officer Denton said as he closed his notebook and tucked it into his pocket. "This looks like the same guy. He's a coward. Targets women living alone. I'm surprised he took a chance on a house with a dog."

"I only got him a few days ago." Mara wrung her hands in her lap. The wolf hadn't returned, and she was terrified he'd been hurt. Or that he'd finally decided to leave.

The officer was still talking. "...usually takes jewelry, electronics, cash."

Mara snorted. "Well, he would have been sorely disappointed here. The most valuable things in my house are my espresso machine and laptop. Outside of that, he would have come away with like fifty bucks."

"Well, you were lucky your dog was here."

"I just wish he'd come back," Mara said quietly. A wave of exhaustion pressed down on her, and she slumped in her chair. "What happens next?"

"I'll check on you tomorrow, but this guy never returns to the scene of the crime. Are you sure I can't call anyone to come stay with you?" Officer Denton took a step towards the door, but he looked so uncertain, Mara tried to force her shoulders to straighten.

"I'm fine. I just...need to rest."

After double-checking all the locks and wedging a chair against the back door, she collapsed on the couch and was asleep within minutes.

The gray light of dawn streamed through the patio doors when she opened her eyes again. Someone was scratching at the front door.

The wolf!

Mara almost fell twice in her rush, but when she flung open the door, the wolf leapt for her and knocked her over as he licked her neck. She wrapped her arms around his sleek, warm body, and he growled.

"It's okay. I'm okay. You're okay," she babbled as she held on to the animal who'd saved her life.

The wolf made a sorrowful sound, grabbed the sleeve of her pajama top in his teeth, and tugged her back to the couch. "What are you doing? Trying to take care of me?"

The yip sounded almost like a yes, and he jumped right up and snuggled against to her.

"I think you saved my life," she whispered. He'd come back, and for just one moment, she felt like everything was going to be okay.

11

Mara

SHE WAS DROWNING. Every part of her was desperate to reach the surface. When her head broke through, she was in the middle of a vast, endless ocean at sunrise.

Waves crashed over her, and she screamed for help, but only the roar of the wind greeted her.

How did I get here?

The wind howled and seemed to say, *"Accept this."*

Accept what? Dying?

"No! I want to live!" Mara cried out.

The wind bellowed harder, and water stung her cheeks. *"Accept who you are."*

Sitting up with a gasp, she sucked in great lungfuls of air and looked around. She was in her bed, the wolf pressed against her, a questioning look in his silvery blue eyes. The whole previous day, he'd stayed next to her, and by the time she'd crawled into bed at night, she'd felt...better.

"Just a dream, buddy," she said. "Need to go outside?"

While he checked all around her yard, Mara programmed a

cup of espresso. She felt good, despite the stress from the break-in, and she was due for a transfusion that afternoon, which guaranteed she'd feel even better tonight.

Her doorbell rang, causing her to flinch and spill a few drops of espresso, and the wolf padded back inside as Lillian came through the front door. He looked up at Mara, a rumbling growl almost a question.

"It's okay," she said, stroking his head.

Lillian gasped as she focused on the wolf. "You still have him? Can you put him outside?"

She shot her aunt a sideways glance. "He won't hurt you. Will you?"

The wolf lay at Mara's feet and tucked his head between his paws.

"I'll stay over here, thanks," Lillian said warily. "I'm with Adam, hon. That's a wild animal. Not a house pet."

"Look at him. Does he look wild to you?" Mara knelt and scratched the wolf behind the ears. His tail thumped against her hardwood floor.

"He looks like he'd kill anyone who tried to hurt you."

Mara laughed. "I think you're right. But you're not going to hurt me so you're safe. You probably do want to sit down, though," she said. "Let me make you some coffee. We need to talk before we go to the hospital."

While the coffee beans ground and the water heated, she fed the wolf, then pulled out a few of the Christmas cookies to munch on. Setting the steaming mug of coffee in front of her aunt, Mara sank into the chair across from her. "Someone broke into my house two nights ago."

"What?" Lillian slammed her coffee cup down. The wolf looked up and cocked his head, but when Mara smiled at him, he went back to eating.

She reached out and took her aunt's hands. Lil had aged a decade since Mara had gotten sick, and somehow, Mara hadn't noticed until just now. Her aunt was doing too much: shopping, driving Mara to appointments, even cleaning her house.

Forcing lightness into her voice, she told Lil everything. Including how the wolf had chased the man away. "I can't explain it, but he's not normal. I think he understands me, and he's definitely been domesticated somehow." The wolf finished his breakfast and padded over to sit next to Mara. He watched Lillian keenly, but his body was relaxed and calm and he laid his head on Mara's thigh.

Lillian glared at her. "You're movin' in with me. You're not stayin' here another night."

"Um, no. I feel better today than I have in months. And this is my home. I'm staying until I can't take care of myself any longer."

"You do look better," Lillian mused. "Look. I'm not happy about him," she said, gesturing to the wolf. "But as long as you don't expect me to take him in when..."

"When I die. You can say it, you know. I've accepted it. Despite my little outburst at Thanksgiving. Sometimes I think I'm the only one who has."

Lillian shifted in her chair, staring into Mara's backyard. "You're so your mama's daughter. That was her way, you know. That directness. Fine. As long as I don't have to take him in when you die, I can't stop you. But if he ends up attackin' you and killin' you, I'm gonna come hunt you down in the afterlife and kick your ass."

Mara laughed. She wrapped her arm around the wolf and leaned down to whisper in his ear. "You'll win her over."

As the nurse pressed a bandage to her arm, Dr. Pendergast ducked his head through the door of the transfusion center. "Mara? Can we talk for a couple of minutes?"

Oh, shit. This can't be good.

Lillian held her hand as they followed the doctor to his office and sat across from him.

He pulled out a sheet of paper and passed it to Mara. "I don't know how to explain it, but your red blood cell count improved this week. Not by a lot, but this is the first improvement we've seen since this all started."

Mara grinned. "Ever since I got back from Orcas, I've felt better."

"How long has this been going on? This feeling better?" The doctor scribbled in her chart and arched a brow at her.

"Two days before Thanksgiving. I went for a couple of long swims and then, I sort of adopted a dog." Mara blushed and looked sheepishly at Lillian. The older woman huffed out a breath, but said nothing. "When I feel bad now, it's truly horrible, like I can barely focus, but as long as I stay hydrated and relax, I feel better than I have in a few months."

"Well, whatever you've been doing, keep it up. Unless you feel you need it, let's try to go a full seven days before you come back in, okay?"

"You got it!" Her cheeks ached from the width of her smile, and she felt lighter than she had in weeks. She was going to buy the wolf some filet mignon on her way home. Maybe she'd buy enough for both of them.

Cade

He paced. Where was Mara? She helped ease the fire burning him from the inside out. He didn't know why he was in so much pain. Flashes of the bad woman screaming, memories of scorching earth, freezing water...

Charm. Werewolf. Elemental.

More words floated in and out of his consciousness with every passing day. What had started as a single word—beautiful—had turned into fragmented thoughts and broken sentences.

Every time Mara spoke to him, a little more of the *man* he used to be bled through.

He paced until exhaustion covered him like a blanket and he curled up on the couch to wait for her.

She came home with two bags of groceries, and the older woman who'd been with her earlier helped her put everything away. The wolf stretched out on the living room floor at Mara's feet while the two of them watched a movie.

The other woman kept looking at him warily, but once she left, Mara fed him something delicious—something even better than he'd had for breakfast—and scratched him behind the ears. He liked it when she did that.

That night, she patted the bed and draped her arm around his side. For a long time, she talked to him. Told him about her doctor's visit, about the call she'd received from the police. They'd caught the man who broke in, and he was in jail now.

The wolf felt more like a man when Mara talked to him, even though so many of the words were still gibberish.

Someday, he hoped he'd be able to hold her in his arms. Talk to her. Tell her how much she meant to him.

He'd never tell her about chasing the man who'd tried to hurt her though. Or let her know how close he'd come to killing him.

But he'd known, somehow, that Mara wouldn't have wanted him to do that, so he'd released the man and started to run. No longer starving and injured, he'd relished in the power he felt pushing himself to his body's limits.

Miles had passed, the sun had started to rise, and he'd realized he had no idea where he was. Then, he'd panicked. He needed Mara. Needed her more than he needed his next breath.

It had taken him hours to retrace his steps, and when he'd picked up the scents he associated with her house and yard, he'd cried in relief.

The wolf rested his head on his paws as Mara's breathing evened out and she fell asleep. Her element seeped into him and eased some of the pain from the fire that held him prisoner.

He had to figure out how to tell her. She could free him. He was sure of it.

Mara

She'd lasted six days. But the night she brought home a small tree and spent the early evening decorating it, everything changed. The ornaments felt like they weighed ten pounds each.

The Christmas music helped—a little—but after the last ornament was hung, she sank down onto the couch and let the wolf hop up next to her. He whined and sniffed her neck.

"You know I don't feel well, don't you?" Mara asked. He yipped at her in agreement. "You're more communicative than my last boyfriend. Of course, he was an asshole, so that's not hard. Some days, I think you're more man than wolf."

His head snapped up and he barked, loudly, before jumping off the couch and pacing back and forth. Mara frowned. "That was a new sound. What was that for?"

His desperate whines and barks worried her, and Mara tried to stand, but her knees buckled.

"Oh, shit. I'm sicker than I thought." Tears started to burn her eyes, and she rested her head in her hands until the room stopped spinning. Wheezing breaths sawed in and out of her chest.

I have to lie down.

Static filled her ears. It started as a whisper, then built up until it was all she could hear. Her thoughts were thicker than molasses. Bracing her hands on her coffee table, she pushed to her feet. But after a single step, she toppled over, only missing the sharp corner by a fraction of an inch.

The wolf ran to her side, sniffed her face, and whimpered. A nudge of her hand, a paw to her shoulder, his cold nose against her forehead.

Mara wrapped her arms around his chest. The roar in her ears turned into a single note, then a second, then a third.

The song. The one she'd heard on and off for months.

"I don't want to die," she whispered, and the wolf's whines grew louder.

He struggled to his feet, bringing Mara up to her knees with him. After a quick glance back at her, he made a low sound in his throat, then took a step towards her bedroom.

He was *helping* her.

They shuffled carefully, slowly, until they made it to the bed. Mara didn't bother getting undressed—she couldn't have even if she'd wanted to—and fell onto the mattress.

The wolf lay down next to her, and Mara buried her face in his fur. He smelled like the outdoors, like her Christmas tree, and like...strength.

The pounding in Mara's head lessened, but it felt like something inside her was itching to escape. Her palms were clammy, and a sheen of sweat broke out on her brow. She was so cold.

Tremors wracked her body, and her tears soaked into the wolf's pelt. He made a surprised sound and licked her arm.

Mara rolled away and reached for her phone. She had to call Adam. Or 911. The phone slipped from her hand, landing with a crack before clattering halfway across the room. It might as well have been a mile.

I can't die like this. Alone.

She moaned softly, too dizzy to move.

"You'll be too tired to get out of bed. Then you'll be too tired to stay awake."

The doctor's words came back to haunt her, and she cried harder. It wasn't supposed to be this fast.

The wolf licked her hand, and she turned back to him. She wasn't alone. But he would be. Soon.

"Do me a favor," she whispered. "When they come—whoever comes—be nice. Or...run. Don't let them lock you up."

The wolf growled a sound she thought might be a "no" and leapt off the bed to retrieve the phone. He carried it in his jaws and dropped it next to her.

The room spun, but an insistent bark helped her focus. He jumped back up onto the bed and pressed to her side.

Animals knew, didn't they? When a person was going to die?

Mara wrapped her arms around him. "Don't leave me," she sobbed. He shook his head and snuggled closer, and if this were the end, at least she knew she was with an animal that loved her.

Seconds, minutes, maybe even an hour later, Mara jerked and the ground rushed up to meet her. The impact jarred her entire body, sending pain through her hip, her shoulder, and the back of her head.

The air was heavy and moist in her bedroom, the only faint light coming from the street lamp outside. It smelled like rain. Had she left the window open?

A strange clicking sound from the bed distracted her from the odd humidity and the dampness covering her palms.

Why am I on the floor?

It took her several deep breaths before she started to wonder more than that. Why wasn't she dead? She felt good. Well, other than the bruises. And the low-grade confusion.

Her headache was gone. Her hands were steady. Mara got to her knees, not trusting her legs to support her, but they did— without any protest.

I was dying. I know I was.

A piece of shattered plastic dug into the ball of her foot. Her broken phone. She hadn't imagined it. Panic tightened in her chest. She needed her wolf.

"Bud? Where are you?" Mara asked as she flicked on her bedside lamp and froze. "Oh, my God!"

On her bed, curled in a fetal position, was a naked, shivering man.

12

Mara

SHE WATCHED the man for several seconds, too shocked to move or speak. Deep scars and burns crisscrossed his toned back. A mane of hair—an odd mix of straw and granite—fell in gentle waves past the nape of his neck.

A mass of corded strength, he had his arms wrapped around his knees and his face buried in her pillow. His teeth chattered, and his entire body trembled violently.

What the hell? That can't be...my wolf?

Except it had to be. The animal was gone, and where else would the man have come from. But how? Werewolves weren't...*real.*

He hadn't moved outside of the shaking, and Mara risked crawling onto the bed. Reaching out, she touched his shoulder. He flinched and cried out, a mournful, pained, and fearful sound.

"Shh. I'm not going to hurt you. Can you move?"

He didn't answer her, but with his teeth chattering so badly, she wasn't sure he *could.*

"Hang on. Let me turn on the electric blanket. Get you warm."

Mara stretched over the naked man to reach the control switch. Her shirt rode up and the bare skin of her waist brushed the man's arm.

The longing sound that escaped his throat made her heart hurt, and she spun the blanket's dial to the maximum.

"I'm going to help you under the blanket now. Relax."

Slowly, Mara slid her hands under his calves, feeling the hard muscles. He was solid, and she lifted his legs enough to pull a corner of the blanket out from under them.

Little by little, she maneuvered his thighs, his hips. She stammered out an apology when she reached his ass, but he didn't seem to notice or care. He was too busy shaking.

Once he was completely under the blanket, Mara sat back on her heels. But after a few minutes, he was still trembling, maybe even more violently than before.

I can't believe I'm doing this.

She draped her own body around his, and he shuddered. Moisture coated her fingertips, and she brushed a lock of hair away from his face.

The tremors slowed.

"Arr...ra?" His hoarse whisper shocked her.

"I'm right here."

He tensed as if he wanted to move, but after a breath, he let his body go limp with a quiet keening sound.

"What do you need? Should I call a doctor?"

The man shook his head and grunted, then hissed a breath between chapped, firm lips. Mara checked his pulse—rapid, but still strong. His skin was cool, his forehead clammy.

"Food?"

After a small nod, he relaxed.

The half of his face she could see was handsome with a strong cheekbone and a light coating of stubble along his jaw. His eyes were closed, and long lashes fluttered.

Mara inhaled deeply. He smelled like her wolf. *I'm losing my mind. There's no way this can be real.*

She pulled away, and he moaned quietly. "I'm coming back. I promise," Mara said as she stroked his arm. "Maybe I'm in the hospital in a coma and this is all some drugged up dream. Either that or the afterlife is some psycho trip."

Staring at the inside of her fridge, she froze with indecision. Broth. That was a safe bet. She poured the chicken stock into a pot, then searched her pantry. Rosemary, cayenne, and oregano would work. Lillian had taught her all about the medicinal properties of herbs one particularly hot summer Mara had spent sick in bed as a teenager.

While the broth simmered, she leaned against the counter and watched the man in her bed. Every few minutes, he shuddered with a hoarse, weak cry, but otherwise, he didn't move.

By the time the broth was ready, he'd managed to turn over with the blanket bunched around his hips. A light dusting of flaxen hair sprinkled over his muscular chest and chiseled abs.

He sniffed the air and his eyes opened. Bright, ice blue orbs stared at her, flecked with hints of gold. The tendons in his neck strained as he tried to sit up, but he grunted and fell back onto the mattress with a frustrated growl.

"Relax. I'll help you." She set the large mug down on the nightstand, climbed onto the bed next to him, and settled against the headboard. "Let's get you sitting up."

He leaned against her, relaxing and turning his head towards her neck. When his chapped lips brushed her skin, a tremor raced down her spine.

Mara picked up the mug and held it to his lips. He drank it all, and she refilled it twice before he laid his head on her shoulder and closed his eyes.

"Hey," Mara said softly. "What do you need now? Rest?"

The man nodded, and she helped him lie down, tucking the blankets around his body. Pain filled the depths of his gaze, and the corners of his eyes crinkled. He worked his jaw open and shut a few times, but didn't make another sound until Mara started to ease herself off the bed.

"St-a-ay," he managed.

The hoarse sound was full of longing, and she cracked a weak smile. "Well, seeing as you're in my bed..." He stared up at her, his gaze pleading, and Mara swallowed hard. "I don't understand any of this. I know you're my wolf."

He choked out a weak sob and tried to reach for her, but the blankets foiled his movements. "I won't leave," she said. "I just have to change. I'll be right back."

Mara hurried into the bathroom and splashed some water on her face. The dark circles around her eyes were gone. She was exhausted, but she felt stronger than she had in months.

After changing into her pajamas, she returned to the man in her bed. "C-c-coo..." he whispered, then groaned, frustrated.

"Cold?"

When he nodded, Mara pulled the blankets around him and brushed his hair away from his face. "No wonder I felt like you could understand me. I still think I'm probably hallucinating this whole thing, but..." She chewed on her lip for a moment, then held his uncertain gaze. "You're not going to turn back into a wolf overnight, are you?"

He shook his head as he closed his eyes, and his face relaxed into sleep almost immediately.

Before she turned off the light, she watched him. There was something so pure about him—as if he had no worries, no fears. Or perhaps he was just too exhausted to care.

He shuddered once, and then lay still. Her wolf. Her wolf wasn't a wolf. Instead, he was one of the hottest men she'd ever seen, but he could barely move or speak. What had happened to him? And who the hell was he?

MARA JERKED awake and found herself staring into the luminous blue eyes of the man in her bed.

It wasn't a dream. Holy shit. He's real.

"Um, you look better. Not so pale," she managed with a weak smile.

He glanced down at his bare chest. "Shit." The rough, deep voice was almost clear, and seemed to surprise him as much as her.

"I take it waking up with just two legs is a bit of a shock?"

Get yourself together, Mara. You need to find out what the hell is going on.

He lifted the blanket, peering down as if he wasn't sure what he'd see. Apparently satisfied, he hugged the wool to his chest. "Ma-ra?"

"Yes. But I still don't know who you are, though."

His brow furrowed, and uncertainty churned in his gaze. "Cade?"

"Cade?" Damn. The name fit him. Sexy, strong.

"Think...so."

"You don't know? How come?" She sat up, tugging her t-shirt down to cover a bit of exposed skin at her hip.

"T-too long...wolf. Mem...ries..." He worked his jaw back and forth and ran his tongue over his teeth. "Words...hard."

Frustrated, he fisted the blankets as he growled low in his throat, so many emotions in that single sound. Anger, longing, frustration.

"You, uh, don't have to talk. Not yet. Are you hungry?" She scooted to the edge of the bed, but didn't take her eyes off of him. She shouldn't trust him. But...he was her wolf. He'd protected her for over a week, had done nothing but make her feel better...

Cade nodded.

"Bacon and eggs?"

His lopsided grin warmed her down to her toes, and she

reached over to cover his hand with hers. Those blue eyes lit up, and something primal churned in their depths.

"Don't get up. I'll be back in a few minutes. If your tongue doesn't work right, I can't imagine your legs will either. Okay?"

At his rough grunt, she dashed for the kitchen, desperate to put some distance between her and the very sexy, very naked man.

Jabbing the button on the espresso machine, she urged the damn thing to heat up faster. The caffeine would help her figure all this out. At least, she hoped so.

The scent of the beans centered her, helped her focus on the one part of her life that was still normal—her coffee addiction.

She arranged the bacon on the griddle, brewed two cups of French roast, and carried one mug back to the bedroom.

Cade was sitting up, his back against the headboard, staring at his hands like he couldn't believe they were real.

"Coffee?"

"God. Yes." The words were slow, a bit awkward, but clearer. She skirted the edge of the bed and held out the mug. But when Cade just looked up at her, unsure, she took one of his hands and wrapped it around the mug, followed by the other.

"Hold. Got it?"

He nodded and raised the mug to his lips. At his first swallow, his eyelids fluttered, and a low, satisfied sound rumbled in his chest. "Missed...this."

Leaving Cade to his coffee, Mara scrambled eggs while the bacon crisped, and then returned with two plates. She sat on her cedar chest a few feet away as he struggled to close his fingers around the fork, but he watched her movements, then mirrored them.

The two ate in silence, though Cade cleaned his plate before Mara had managed even half of hers.

He worked his mouth with a hand on his jaw, and his fingers

rasped against the stubble. The silence between them grew until it was almost overwhelming.

"You helped me," he said slowly.

"How?" Mara passed him her plate, no longer hungry, so he could finish the last slice of bacon and her eggs. "This doesn't make any sense. How were you turned into a wolf?"

Cade set both plates on the nightstand. "No. Am wolf."

"What? You're *definitely* not a wolf."

"Werewolf."

Mara shrank against the wall, wrapping her arms around herself tightly. "Shit. No. Werewolves...don't exist. You can't exist."

Cade tried to sit up straighter, but failed and slumped back against her headboard. He clutched the blanket tightly. "Won't hurt you," he said. "Never. You saved me. Elemental." The last word seemed to be a struggle, and he sighed as he closed his eyes.

"What's an elemental?" Wary, Mara inched closer, finally sliding a hip onto the bed.

"You." Cade forced his eyes open and stared over her shoulder, like he couldn't find the right words. "Have, uh, water. Fire... did this...to me."

She shook her head. Despite how sincere he sounded, there was no way she was an elemental. "I think your brain is still a little addled."

"No. Not about...this."

Running a hand through her hair, Mara gave it a tug, using the light pain to try to focus her thoughts. "One of my aunt's friends does keep telling me I'm a...'water soul.'"

Cade nodded, as if that were a normal thing to hear. "You are."

"Yeah, right," she said with a snort.

"Knew when...I found you. Hid in your car. Smelled like rain." Frustration creased his brows, and though his words were clearer now, he huffed and had to try three times before he could continue. "F-fire did this. To me. The wolf. Water—you—helped me."

"How?"

"How what?" His hand went to the back of his neck, and he grabbed a fistful of hair and pulled, hard.

"How did I help you? All I remember..." She shuddered. "I thought I was going to die. You—the wolf—helped me in here. I don't think I could have gotten up off the floor without you. But after I laid down, I don't remember much of anything. I woke up when I hit the floor."

Cade shifted his legs under the blankets, grimacing. "Worried. About you. Humid. Then, ice cold. When you broke the charm. Screaming. Mine. Power was over-wh-whelming."

Her chest tightened. "No. This doesn't make any sense. I'm in a coma somewhere. Werewolves aren't real. Neither are elementals. There has to be another explanation."

Cade shot her a look that said, *"Really? And that would be?"*

"Shit. What am I supposed to do now?"

With a hard swallow, Cade stared down at his hands in his lap. "Help me? I need to, uh, get up. Move. Remember how...to walk...on two legs. And—" He glanced at the bathroom door and his cheeks flushed a deep red. "Um. You know..."

"Oh." Mara approached warily, and Cade swung his legs over the side of the bed, still clutching the blankets tightly to his waist. Mara was suddenly very aware that he was naked, and her own cheeks caught fire. "Wait. You need clothes."

Rummaging in her closet, she came back with her old robe. It was all stretched out and at least three sizes too big for her. While it would certainly be too small for Cade, she didn't have anything else.

He needed help getting his left arm into the sleeve, but managed the right on his own. When he tried to fumble with the belt, though, he failed, and a frustrated growl built in his throat.

Mara slid her fingers over his. "Let me."

Once she was convinced he was covered well enough, she draped his arm over her shoulder and helped him to his feet. He swayed against her, but steadied after a few shuddering breaths.

The trip across the room and to the bathroom door took long, stressful minutes. Each step seemed to be like running a marathon for him, but when they reached the threshold, Cade withdrew his arm from her shoulders. "Can manage."

Oh, thank God.

Leaning against the wall, she tried and failed to make any sense of what had happened. If she hadn't *known* she'd passed out holding the wolf, she'd never have believed anything that had happened since.

Cade had to be insane. *She* had to be insane. Maybe everything she'd seen the past few weeks had been conjured by her dying mind. But that didn't explain Adam and Lil seeing the wolf.

The door opened, and Cade leaned against the bathroom counter. She draped his arm over her shoulders again and they made their way out into the living room. Mara wanted him to rest on the couch, but despite breathing heavily, he didn't want to stop.

"Not yet. More."

With every step, he steadied. By the time they'd taken another loop, he was only holding her elbow for support.

"Okay. That's enough for now," Mara said as she guided Cade into one of her well-worn chairs.

"Food helped. Coffee too. Shit. Having a human mouth again feels so weird." His words were still slow, but at least now they were clear.

"A complete sentence. That's another improvement." She made them both more coffee, then sat down across from him.

"You saved my life." Cade took a sip of coffee, searching for his next words. "The wolf...he was dying. *I* was dying inside of him."

"How does it work? The two of you. You're separate? Where is the wolf now?" Mara chewed on her lower lip, both desperate to know and not wanting to at the same time.

"He's inside. Not caged. Not trapped. He just...*is*. When he takes over, I'm the one inside. Not trapped. Not before all...this."

Mara took a few seconds to process Cade's words, watching his movements. His eyes. "You remember when he was in control?"

"Some. My brain feels like Swiss cheese. More holes than memories." He grinned. "I remember seeing you before I got into your car. Nice bikini."

Choking on her coffee, she blushed. "Orcas Island."

"Shit. I was so close." He seemed to deflate, and Mara ached to touch him.

"What is it?"

"My pack. The other werewolves I was responsible for. Pretty sure they're all dead. The woman who did this to me killed them." He drained his mug and stood up, wavered for a minute, and then shuffled over to the sliding glass door.

Pressing his fist to his chest, he winced, then took a deep, shuddering breath. "I shouldn't stay here any longer. I don't want to put you in danger. I need clothes. If she finds me here, she'll kill us both."

"She?" Mara followed him, stopping a few feet away.

"A fire elemental. She's the one who trapped me as my wolf. She explained how, but I can't remember. It hurt. All the time." His voice cracked. "I felt like my blood was boiling."

"Who is this woman?" She risked laying her hand on Cade's shoulder. He leaned into her touch for a moment, closing his eyes.

"No one you ever want to meet. Please, Mara." Cade turned and took her hands. "You saved my life. You stopped the man from euthanizing me. You fed me when I couldn't even move." With a sigh, he shook his head. "There's a lot—even from the past few days—that's still a blur, but I know you saved me. Help me disappear. I need clothes. Maybe a hundred bucks so I can get a bus ticket and some food for a day or two."

Cade's grip was strong, and the heat from his body rolled over her. Under the flannel, the muscles of his chest flexed and his biceps strained against the sleeves. He stared at her Christmas tree. "She trapped me back in summer. It's been *months*. I couldn't stand it if she found me here and hurt you."

Mara tightened her grip on his fingers. "She'll have to hurry. I'll probably be dead in a month."

"What?" Cade's voice came out rough, a growl that sent chills down Mara's spine.

"I'm dying, Cade."

13

Cade

HE PULLED Mara over to the sofa. Confusion twisted in his gut and he couldn't let go of her hands if his life depended on it. "Explain."

Mara shrugged and leaned back against the cushions. Her voice took on a hint of exhaustion. "I've been sick for a while. My blood doesn't carry oxygen like it should. You knew it—when you were a wolf. Every time I started to feel worse, you'd whine and you wouldn't leave my side."

Cade stared down at their linked fingers. "The wolf operates on instinct. Short-term memories are the strongest." He let his eyes unfocus, staring out the window into Mara's backyard. He remembered sniffing around the fence. Marking his territory. "Last night, I was scared. You fell. Most of the rest of it is fuzzy. But you didn't smell right."

"Well, that's...the strangest thing anyone's ever said to me," she said with a little laugh. Her smile lit up the room, and he wanted to see it every day. "You made me feel better. When I touched you, whatever's wrong with me faded a little."

Cade narrowed his eyes and brought her hand to his nose. Inhaling deeply, he frowned. "You don't smell sick now. You're balanced. Like spring rain."

"Good to know." She laughed again. "But whatever this reprieve is...it's temporary."

"You're not sick," he insisted.

"You want to see my medical file? Talk to my doctor?" She jerked her hand away and glared at him.

A fiercely possessive flash of emotion twisted his heart in a vise. "Yes."

"Cade—"

"How do you feel now?" he asked.

"Fine. Better than fine. I haven't felt this good in months. But it won't last. It never does."

"You're not sick. I'd know." *And I'd fix it.* His thoughts started to muddle, exhaustion weighing him down and chills wracking his body.

"Cade? Are you okay?" Mara curled her fingers around his arm and leaned closer.

"Cold," Cade said. "Tired. Not used to this body."

Taking the blanket from the back of the couch, she wrapped it around him. "You need clothes. There's a Target right up the road. If I go shopping, will you promise me you won't leave before I get back?"

A hint of a smile quirked his lips. "I promise. I'd rather not get arrested for indecent exposure."

Mara handed him a pad of paper and a pen. "Write down your sizes for me while I take a quick shower and get dressed."

HE SAT on the couch for a long time, holding the pen and trying to remember how to write in anything other than chicken scratch. He wore a size twelve shoe, but that's all he could remember.

He'd been so scared the night before. Her element had seeped into his pelt, cooling and soothing him. And then...pain. Agony. Howling that turned into screaming.

Thoughts hadn't formed until Mara had talked to him. Her touch calmed his frantic mind, and even though he still hadn't understood all the words and could barely answer her, she'd known what he'd needed.

Glancing down the hall, he ached for her to come back. Nothing felt right without her next to him. His muscles trembled from simply sitting up, and he was hungry again. Starving, actually. And so very tired.

When Mara emerged from the bathroom wearing jeans and a soft green sweater, he offered her the paper, his hands trembling. "I don't remember."

"It's okay. Come with me." Mara took his hand and led him back into the bedroom. After rummaging in her dresser, she came away with a flexible measuring tape. "Arms up." The tape wound around his waist, and she hummed. "Twenty-nine. Skinny one, aren't you?"

"She starved me," he whispered. "If you hadn't been there, I don't think I would have lasted another few hours."

"Well, then, maybe a larger size and a belt for you. And some chocolate."

She took all of his measurements and had him write them down. Every letter and number was easier than the last, but there were still so many things he'd forgotten. Like the evil woman's name.

Mara tucked the paper into her pocket, but before she could leave the room, he grabbed her wrist. "How far are we from where you found me?"

"We're in Seattle. Three hours or so. Ninety minutes by ferry and the same by car. Why?"

Uncertainty roughened his voice. "The elemental who did this to me...I don't know where she is. What if—?"

"Target is less than two miles away. I'll be back in under an hour. Besides, how would she even find you?" She angled a glance at him like he was being ridiculous, but Cade shook his head.

"I don't know. But that's the problem. *I don't know.*"

Mara smiled, and his heart skipped a beat. She wore no makeup, and her red hair tumbled loose and long over her shoulders. The scoop neck of her sweater exposed a creamy expanse of skin and a wire-wrapped crystal rested in the delicate hollow of her throat. He stared at it, seeing the swirling colors of the sea after a storm. Unable to stop himself, he stepped closer.

"I...don't go."

Mara rested her hand over his heart. His fingers still curled around her wrist. "Relax, Cade. You can't live in my old robe, and you certainly can't leave wearing it. My hot water heater is amazing. Take a long shower. It'll warm you up and make you feel better. When I get back, we'll figure out what to do next, okay?"

"I don't like this."

Mara turned, picked up the pad of paper and pen, and scrawled a series of numbers on the top sheet. "You remember phones?"

"Um, yes. I think so."

"That's my cell. If you need anything, call. I can be back here in ten minutes." Running her fingers over Cade's hair and then cupping the back of his neck, she leaned in slightly, and the impulse to kiss her was so strong. But she just touched her forehead to his. "Relax. There's no way she'll be able to find you here."

NOTHING MADE SENSE TO HIM. Least of all his own thoughts and emotions. He shivered and headed for Mara's bathroom.

Cade barely recognized his own body. At least a dozen new scars covered his torso, legs, and back. His hair was longer than he remembered, and his cheeks were almost hollow. But the face that stared back at him in the mirror was vaguely familiar.

By the time the hot water had started to cool, his body felt less foreign, and he smelled like Mara's soap, which comforted him. But after he dried off and wrapped himself in Mara's robe again, his stomach growled insistently, and tremors wracked his body. He needed more food and rest. With a single longing look at Mara's bed, he trudged out to the living room and wrapped himself in the blanket on the couch. Within minutes, he was asleep.

Mara

When Mara pulled into her driveway an hour later, Jen was just getting off her scooter in front of the house.

"Hey, Mar. It's Senior Cut day. Are you headed to the hospital? I thought I could drive you and we could grab lunch after. I want to try that new Mexican place on the west side of the lake."

"I..." *Shit. I forgot all about my transfusion appointment.* "Um, I can't have lunch with you today," she said as she juggled her purse, her keys, and the bag of clothing.

Jen reached for the bag and gaped. "What the hell?" She withdrew a four-pack of boxer briefs and waved them in front of Mara's face.

"Give me those," Mara snapped.

"Nu-huh. Not until you tell me why the hell you have these. You're *sick*, Mara."

"Don't you think I know that?" Her voice rose an octave and

took on a defensive tone. "Hand over the underwear. What I do with those is my own business."

"If you're seeing someone, it's definitely my business. You didn't say anything to me at lunch the other day. Did you pick up some guy off the street? And what? You're buying him clothes now?" Jen jammed her hands on her hips and narrowed her eyes at Mara. "I know you've checked out already, but that doesn't mean the rest of us are going to give up on you. Don't be stupid and reckless."

Her retort was on the tip of her tongue when her front door swung open. Cade drew himself up to his full height, still wrapped in her purple robe, his blue eyes smoldering. "Are you all right?" he demanded.

Jen's jaw hung open, and Mara took the opportunity to snatch the underwear from her hand. "I'm fine. Jen was just leaving."

"I—no. I wasn't." Jen sidestepped Mara. "You know she's dying, right? She's supposed to be taking it easy. Who the hell are you and why is she buying you underwear?"

"She's not dying. She might have been before, but she's not now," Cade said firmly.

"Because I'm not here at all," Mara muttered. "You—" she slapped Cade in the chest with the package of boxer briefs, "— take these." Turning to Jen, she drew in a deep breath. "And you? Go home. If you tell Aunt Lil, Lisa, or Adam about him, I'm personally writing you out of my will and I know you want my espresso machine. We'll talk *later*. Like tomorrow. Or Sunday. Until then, you're going to treat me like the adult that I am."

"Mara, he's hot and all, but don't sacrifice what little life you have left for a one-night fuck. You know the doctor doesn't even want you *driving*, let alone banging some random guy."

Cade growled and took Mara's arm. "I don't know who you are, lady, but where I come from, friends don't speak to one another like that." He pulled Mara against him, his abs shaking, but he kept his voice strong. "Don't expect me to stand here and let you insult her."

"Who do you think you are, jerkwad? I'm her best friend—"

"He lives across the street," Mara said quickly. "And there was...uh..."

"My roommates are assholes," Cade said. "Mara let me sleep on her couch last night."

"I'm not *banging* him," Mara snapped. "But even if I were, I wouldn't need your permission. Go home."

Jen's cheeks turned bright red, and Mara couldn't believe Cade had come up with that half-assed excuse so quickly. Against her back, his abs shook with the effort of merely standing, and she let him lean against her.

"What about the hospital?" Jen asked.

"I can drive myself. I'll call you tomorrow." Mara backed Cade into the house, keeping her arm tight around his waist. As soon as she'd set both the deadbolt and the chain, she helped him back to the couch where he half-fell, half-sank onto the cushions.

Dark circles braced his bloodshot eyes, and Mara pressed her fingers to his neck and checked her watch. His pulse was racing, and his skin clammy.

"What's wrong?"

"Hungry. Shifting takes a lot of energy."

Mara kicked herself for not feeding him more before she left. "Can you get yourself dressed while I make you a sandwich? Or do you need help?"

"Can manage. In a minute. Who was that?" Cade closed his eyes and let Mara intertwine their fingers. His thumb dragged back and forth over the inside of her wrist, soothing her.

"Jen's my best friend."

Cade stifled a snort. "Have any enemies I should know about, then?"

Sinking back next to him, she let her head rest against his. "I know. She's not usually that bad. They're just overprotective."

"They?" He tightened his fingers on hers.

"Jen, my Aunt Lillian, Adam, and Lisa. They take turns bringing me to my transfusions. And pretty sure each of them has insisted I move in with them at least twice in the past month or so. But I like being on my own. They'd smother me to death while trying to keep me from dying."

Mara laughed at her own joke, but Cade growled and sat up straighter. "You're *not* dying."

She didn't bother protesting. He was so adamant, but Mara knew better. She'd have her blood test today and she knew what the doctor would find.

"Come on. Get dressed, and I'll make you all the sandwiches you can eat."

Cade

He didn't want to let go of Mara's hand, but when she dumped the bag out onto the bed, the sight of actual clothing staggered him.

"Too much," he managed over the lump in his throat. He'd never take basic necessities like shelter, food, or his humanity for granted again.

"It's Target. And I don't really need to worry about money right now," she muttered, almost as an afterthought. "If anything doesn't fit, let me know. You okay with grilled cheese?"

"Yes." Cade snagged her wrist and held on tight. "Honey, I can't repay you for this." The term of endearment slipped out before he realized it, but he liked the way it sounded. Honey.

Mara blushed. "I didn't ask you to. Now get dressed. That robe doesn't exactly fit you."

When she left the room, he stared down at his body. *Shit.* His dick tented the soft purple cloth. Being so close to his beautiful Mara was too much when he was still so weak.

She's not mine.

The reality slammed into him, and he sank down onto her bed, all his lustful thoughts shuttered in a heartbeat. A flash of memory hit him. The bad woman had someone with her. A young man with control of the earth. Cade wracked his brain for more, pressing his fists against his eyes, but though he could almost see them, almost hear their voices, he didn't know their names.

He hated all these holes in his memory. The wolf thought in images, operated on instinct. Add in the fire charm, the starvation, and the isolation, and most of his thoughts from his time trapped inside his beast were nothing more than wisps slipping through his fingers.

14

Cade

THE CLOTHES FELT good against his skin. Reassuring. Normal. He had trouble with the buttons on the flannel shirt, but forced his fingers to obey and push the small pieces of plastic through the holes.

Thank God the shoes didn't have laces to maneuver. As he reached the hallway, he stumbled, and Mara caught him when his knee buckled.

"Sit down. I think you've had enough of being upright for a while." She led him back to the couch and eased him down. "Grilled cheese and tomato soup coming right up."

Less than two minutes later, she sat down next to him with food that smelled so good, he almost moaned. He didn't care that the soup was probably out of a can.

Mara picked at her own sandwich, her green eyes flicking to him often.

"Ask," he said between bites.

"How did you, um, become a werewolf?" She seemed to

shrink back against the couch cushions as she worried the hem of her sweater.

"I was born one. A lot of us are. Some...if a person is bitten during the full moon, they can turn."

Mara's lower lip trembled slightly. "Look, I believe you. The wolf was with me, I fell off the bed, and then you were there. But I feel like I'm losing my mind. Werewolves and elementals? Are witches and vampires real too?"

"Yes."

Mara choked on a sip of water. "Really?"

"I can turn into a wolf at will," he said simply, though the very idea of ever giving his beast control again made him so nauseous he wasn't sure he could finish eating. "Why are vampires so hard to believe in?"

Mara set her plate down. She'd made him two sandwiches, and he'd finished everything while she'd barely managed two bites.

Cade leaned over and returned the plate to her lap. "Eat. You look like you're wasting away."

"I haven't had much of an appetite lately. Or any energy to cook." She tore off a small piece of the grilled cheese and shoved it into her mouth. "Happy?"

"No." Dammit. He wanted—needed—to take care of her. Cade watched her until the sandwich was gone, set down his empty plate and strode back into her bedroom. When he came back, he had three of the chocolate bars she'd bought him.

Mara rolled her eyes but accepted one of the bars. Not until they'd finished every bite did his lips quirk. "Now, I'm happy."

"You sound like Adam."

Cade stifled his growl. Adam had wanted to euthanize him, and even though he probably would have euthanized a wolf in his condition too, he didn't want this Adam anywhere near his Mara.

"I don't like him. Why are you with him? And where the hell

is he?" Cade clenched his fists on his thighs. He wanted to tell Mara he didn't want her around Adam again, but he didn't have any claim on her.

"Oh, God." Mara slapped her hand over her mouth, but the laugh escaped anyway. "I'm not *with* Adam. He's been married to Lisa for ten years. They have two little girls: six and four. He's a vet down at the equestrian center. Plus...he's not my type. Way too high strung."

"There's...no one else?"

A blush tinged her cheeks the most amazing color. "No. Dating's too hard when you can't stay awake for more than a few hours at a time. And the whole dying thing? It's kind of a buzzkill."

Cade frowned. "You're not—"

"Enough. You can tell me I'm not dying until you're blue in the face, but that's not going to make it true. So while I still feel good, we should figure out what you're going to do now."

"I need to go." Picking up the dishes, Cade carried them into the kitchen and started to wash them.

"Where?"

"I don't know. Somewhere I can be alone. Find a job. Start over." The act of cleaning the plates kept his hands busy and distracted him from thoughts of leaving Mara. He'd need to rest again soon.

He couldn't ask her for anything else, even though he was still hungry. She'd been so kind to him. If she agreed, he'd sleep another few hours, then run. His pack was gone—as was his family back in Barstow. At least he thought they were. Those memories were still fuzzy.

"Cade?" Mara touched his arm, and her warmth seeped through the flannel shirt. "Where'd you go?"

"Trying to think. It's...hard. My brain isn't working right yet."

"And you think leaving is a good idea? What's your last name? Do you know how to buy a bus ticket? Make change? Do you remember how much a hotel room should cost? What are you going to do if you run into the woman who did this to you?"

Cade shut the water off and dried his hands on his jeans. "I know my last name," he muttered, staring down at his feet. "The rest is pretty fuzzy."

Her green eyes filled with understanding, and she offered him her hand. "Come sit down with me. I'm not sending you out into the world like this. Let's see if we can fill in some of these holes in your head."

Being close to Mara on the couch was pure torture. Her scent was intoxicating. Almond blossoms, coconut, spring rain... He knew those scents—could pick out each of them by name.

"Last name?" Mara asked, pulling him out of his thoughts as she picked up her laptop.

"Bowman." His gaze locked onto her lips.

"You lived in Bellingham."

"Yes." Leaning closer, Cade took a deep breath, letting her scent wrap around him and soothe his beast.

"Oh, God." She clicked on a newspaper article from May.

Cade Bowman, local artist and woodworker, has been presumed dead by the Bellingham Police Department after his apartment building collapsed and burned over the weekend. None of the building's residents have been located, and investigators believe the intense heat of the blaze destroyed any identifiable remains. Liam O'Sullivan, Peter Shea, Olivia Parker-Grantham, Shawn Grantham, Christine Smart, and Oliver Case were all registered tenants of the building and are presumed dead.

Oliver Case served as the Whatcom County Sheriff for the past eight years while Liam O'Sullivan ran Build It Construction. A neighbor, Margaret Othello, reported seeing a dark-haired woman in the street shortly before the building caught fire, but the woman has yet to be identified. Anyone with information on the origins of the fire should contact the Bellingham Police Department.

Cade stared at the screen until it blurred, then wiped a tear from his cheek. His pack. Gone.

"Who were those other people?" Mara's soft voice and her warm hand on his thigh sent another tear spilling over.

"My family. I think...they were all my pack. I can't see their faces, but I *know* them. Liam was my beta. Livie. She was mated to Shawn."

"What about blood relatives? Your mother and father? Are they alive?" Mara arched a brow. "What were their names?"

"No. They died a long time ago. I can't...I..." Cade dropped his head into his hands. "I don't want to remember."

When Mara wrapped her arms around him, he couldn't stop himself from holding onto her like she was the only thing anchoring him to this life—this world. Maybe she was. He didn't have anyone else.

"Mara." Cade started shaking. How could he leave her? She was his whole world.

"It'll be okay," she crooned as she ran her hands up and down his back. "Take a deep breath. You're safe here."

His wolf wanted her. The beast reared up, demanding to be heard, but Cade shook his head and pulled away.

"Tell me about Liam." Mara searched for his name and found a photo from his obituary. Reddish hair brushed his shoulders and his eyes were full of sadness and pain. They'd always been like that. Another memory bubbled to the surface.

"Yer goin' to want to be there. I'm puttin' ya' up for alpha."

Liam had told him that the day Mike—their former alpha—had been killed.

"He's—he was—a good man. We used to have beers after work. He liked to bowl." A smile tugged at his lips. "But he was terrible at it."

Mara chuckled. "Sounds like me back in college. Want to keep going?"

"Yeah."

She brought up pictures of Livie, Shawn, and Ollie before Cade's eyelids started to droop and then they were suddenly too heavy for him to even keep open. He turned towards Mara and rested her head on her shoulder.

"Cade? What's wrong?" Her panicked voice squeezed his heart, and he tried to respond, but he couldn't manage the energy. His abs trembled from the effort of merely breathing.

"Cade!"

"R-rest," he grunted.

Her relief seeped into him, and when she draped his arm around her shoulders, he leaned heavily on her and let her help him back to her bed. After she'd removed his shoes, she reached for the button of his jeans, but he stopped her.

"Don't be ridiculous," she said. "I'm a nurse. Well, I *was* a nurse anyway. And you were naked in this bed last night."

His cheeks flushed hot, but he let her help him with the jeans. At least he managed the shirt on his own. Left in only the boxer briefs, he curled onto his side, hoping she wouldn't see his dick straining against the cotton.

Being this close to her with her hands on his skin was driving him mad. She smelled so good. Like she was his—only his.

"I'm sorry," he whispered as she tucked the blankets around him.

"For?"

"My body isn't used to its human form. I haven't had to walk on two legs or breathe with these lungs in months."

"Cade, you were mostly dead ten days ago. You're going to be weak for a while." She smiled and rested her palm flat against his heart. "You need to stay. At least for a night or two. Until you get your strength back."

"One night. We heal quickly—werewolves do." His eyelids drooped. He was so tired.

"We'll see about that. I have to go to the doctor for some blood work and run a few errands. All I've got in my fridge is eggnog, grilled cheese fixings, and the meat for your wolf. But if you feel like getting up, help yourself to anything I have. I'll be back in a few hours and we'll do some more work on your memories. I'll cook you dinner tonight, and the rest...we'll figure it out."

Cade closed his eyes and nodded. As he drifted off to sleep, he felt Mara's tender caress against his cheek.

Mine.

15

Mara

Thoughts of Cade consumed her the entire drive to the hospital. She'd felt such a connection to the wolf—like he'd understood her in a way no one else had. Now that he could speak, that feeling had only intensified.

Her heart ached for what he'd been through. Seven months. She couldn't imagine how awful it had been to be trapped as an animal for so long. Had he known? The time he'd spent with her as a wolf, had he been trying to tell her who he was the whole time?

She didn't want him to leave—if for no other reason than she felt better around him. But it would be ridiculous for him to stay. He'd had a life before.

Shit. I never even asked if he was married.

Though, in his current state of confusion, Mara figured he might not know.

By the time she'd given three vials of blood to the lab, crossed the skybridge to the medical offices, and changed into the thin, paper exam gown, her mood had soured. Dark clouds obscured the winter sun outside the high windows of Dr. Pendergast's office, and she scowled at them. She couldn't help feeling like the Universe was foreshadowing something. Maybe the news that she was getting worse—despite how good she felt.

After two raps on the door, Dr. Pendergast breezed in. "How are you feeling today, Mara?"

"Great. Really. I haven't felt this good in months."

The doctor raised a brow, but then almost did a double-take. "You look better. Your color's improved." He palpated her lymph nodes, listened to her heart and lungs, and went through the usual litany of tests and measurements.

"Your nail beds aren't blue, your heart rate is exactly where we want it to be, and the low-grade fever's even gone. What happened?" He seemed as confused as she was.

With a shrug, Mara hugged herself tightly to ward off the chill from the air vents above her. "I don't know. Last night...I think I overdid it. I barely made it to bed. I think I might have even passed out for a few minutes. But..." She chewed on her lip for a moment. There was no way she could tell the doctor about Cade. "I woke up a few hours later and I felt...normal. Good even. It's lasted all day."

The doctor stripped off his gloves and picked up the phone. "This is Benjamin Pendergast. Do you have the red blood cell count for Mara Taylor yet?" After a long pause, he continued. "Are you sure?"

Mara held her breath as he listened for another moment. "Huh. Run it again. Do the whole panel."

When he turned back to her, the look on his face was one of pure shock.

"Well?"

"Your hematocrit levels are almost normal. Everything's almost normal. So close, in fact, I want them to run the tests again." Leaning back against the counter, the doctor shook his head. "According to your test results, you're healthy."

"Shit. Really?" She wanted to laugh—or jump off the table and hug the doctor. But that...could be embarrassing.

"I want you back here on Monday for another blood sample. And *don't* overdo it this weekend. But we won't transfuse you until we get the next round of test results back."

Dr. Pendergast paused with his fingers inches from the door handle. "I don't know what made you sick in the first place, so I guess I shouldn't be surprised I don't know why you're suddenly better. But I hope this isn't a fluke."

"I'll take whatever flukes the Universe wants to give me at this point," Mara said with a smile. "Thanks, doc."

ON THE WAY to the grocery store, Mara popped an earbud in and dialed her aunt.

"Hey, Aunt Lil."

"Mara. How are you feeling today?" Her aunt sounded tired, and Mara hated that she'd had to rely on Lil for so much the past few months.

"Good. Really good, actually. But I'm not going to make it over for dinner tonight. Something...uh...came up."

"Mara...don't lie to me. You're feeling worse, aren't you? I'm coming over."

"No!" Mara pulled into a parking spot and sighed. "I'm not home, and you can't come over."

"Yer in the hospital, ain't ya'? Dammit, Mara. Yer too independent for yer own good." Aunt Lil's voice rose half an octave, and her southern drawl intensified. "Don't expect me to take care of that wolf for ya'."

"Oh, for fuck's sake. I'm fine."

"Language!" Aunt Lil snapped.

Taking a deep breath, Mara rested her head on the steering

wheel. Aunt Lil wasn't going to believe her. "My blood work came back almost normal today."

"What?" Lillian screamed.

Mara winced and pulled the earbud halfway out of her ear. "Okay, I might be deaf now. But as of today, I'm not about to die, and I have some things to take care of. But I need to ask you a couple of questions. Eleanor. She kept telling you I was a water soul. What *exactly* did she mean by that? Did she ever use the word *elemental*?"

Her aunt was quiet for so long, Mara checked the screen to make sure they were still connected. "Aunt Lil?"

"This isn't a conversation we can have over the phone."

If she rolled her eyes any harder, she feared they'd come right out of her head. "Fine. Tomorrow?"

"I'll be over at noon with sandwiches." Her aunt hung up before Mara could argue.

After going through Whole Foods in a rush, she headed home, half expecting Cade to be gone when she got there. Relief washed over her when she found him pacing her living room.

"Feeling better?"

"Trying to get my stamina back. The more I use my muscles, the better." He took the bag of groceries from her and set it on the kitchen counter. "I was worried."

The crumpled paper with Mara's cell phone number was clutched in his hand. He tucked it back into his pocket.

"I was gone all of three hours. Hospital visits are never quick. I don't know why we, as a society, allow doctors to keep us waiting forever, but—"

Cade cut her off. "What did the doctor say?"

Mara shook her head. "I don't know how to explain it. Neither does he. But at least for today, you're right. I'm not sick. My blood work came back normal." She pulled out the packages of steak and the wine, waving the bottle at him. "So we're celebrating."

Cade looked longingly at the steak and his stomach growled.

Mara tossed him one of the paper-wrapped sandwiches. "No steak until dinner. Eat these. I got you two."

He tore into the sandwich so fast she laughed. Between bites, he gave her a sheepish grin. "Werewolves eat a lot."

"Obviously. And I thought your wolf was ravenous."

"When I used to shift and run with my pack, we'd each put away a couple of pounds of meat afterwards." Cade crumpled up the first sandwich wrapper and leaned back against the counter. "Fuck. I remember the forest where we'd run. I can't see their faces, but...I can almost hear them."

Mara grinned and passed him the second sandwich. "In Bellingham?"

"Yeah." He paused before taking a bite. "I can't pay you back for this," he said.

"You can do the dishes tonight," she replied.

Despite how enthusiastically he ate, his manners were impeccable, and he didn't spill a single crumb. As he reached around her for a napkin, his hand brushed her arm, and a jolt of electricity curled her toes in her boots.

Using the tub of chocolate chip cookies as a distraction when he finished the sandwich, she took a step back. "Dessert?"

"You know how to treat a man," he said as he shoved half a cookie into his mouth.

Mara's heart melted at his lopsided smile. The left side was a little higher, a little wider than the right. His chapped lips would be rough if she kissed them. Blushing, she turned away before she could do exactly that.

"We should try to work on those holes in your memory a little." She slipped around him and headed for the couch.

Cade brought the box of cookies with him when he sat down next to her, and his scent wrapped around her, all strength and sea air and comfort.

She typed his name into Google and scrolled past the references to his death to find an article in *Seattle Magazine*.

Cade Bowman's work for the Gates Foundation has drawn frequent crowds since his death in a fire in his hometown of Bellingham. The two-story wood installation, carved from three pieces of oak felled by lightning in 2011, evokes Seattle's marine past and industrial future.

"Oh, Cade. This is gorgeous," Mara said as she clicked through the pictures accompanying the article. "You did this? By hand?"

The massive design featured waves crashing against a rocky coastline. Pike Place Market's profile filled one corner and Mt. Rainier the other.

"I want to see this in person," Mara said.

"I don't."

Mara stared at him in disbelief. "Why not?"

"Dunno." He shrugged, and the look on his face...nothing but confusion, frustration, and pain.

Unwilling to push him too far, Mara switched up her search and typed in Liam's name. Only a handful of results came through, and she found one from a Dublin newspaper.

St. Andrew's Wayward Youth will be packing their bags and moving to East Dublin after the holidays. The O'Sullivan family estate, which had been earmarked for the youth home, was pulled off the market suddenly in June.

"That O'Sullivan place woulda been just grand for the wee ones, but after we got an anonymous angel donation, we went straight for the Murphy house. Bigger, closer to town, and a larger piece of property," said Mary Leary, Director of St. Andrew's.

Barristers for the O'Sullivan estate have so far not given an official statement, but there are rumors that the estate was sold privately.

Liam O'Sullivan was the last surviving member of the O'Sullivan family. He died several months ago in a tragic apartment fire. His will has not been released and repeated calls to his family barrister have not been returned.

Two photos accompanying the news article depicted the

Murphy house and the O'Sullivan estate. The latter was captioned, "Has a private sale already gone through?"

One of the windows was open, and a face peered out, half-obscured by a curtain. "Who is this?" Mara asked. "Do you recognize him?"

Cade bent down and squinted at the screen. "Make it bigger?" Mara zoomed in.

"Oh my God. That...looks like Liam."

Cade

Could Liam really be alive? Or was his memory playing tricks on him? The man in the picture looked like Liam, but if his beta had survived, why wouldn't he have left some trail Cade could follow?

Or...maybe he had. If so, it would be in Bellingham.

He and Mara spent the next two hours searching for more photos and news articles, but came up empty.

The phone number for the O'Sullivan Foundation had been disconnected, Cade couldn't remember the names of any of Liam's extended family, and as it was the middle of the night in Ireland, they couldn't reach anyone in law enforcement who knew anything.

"What about Livie?" Mara asked.

"She...doesn't have family she talks to," Cade said quietly. "She was adopted as a baby. No one knew she was a werewolf until she had her first shift. I think..." He ran his hand over his jaw, trying to remember her voice. "She ran away from home at seventeen. Mike sort of adopted her after that."

Mara threaded her fingers through his. "You're smiling."

"It feels good to remember. Anything."

Turning his hand over so she could trace the lines on his palm, Mara asked, "What happened here?"

Scar tissue covered his hands, but the tips of his fingers were mostly intact.

"Don't ask me that," he muttered and tried to pull away, but Mara held on tight.

"I *am* asking. Tell me. You need all of your memories back. Good and bad. What happened to you?"

Tears stung the corners of his eyes. "The ground...was like lava. Where she kept me. Every time I tried to escape...I burned." He shuddered, and Mara pressed closer to him. "The scars...the wolf's paw pads burned over and over again. I can't feel... anything there."

"Cade? Look at me." She cupped his cheek and held his gaze. "You're safe. You're with me. And you're a man. Breathe for me."

He tried, but his chest didn't want to cooperate. Not until Mara scooted even closer. His heart raced, and he wanted to hold her, to just wrap his arms around her and forget about everything else. But he couldn't. She was right. He needed all of his memories back.

"Tell me about the woman who hurt you."

He closed his eyes and focused on Mara's touch. "I think...I can see her. A little. Dark hair. Green eyes. Tall. But that's it. Her voice though. She called me *dog*." He spat the last word before pushing to his feet and starting to pace the room. "There's fire. And screaming. A cage. She kept me in a fucking cage. I had to dig my way out." Clenching his burned fingers, he remembered the feel of the charmed earth.

"It hurt. I ran. I knew I was going to die." The bone-deep, chilling fear of the bad woman standing over him, hands glowing, about to end his life...he couldn't stand his memories a moment longer and clutched his head in his hands.

Mara was at his side almost immediately. "Cade? You're safe here."

He jerked away from her. "No. I'm *not*. She's out there. And I can't even see her face. She could live next door and I wouldn't know. All I can remember is the fire and that fucking cage. Nothing in between. I can't do this. I don't want to remember. Not my pack dying. Not whatever she did to me."

His Mara's voice was so full of pain. "I don't think you have a choice."

"I should have let her kill me!" Cade spun on his heel, raced for her front door, and fled, his shoes slapping against the concrete. He heard Mara following him, but he veered around a corner.

"Cade!"

He ignored her desperate cry. No coat, no wallet, not a cent to his name. He didn't know where the hell he was going, but it didn't matter. All he cared about right now was putting some distance between him and the return of his memories.

16

Mara

SHE PACED FOR A BIT, trying to decide whether to try to find Cade, but with no idea where he'd possibly go, she'd just be driving around aimlessly. Instead, she paced and worried.

By the time the sun kissed the horizon, she'd opened a bottle of wine and poured herself a healthy glass.

"To my health," she said, toasting the air. Did a toast still count if you didn't have anyone to toast with?

Though worry dampened her spirits, she hummed to herself as she seasoned the steaks, diced the potatoes, prepared the kale, and sunk her hands into a bowl of flour and butter. It had been so long since she'd made a pie, and having the energy to bake...it was liberating.

Wendy, her adoptive mother, had been a gourmet cook. Until she'd had a heart attack one summer when Mara was sixteen. Right in the middle of making her famous fried chicken.

Wendy had been the only mother she'd ever known, and had adopted Mara when she was only six months old.

More than once after her mysterious illness had reared its

head, Mara had thought about reaching out to her older sister. But the only time she'd met the woman—when she'd been home from college on spring break—Katerina had frightened her. Her sister had talked about the man who'd killed their birth mother, then told Mara that he'd died in a car accident.

But the glee in Katerina's voice when she'd recounted that story had left a sour taste in Mara's mouth.

"One day, little sister, you'll understand, and you'll love me. I know it."

Shaking her head, Mara returned her attention to the pie. Once it went into the oven, she lit candles around the living room, desperate for the soothing, flickering light and warm scent of vanilla to calm her nerves. With every strike of the match, though, a vague sense of discomfort twisted in her belly.

The wind kicked up, rattling the windows. A storm warning buzzed on her phone, and she jerked, pressing her hand to her heart. For a split second, she'd hoped it was Cade calling her.

Darkness shrouded the windows, and he still hadn't returned. Would he ever? Every time she closed her eyes, she pictured him cold and alone, so she turned to the television for distraction. A dark crime drama seemed to fit the weather, but it did nothing for her nerves.

Halfway through the show, the first sharp pelting of rain against her kitchen window was followed almost immediately by the doorbell.

Oh, God. Please be Cade.

He stood on her porch, arms right around his torso, shivering. In the glow from her porchlight, his hair was tousled and shining, and a few rain drops clung to the strands. "Can I, um, come in?"

Mara lunged forward and wrapped her arms around him, pulling him into the house and holding on tight. "I thought you'd be halfway to Canada by now," she said softly as she inhaled his scent and realized just how worried she'd been.

Cade's deep voice rumbled in his chest as he nuzzled her

neck. "I made it to the far side of the lake. But then...I couldn't remember my way back here. Nothing smelled right."

His breath warmed her skin, and desperation threaded his tone. "I was scared I wouldn't find you again."

He felt so damn good. Hard and strong and full of life. Like his wolf had been. But now he smelled like her lavender soap and the woodsy deodorant she'd bought him.

"You found me," she said over the lump in her throat.

The dinging of her kitchen timer forced them apart, and Mara pulled the pie out of the oven. But as soon as she set it down, Cade was right behind her.

His arms caged her against the counter, and she shuddered at the closeness and how very much she ached for him.

Now or never.

Feeling reckless, but more sure of herself than she'd ever been, she brushed her lips to his. He tasted of chocolate and coffee, and deepened the kiss as he pressed his body to hers.

His tongue begged for entrance, tracing the seam of her lips, and she yielded, the dance they'd been trapped in all day building. He ground his hips against her, and his hands slid down to cup her ass.

Need raced through her entire body, dampening her panties and her palms. She'd never felt like this before. Both in control and completely helpless at the same time.

The stubble on Cade's upper lip rasped against her skin, and he lifted her so she could wrap her legs around his waist and settle against his chest.

More.

The satisfied growl from his throat spurred her to run her hands up his back to tangle in his hair.

As he slipped his fingers under her sweater, his callouses sent shivers through her. He'd just started to fumble with the clasp of her bra, his erection pressing against her mound, when her mobile phone rang, and Mara yelped.

The distraction sobered him immediately, and his eyes widened. "I can't. I'm sorry," Cade managed as he set her down and skirted the kitchen island. "That was a mistake."

Mara's cheeks flooded with heat as she fumbled for her phone and hit Ignore. Jen could leave her a message.

"A mistake?" She licked her swollen lips, still tasting him on her. "We..." Turning away, she scrubbed her hands over her face, kicking herself. He'd wanted comfort. As a friend. Nothing more. "I'm sorry. I thought... It seemed like you... Shit. I was wrong."

"No!" The sharp word almost sounded like his wolf's bark. "God, honey. That's not it. Not even close." Mara shifted her weight from foot to foot as he ran a hand through his shaggy hair. "You're gorgeous. And smart and kind. And I wanted to kiss you like I've never wanted anything else. But wolves—alphas anyway—don't have casual sex. I won't use you to scratch an itch. You deserve better."

Cade grimaced and adjusted himself, his erection obvious through his jeans.

"Oh." Mara moved towards the stove and started heating the pan for the steak and potatoes. With her back to Cade, it was easier to be vulnerable. "It's been a long time. And I feel like I know you—even if you don't know yourself. Plus, you've got that whole damaged vibe working for you," she said with a wave of her hand.

Behind her, Cade choked out a laugh. "Damaged vibe?"

Tossing a glance over her shoulder, she almost smiled. "Oh, you know. Women like to fix things. And you need some fixing."

"You can't fix what's wrong with me. I'm a danger to you, and the longer I stay, the greater the risk." His luminous blue eyes filled with pain, and she reached for her wine, taking a healthy sip.

"We're not talking about that right now," she said. "Dinner will be ready in twenty minutes."

Cade hovered in the doorway, his hands shoved into his pockets. "Can I help?"

"You can set the table," she replied, angling her head at the cabinet next to her. "Dishes up there, silverware in the first drawer. And pour yourself a glass of wine. We're celebrating, remember?"

If only everything she'd wanted to celebrate didn't feel like it mattered anymore. His pain, the mountain of guilt he carried on those strong shoulders made her heart hurt.

Squeezing her eyes shut for a brief second, she shoved those emotions deep inside and focused on the task at hand. Making them both a meal.

Cade

"A mistake? That's the best you could do?"

If he could kick himself any harder, he'd leave bruises. Kissing Mara wasn't a mistake. Well, except for how hard and painful his dick was at the moment.

The mistake had been stopping. If her phone hadn't rung, he might have mated with her before he'd even asked her last name. His wolf wanted her. *Needed* her.

Two weeks of sleeping close to her at night, breathing in that intoxicating scent, seeing what a good and pure heart she had... Add in his own insecurities, and he wanted nothing more than her arms around him, her lips on his, and to lose himself inside of her.

As she cooked, Cade's stomach growled insistently. He hoped this constant need to eat would go away soon. How was he going to survive on his own when he had to eat every three hours to avoid passing out?

He'd come to a sobering realization sitting on a park bench at the edge of Green Lake. He had to go back to Bellingham. See where his pack had died. Maybe if he saw his shop or walked through the woods where they used to run, he'd remember more.

It was too dangerous to let his memories return at this frustratingly slow pace. The fire elemental could find him before he even remembered her name. All he wanted to do was stay with Mara, but he couldn't.

At least the bad woman would never trap him as his wolf again. Because he'd never shift again. The beast inside him railed at the decision, but also understood. The fire bitch would have to kill him as a man. He'd die, but he'd die on two legs, able to think and speak.

"Cade?" Mara's voice pulled him out of his morbid thoughts. "Think you can manage a bread knife?"

"Maybe?" He picked up the blade sitting next to a loaf of bread on the cutting board. After a moment with the handle in his right hand, he switched it to his left. "Huh."

"What?"

"I think I'm ambidextrous." Grinning, he made a quick, deft slice through the crusty loaf, then another and another before setting the cutting board on the table. "What else?"

Mara moved to one side of the stove. "Get the steak out of the oven and set the pan on the front burner."

"I used to like to cook."

Every hour brought new realizations, new memories. Even this simple act of helping Mara in the kitchen opened doors in his mind he'd thought locked for good.

A sudden flash of a bubbling dish of lasagna behind his lids, and a voice. *This is great, boss-man. Where'd you learn to cook like this?* Livie. He could almost see her smile.

"Then you get to make dinner tomorrow. Top off our wine glasses and sit down. I just need to let the steak rest and we're good to go." Grabbing a dish towel, she wrapped it around the handle of the hot pan and started spooning butter over the steaks.

"I worried about you," she said, so softly only his enhanced senses could have picked up her words. "I wasn't sure I'd see you again."

Cade balled his hands into fists on his thighs. Hurting her...it was unacceptable. "I wasn't thinking straight. It's...the moon."

"What about it?" Mara transferred the steaks to a plate and leaned a hip against the counter.

"It messes with me. Especially when it's new, like it is now. I don't know how to explain it."

Bringing the various serving dishes to the table, Mara took a seat next to him and slid her fingers over his. Gentle. Tender. In a way Cade didn't deserve.

"Try."

"We're weakest this time of the month." With a shudder, he squeezed his eyes shut. "I think she trapped me during the new moon. The fire elemental."

Twisting his hand, he threaded his calloused, half-numb fingers with Mara's. His heart pounded, and it took him several long breaths to calm it down. "When I had a pack, I used to break up fights this time of the month. I'd close my shop. Being around sharp tools wasn't always a great idea."

She chuckled as she served him a steak the size of half the dinner plate, then poured shallot butter over the top. After his first bite, he groaned. "Shit, honey. This is amazing."

Smiling, Mara blushed. The candlelight turned her face a pale pink, and her green eyes sparkled. Her steak was half the size of his, but at least she was eating.

Emboldened by the meal—and Mara's closeness—he cleared his throat. "I asked before. Kind of. But, you don't have a boyfriend? How come?"

"No one wants to go out on a date with a dying woman. I'm not—I wasn't—a good investment." Draining half of her wine glass, she set it down with a little more force than necessary, and it almost toppled over. She shoved her hands under the table, but Cade had noticed the tremor to her fingers.

"I didn't mean to pry." The last thing he wanted to do was to cause Mara more pain.

"And you?" Mara asked. "Your, um, obituary said you were thirty-one. Are you still? Or thirty-two? You're not married?" She bit her lip and held her breath.

Scrubbing his hand over his chin, he shook his head. "I don't know how old I am—I mean, when my birthday is. Spring, I think? I'm not with anyone. Werewolves know. When we, um, mate...it's not just emotional. Its physical. I'd know. And I never would have kissed you. I couldn't have even thought about it."

"That's some moral code." Mara whistled.

"Wolves mate for life. It's who we are. Who...I am." He shoved half a slice of bread into his mouth so he wouldn't end up with his foot in there instead. This conversation was dangerous. It made him want...more. With Mara.

His plate was almost clean by the time he risked another question. "What about your family?"

"I was adopted when I was six months old." She fiddled with a piece of steak on her plate, pushing it around in the butter. "My birth parents are both dead. But my adoptive parents—they were amazing. Until my mom had a heart attack and died when I was in high school."

Cade reached over and brushed his fingers over her thigh.

"After that, my dad shut me out and started drinking. He died ten years ago. Aunt Lillian...she became my mom and dad then. Helped me apply to colleges, moved me into my first dorm, nursed me through my first breakup." Smiling sadly, Mara patted his hand. "She's awesome. Even if she did turn a little overprotective when I got sick."

Cade couldn't blame the woman.

Over pie, Mara told Cade all about her childhood in California and her last serious relationship with an asshole named Roger. After they'd done the dishes, they moved to the couch. Cade was tired, but he had to tell Mara what he'd decided.

He took her hand and relished the warmth of her touch. "I have to go to Bellingham. I know it's a lot. You've done so much for me already. But can you help me get a bus ticket? And maybe a duffel for the clothes you bought me?"

"You're leaving." In the candlelight, her eyes blazed, and her voice took on a hard edge. "And I'm just supposed to let you go to the one place *she's* most likely to find you? Alone? With no resources or transportation of your own? With no defenses beyond your wolf?" She jerked her hand away.

Cade couldn't tell her he wouldn't even have his wolf. The very thought of shifting again terrified him. "Please, Mara."

"No. Not happening. If you want to go to Bellingham, I'll take you."

"It's too dangerous." Cade pushed up and started to pace the room, but the wine and his still-healing body conspired against him, and he stumbled. Crashing to his hands and knees, he narrowly missed slamming his head into Mara's coffee table. Falling onto his ass, he grunted, "Fuck."

"Yes. It's definitely too dangerous," Mara snapped as she sank down next to him and wrapped her arm around his shoulders. "For you to go alone in the state you're in. I made up the guest room for you. We'll talk more about this in the morning."

Keeping her arm around his waist, she helped him up. His wolf calmed just by being near her. After she tugged back the blankets, she eased him down. "There's a toothbrush and tooth-paste in the bathroom. If you get hungry, the cookies and pie will be on top of the fridge."

Cade grabbed her wrist before she could escape the room. "Wait."

Under his fingers, her skin was soft and her pulse thrummed

steadily. He brought her hand to his lips and frowned. "How do you feel?"

"I'm a little tired."

"You don't smell as much like rain as you did earlier."

Mara's lips pressed into a thin line. "You really know how to talk to a woman," she said flatly. "No wonder you're not mated." She tried to pull away, but Cade held on tight.

"No. Goddammit, honey, you're getting sick again. I can smell it. Every time you got weak, my wolf knew. *I* knew. You're not there yet, but you're not as strong as you were this morning. What the hell is going on with you?"

"I'm dying. I told you that." Wrenching her wrist free from his grip, she stalked out of the room. "Good night, Cade."

17

Mara

Her bed felt empty without the wolf next to her.

"Get over it," she muttered, turning over so violently she tangled her legs in the sheets as Cade's words ran on a loop in her head.

You're getting sick again.

"I feel fine. What the hell does he know?"

Trudging into her bathroom to refill her water bottle, she swore under her breath as her hands trembled. The bottle slipped from her grasp and landed with a dull thud on the bath mat. "Shit."

Cade was right. Her episodes always started with trembling hands. Then a headache. Then exhaustion. She drained half the water bottle and her hands steadied. At least that was something.

The clock ticked past one. Then two. Still, she hadn't managed to fall asleep. Apparently, neither had Cade. Her floorboards creaked in the kitchen, then the living room. Was he pacing? He'd been so exhausted he hadn't been able to keep his eyes open two hours ago.

Padding down the hall, she found him leaning against the counter with a cookie in his hand and his back to her.

"Can I have one?" Mara asked.

He yelped, the sound so much like his wolf, and almost dropped the half-eaten cookie.

"I didn't mean to startle you." She slid her hand along his forearm, her gaze drawn to his bare chest, the sprinkling of hair covering the corded muscles, and his obliques cutting a deep *V* that disappeared into low-slung jeans.

She should have bought him pajamas. Or a parka. Something big and shapeless to hide all those muscles.

Cade passed her the box, moved away, and brushed his hands over the sink. But he didn't turn back to face her.

"What woke you?" Mara asked.

"Memories."

Mara wrapped her arms around his torso. He stiffened and tried to pull away, but she held fast, pressing her cheek against a long healed burn on his back.

"I can't," he said, his voice practically a growl.

"What? Let someone comfort you?"

"Do this. Be close to you without...more. I don't even know your last name. And despite your assessment of my current level of health, I'm going to have to leave soon. Don't make it harder than it's already going to be."

"What?" Mara released him and backed away. He turned around, and she flicked on the light to get a better look at his face.

His stubble had been rough when he'd kissed her, and she'd liked the slight burn. And his eyes. Haunted, but strong.

"Wolves are instinctual creatures. I want you, Mara. And it wasn't only the nightmare that woke me. The bed feels..."

"Lonely. I know. There's a remedy for that." She looked up at him through lowered lashes, needing him close to her.

"No. I mean, yes. There is. But I can't sleep with you. I'm sorry

I said anything. Good night." He turned, strode back into the guest room, and shut the door.

"Taylor. My last name is Taylor," she whispered as she headed back to her room.

———

DREAMS HAUNTED HER. Flames burning her skin, a smokeless conflagration she couldn't escape. Until the mattress dipped, and a warm, hard body wrapped around her.

"One night," the rough voice whispered in her ear. "One last night I'll get to hold you."

Mara didn't reply. She wouldn't risk spooking him. He sucked in a shaking breath and buried his nose in her hair.

Stay.

She ached for him to do more than hold her, but in under two minutes, Cade's breathing evened out, and slept. If this was all she could have of him, she'd take it. One night held safe in his arms.

———

WHEN SHE OPENED her eyes in the morning, the sheets next to her were cool and the guest room door was closed again. After a shower and way too much time debating what to wear, Mara found Cade, his own hair still damp, in the kitchen cooking breakfast.

Eggs sizzled alongside slices of bacon, and he sipped coffee while he watched the pan.

Clearing her throat so she wouldn't startle him, she leaned a hip against the door jamb.

His smile didn't reach his eyes. "Morning, honey. Uh, Mara. Hungry?"

"No. But I'll eat." She headed for the espresso machine, but he waved her off.

"Sit down. You look tired." Concern laced his tone, and she sighed. She *was* tired, and her hands weren't totally steady.

She couldn't figure Cade out. He belonged in her kitchen. Comfortable. At ease. Like he wanted to stay. Tugging at the hem of her tight red sweater, she took a seat and hid her hands under the table. Faint, dark smudges had braced her eyes this morning, and she'd spent extra time with the concealer, hoping Cade wouldn't notice.

The mug of coffee he set in front of her was life itself, and she smiled up at him. "Thanks."

That moment was all he needed to see what she'd tried to hide. "Mara. Shit." Crouching down, he cupped her cheek and brushed his thumb under her right eye. "You're not going to Bellingham with me."

She jerked away. "We had this discussion last night. My way or no way at all. And you want me there."

Stalking back into the kitchen for the plates, he almost growled. "No. I don't."

"Really? My purse is sitting on the counter. There's a twenty in the little bowl next to it, along with my keys. If you'd really wanted to go alone, you could have taken what you needed and left."

The bacon was perfect, but with her stomach in knots, she couldn't manage the eggs and dumped them onto Cade's plate.

"I need to call Aunt Lil before we leave. Eat more. You know you want to. We'll hit up a coffee shop on the way out of town to get some snacks for the trip."

Before he could protest, she'd shut herself in her bedroom and dialed Lil.

"Mara, hon, I'm bringing Eleanor with me today. We'll be there around noon," Lil said as soon as the call connected.

"Can we do this tomorrow instead?" Pinching the bridge of her nose, she prayed her aunt wouldn't be too upset.

"Hell no. You've been actin' odd all week. What in tarnation is goin' on? If Eleanor's right, she could save your life, and you're just goin' to ignore her?"

"I'm not going to die today. Probably not tomorrow either." She pushed to her feet and started to pace. Out in the kitchen, she heard Cade cleaning. "Just...do this for me. Please."

"Fine. No matter that Eleanor drove all the way from Cannon Beach to see you. I'll put her up tonight and we'll be over tomorrow for breakfast. But you're goin' to have to put the wolf outside when we're there. I don't trust that thing."

"I will." Mara stifled her snort. There was no way Cade would shift and sit in her backyard the whole time. If he was still here, he could hide in the guest room.

A LITTLE BEFORE TEN, Mara and a very nervous Cade got into her little car. He hadn't said a word to her as she'd gathered her things, and that was probably for the best. If he tried to stop her again, she was going to have some harsh words for him, and she didn't think she had the energy to spare.

Angling into a parking spot next to the local running store, she fixed Cade with a hard stare. "Stay here."

She returned with a black knit cap, a pair of sunglasses, and a windbreaker for Cade. Along with two Americanos, two cinnamon rolls, and a cherry scone from the coffee shop next door. "Put on the hat and the sunglasses. They should help if the fire elemental is poking around. Your hair and eyes are *way* too distinctive."

Cade ran a hand through his shaggy straw and steel hair and shook his head. "Why are you doing all of this for me?"

"Because the wolf saved my life." Turning in her seat, she gave him her full attention. "When I was on Orcas that last night before you crawled into my car, I prayed. I asked whatever god or goddess is up there for one thing. '*Let my life have mattered.*' That's all I wanted. This is a way to have mattered. I don't care what you say I smell like. I'm still dying, and anything I can do for you before the end is important to me."

Cade reached for her so suddenly, she didn't have time to pull away. Despite the console between them, he held her close, his face in her hair. "You matter, honey. You matter to me."

Cade

With the sunglasses hiding his eyes, he was able to keep his gaze on Mara's face as she drove. She'd tried to cover the dark circles under her eyes, but he knew they were there.

She didn't smell sick yet, but she was weaker today. Her water element was *leaving* her. Damn the holes in his memory. He didn't think that should even be possible.

Mara tried to draw him into conversation, but he couldn't answer any question she asked. Favorite foods. Brothers and sisters. Sports.

Eventually, after polishing off one of the biggest cinnamon rolls he'd ever seen, Cade let the motion of the car lull his healing body to sleep.

When he jerked awake, it was to the sense something was very wrong. The car was parked, and Mara wasn't inside. Sitting up straight, he looked around wildly.

"Fuck." In front of him, an empty lot was all that remained of his apartment building. Rain danced over the windshield, and as he caught sight of a greenbelt to the left, his fingers tingled with the desire to shift. To run.

Where was Mara? He needed Mara.

Shrugging into the windbreaker, he got out of the car and inhaled deeply. Fresh pine, dirt, rain, rotten wood, and Mara. She couldn't be far.

Following his nose, he reached the corner of the lot. There were four other apartment complexes close by with too many people and too many scents.

Turning, he shuddered in relief as he saw her across the street talking to an elderly woman silhouetted in the door of a townhouse.

"Mara? Honey, don't leave me like that. Not with—"

"Cade? Is that you, boy?" The older woman stepped closer. Well past eighty, her steps were uneven, but she shuffled forward and poked him in the chest. "Take off those glasses."

He didn't have much choice. Not by her tone.

"Well, shit. It is you. What is your game, girl? He ain't dead." She arched a white brow at Mara.

Throwing up her hands, Mara hunched her shoulders and her cheeks pinked. "I'm sorry, Maggie. Cade didn't want anyone to know he was alive. There might be, um, someone after him."

"Maggie." His neighbor. He remembered. Only a month before he'd been trapped as his wolf, he'd made her a headboard. She used to bring him casseroles.

"Well, don't just stand there," Maggie snapped. "Come inside before I catch my death of cold."

———

MAGGIE BUSTLED about the kitchen and refused any help. "I'm old. Not dead," she said. "I can still make tea for guests."

Cade and Mara sat on a quilt-covered loveseat with their fingers intertwined. He couldn't seem to let her go. "How did you know to come here?" he asked.

"I didn't. I went to the complex next to your old apartment building and tried to find the manager. Maggie was waiting for me when I headed back to the car. She had a frilly, pink umbrella I think she wanted to use as a weapon. When she asked me what I wanted, I made up a story."

Maggie shuffled in with three mugs of tea on a tray. "She said she was a reporter from Seattle doing a piece on your death. I take it that's a lie? The reporter part. I can see you ain't dead."

Cade ran a hand over the back of his neck. "After the fire, I lost my memory. Mara's helping me. I don't remember most of my life before. Bits and pieces. I came back in the hopes...I'd be able to fill in all the holes. But someone's after me. Someone bad."

"That dark-haired bitch shooting fire from her hands?" Maggie took a calm sip of tea while Cade nearly choked on his.

"You...saw her?"

"Sure did. Cops didn't believe me when I said the fire wasn't natural. Tried to tell me I was in-*sane*." She enunciated each syllable as if she couldn't believe anyone would dare question her word.

"I can't remember who she is," Cade said. "But she wants me dead." He squeezed Mara's fingers. She was everything to him, and if he couldn't find answers, she'd never be safe. "I don't remember anything other than fire and my, um, my friends screaming. I don't know how the woman got me out of town or where she took me—other than somewhere on Orcas Island."

"Where's that little blond dynamo who lived upstairs from you?" Maggie asked. "I haven't seen her in a month. She could help."

"Livie?" Cade drew in a sharp breath. "A month? She's alive?"

"She was on the full moon." Maggie shrugged. "Comes around every four or six weeks. Sits in a car across the street for a couple of days. I always try to bring her tea, but she drives off when she sees me coming. I get the idea she doesn't want anyone else to know she's here. But I figure you're her pack leader or whatever it's called. You deserve to know."

"What...what did you just say?" Cade asked.

Maggie rolled her eyes. "Oh, please. I'm not stupid. You lot always disappeared at the full moon. That beau of hers even looked like an animal half the time. You wolves were always thick as thieves. This one's different, though. She one too?"

"No," Cade and Mara said in unison.

"Huh. You're hanging onto her like she's your everything." Maggie drained the last of her tea and relaxed against the cushions.

She is.

"She's an elemental," Cade said. At Maggie's confused expression, he explained. "The woman who shot fire from her hands? She's one too. But Mara's element is water."

"Huh." Maggie shook her head and glanced over at a large grandfather clock in the corner. "The ladies are coming for bridge in half an hour and I need to put cookies in the oven. Any more holes I can fill in for you?"

"No, ma'am." Livie was alive, and she'd been here. That was enough to keep him going.

"Help an old lady up now, young man. And don't be a stranger. You hear me?"

"Yes, ma'am."

Mara wrote down her name and phone number for Maggie. "If they do come—his pack—give them this. I'll do my best to keep him safe until we find them."

18

Cade

THE RAIN SOAKED into Mara's red locks, making them shine. She was stronger now, her element flaring to life in the damp weather. Even her eyes were bright and clear again.

He wanted to lose himself in her scent, and he did for a moment. With his arm around her waist, he held her close. "The fire elemental lied to me. She told me she'd killed them, and every night, I'd have nightmares. Hear them scream. See them burn. This…it's more than I could have hoped for."

"What next?" Mara asked as she wriggled out of his grasp. Disappointment crushed his heart, but only for a moment, because she took his hand and grinned up at him. "Where to?"

"My shop. If it's still there, I want to see it." Cade stared from one side of the street to the other. "I don't know what direction."

"Maggie told me the way." Mara led Cade down the street, her small, delicate fingers clutched in his. Her hair was heavy and sodden, but she didn't seem to care.

"You're going to catch a cold," he said, draping an arm around her shoulders.

"I love the rain. And I've never had a cold." She snuggled into his body, cool against his warmth. "This is nice. You run hot?"

"Yeah. About a hundred, most of the time. We all do." He paused under an awning and turned her away from him. Gathering her hair in a thick twist, he wrung out the water, then pulled the hat from his head and tucked her hair inside, smoothing the wool down over her ears. "That's better."

"Your hair," she protested, her eyes wide.

"If she's here, she's going to find me no matter what my hair looks like. Besides," he said, tracing a knuckle over her cheek. "It looks better on you."

After another block, they took a quick right. The buildings were closer together here: quaint little restaurants, a local market, a bookstore, and a law office. Memories assaulted him. Drinks with Liam. Coffee at the roaster the pack owned.

"The bowling alley is down Third," he said, pointing. "The bank is two blocks north. The lumber yard is a mile south." He didn't care that he was rambling. He was so happy he remembered *anything.*

A block away from his shop, he quickened his steps and started leading her to a dark green building. The shingle hanging over the door had two hand-carved pine trees on either side of the name: *Bellingham Woodworking.*

But there was also a notice on the door and a heavy chain with a padlock securing the handle.

For Sale at Auction - December 14th

"Shit."

"You were dead," Mara said quietly. "But...we'll find a way to fix it. Maybe I can call the agency running the auction and they can let us in."

"There's a back door," Cade said. "The lock never worked right. Maybe it's not secured like this. Come on." With Mara's hand in his, he pulled her around the back of the building. "Can I see your keys?"

The rear door was unchained, and Cade pulled the handle up, jabbed Mara's house key against the lock, jerked the hardware to the left, and the door popped open.

Without even thinking, he flicked on the lights and moved through the shop that had been his second home for more than five years. The scents, the feel of wood dust under his feet, the hand-carved toys resting on his workbench—everything came flooding back to him at once.

Mara picked up a train engine the size of a deck of cards. "Cade. The detail on this is amazing!" She spun the wheels, a look of pure awe gracing her features.

"I worked on that my last day. It was supposed to be a ten-car set. The mayor's kid. Her birthday." Cade eased the car from Mara's hand and rolled it along his bench. Not quite perfect.

Picking up a bit covered with sandpaper, he ran it over the back wheel until the grain of the wood shone through.

Sawdust coated his fingers, and he took a deep breath. The sweet, comforting aroma wrapped around him.

Mara pressed closer to him, resting a hand on his shoulder, her touch calming the whirlwind of memories and grounding him.

When he rolled the car again, it was perfect. "There's a second one around here somewhere." He rummaged in a bin on the workbench and came up with a caboose, then closed Mara's hand around the car. "You said something about kids. The man. Adam. He had kids. Take these."

"But—"

"The job was due months ago. I can't stay here, Mara. This is probably the last time I'm ever going to see my shop. Take them." His voice cracked, and he turned away. Everything he was— everything he used to be—was here. And in a few minutes, he'd leave it forever.

Mara tucked the toys into her jacket pocket, and her voice, when she finally spoke, was quiet. "You're going to stay dead."

"If I can." He turned back to her and shoved his hands into the pockets of his jeans. "It's the smartest thing. I remember some of it now. She was hunting me. Something to do with my father."

Mara was so close, and her intoxicating scent, her kind green eyes, and most of all, her beautiful soul called to him. She'd saved his wolf when she should have run screaming from him.

"Come here," he said, his voice low and hoarse.

It only took two steps. Cade wrapped his arms around her and dipped his head, his lips inches from hers.

"Cade. We can't. You said—"

"If I don't kiss you right now, I'm going to regret it for the rest of my life." Her breath whispered over his lips and she ran her hands through his shaggy hair. Then his rough, chapped lips brushed the soft swell of her mouth. A tiny sound, almost a moan, hung between them.

"Oh my fucking God."

The harsh exclamation from the back door startled them both, and Cade swept Mara behind him.

The petite woman in the doorway looked so much different than his memories of her. Thick, reddish scars covered her left cheek, and one of her eyes didn't open fully. Her left arm hung awkwardly at her side, and she'd aged a dozen years in the seven months he'd been gone.

"Livie."

The little wolf launched herself into his arms, and he caught her with an audible *oof*. Mara stepped back and out of the way, a hint of sadness welling in her eyes.

"I knew it," Livie sobbed. "I knew you were alive somewhere. No one believed me. They said I was stupid for coming back here. Every fucking month. Shawn hated it. He practically forbade me from coming this time. But I knew. I had to."

Cade swallowed hard as he set her on her feet. "Shawn's alive too?"

"We're all alive. Bill was the only one who died." Her tears soaked into the collar of his shirt, and she nuzzled his neck in a familiar, submissive gesture, needing solace from her alpha.

Cade rubbed his hand over her nape, gripping her blond hair tightly for a beat, then letting go. He stepped back and touched the scars on the side of her face. "Shit. I'm so sorry."

He looked her up and down, sensing something off. Something besides the scars and whatever had happened to her arm. Jeans. Black boots. A loose black sweatshirt, her good arm bracing the small of her back.

"You're...pregnant."

Beaming, Livie rubbed her belly. "Five months. Little guy's kicking up a storm today. How the hell did you get here? And where have you been?"

"It's a long story." Cade glanced over at Mara. A pained expression tightened her features, and she hugged herself tightly.

Livie sniffed the air, then whirled towards Mara. "What are you doing with a fucking elemental?"

"I'm not—" Mara started, but Livie had her pinned against the wall before Cade could stop her, hands around Mara's throat.

"Get the fuck off of her! She's mine!" Cade roared. Grabbing Livie's good arm, he pulled with all of his strength, but he was still too weak, and barely managed to loosen her grip.

Mara wheezed and gasped, and the air in the room grew heavy. Droplets of water fell all around them, several slithering down the back of Cade's shirt.

"Mara, honey. It's okay. Livie, let her go, goddammit. Now! That is an order!" He punctuated every word with another tug on her arm.

Everything slowed, and a percussive force shoved Livie and Cade back, drenching them with frigid water. Mara stood alone, her chest heaving with every breath. Water dripped from her fingers, her chin, and the tip of her nose.

"Cade?" she whispered, then collapsed.

19

Cade

RUSHING TO MARA'S SIDE, he scooped her into his arms, sank down onto his ass, and smoothed her hair away from her face. "Mara? Honey, wake up, please."

Livie sulked across the room. "She's an elemental, boss-man. What if she's working with that bitch, Katerina?"

Katerina. Katerina Olmstead.

"You're going to pay, dog. You'll die, but you'll suffer first."

She'd blamed Cade's father for her mother's death. He shivered, the icy water combined with his still too-sparse frame chilling him to the bone. Too many memories all at once, and fuck. He needed Mara to wake up.

"Get away from her. Please," Livie said.

"She's not working with Katerina." Cade couldn't keep the growl from his voice. "She saved my life, Livie." He pinned her with his stare and lowered his voice further so the petite werewolf would understand just how serious he was. "I had one rule. One fucking rule. We never attack without provocation. And you break it by trying to kill the woman who saved my life."

"I don't understand." Livie cradled her swollen belly and sank down into her usual chair at the front desk.

"Neither do I. Not entirely. I was trapped as my wolf this whole time." He rubbed Mara's back, pressed a kiss to her neck, her forehead, and tried to warm her with his own body. "Katerina...she worked some sort of charm that stopped me from shifting. I spent the past seven months in a fucking cage on Orcas Island. She starved me, burned me..." His voice cracked. He hadn't even admitted everything to Mara. And she needed to know before he could tell Livie.

After a deep, shuddering breath, he continued. "I was dying. I don't remember what happened. How I escaped. Except I had to dig my way out. My wolf hid in Mara's car. God. I hurt. Every part of me hurt. But when Mara touched me, it was better.

"She healed me—the wolf. Fed him, treated his wounds. But I still couldn't shift back. Two days ago, somehow, her water element broke the charm, and I was...me again. One minute I was a wolf, the next...I was a man. I couldn't move. I was too weak, too confused. Mara didn't even know she *was* an elemental."

Cade leaned down and brushed a kiss to her forehead. "Come back to me, honey. Please."

"Oh, my God. Have you claimed her?" Livie asked. She tugged at her right ear, a nervous uncertain gesture.

"No. Yes. I don't know. I don't have all of my memories, Livie. Too long as a wolf. It changes you. When I shifted back, I couldn't speak. Couldn't remember...anything. She's mine. That's all I know. We kissed yesterday, then just now, and it felt like coming home."

Livie pushed herself up and waddled awkwardly over to Cade and Mara. As soon as she knelt down, though, Mara jerked away and blinked her eyes open.

"Get away from me," she rasped and tried to fight her way out of Cade's arms.

"It's okay, honey. You're safe. Livie won't hurt you again."

"I'm sorry," Livie said, backing away and keeping her gaze lowered to the floor. "Cade's like my big brother and father in one. When I smelled you, instinct took over. Elementals aren't common. I just...I assumed you were with the bitch that did this," she gestured to the scars on her face, "and hurt Cade."

He smoothed Mara's hair, fighting his desperate need to bite her neck and bury himself inside of her. Livie's attack had provoked a visceral and immediate reaction. The overwhelming need to claim her.

He almost dropped her when he realized the truth. His wolf had already claimed Mara. She was his mate, and the beast inside him knew it.

"Why am I wet?" Mara shivered in his arms, and her eyebrows furrowed, her gaze cloudy and her words slightly slurred.

"Your water element, honey." He tucked a lock of hair behind her ear and tightened his hold on her. "You were in danger. I think...it took over. Like the other night when you were..." He couldn't say the word.

"Dying," Mara whispered.

Cade's wolf railed at the word, and the man in control forced out a slow breath. "Yeah. You...your power knocked us back and soaked the room. If we'd been outside in the rain, you might have drowned us."

"I want to go home," Mara said quietly. "I need...I feel strange. My skin...hurts. And I'm so tired. I can't...I can't drive like this." She lifted her hand, staring at her shaking fingers, and a sob caught in her throat. "No. No, no, no."

"I'll take you home." Cade glanced up at Livie. The blond wolf watched Mara, but there was no malice in her eyes, only confusion. "Livie, do you have a car?"

"Yeah. Why?"

Cupping Mara's cheek, he breathed deeply. Her element filled the room, but he didn't like the way she stared off into space like her entire world was ending.

"Mara, I can't just abandon Livie here. She's my pack, and she knows more about the fire elemental than I do right now. I need her. I need all of them."

Tears tumbled down Mara's cheeks. "You have to go. I...understand. Just help me to my car. I'll take a nap. Or if there's a hotel—"

"You're not getting rid of me that easily," he said, pressing a kiss to her forehead. "I want Livie to follow us. Until you're better, I'm not going anywhere." Cade met Livie's gaze for a brief second. "And maybe not even then."

She felt so good in his arms, but she was freezing—and so was he.

Her pupils were saucers of black with only a rim of emerald remaining, and her lower lip trembled. "What do you mean?"

"Livie would need to stay with you, Mara."

"She doesn't like me."

Livie bowed her head and rested her right hand over her heart. "Cade says you're no threat to us, and I believe him. You saved his life, and so I owe you mine. My wolf will protect you both."

Mara nodded and rested her head on Cade's shoulder. "Fine. She can have the guest room. You can sleep...on the couch."

Cade wanted no part of sleeping on the couch, but until she invited him back into her bed, that was where he'd stay. He sent Livie to get Mara's Prius and once he'd wrapped her in an old sweatshirt he found in the back, he packed up the last few things he wanted from the shop.

A burled wooden box the size of his palm, hand carved, meticulously polished went into a bag. He wanted Mara to have it —whatever happened between them.

He also found his emergency pack: a passport, three hundred dollars, and a prepaid credit card with a two thousand dollar limit. When he'd taken over as alpha, he'd insisted every one of his wolves have the same type of go bag—just in case.

"Boss-man? Where am I going?" Livie asked as she tossed him Mara's keys.

"I'm at 1029 Northeast Eighty-Second in Seattle," Mara said, lifting her head and staring around the dusty shop.

"Gotcha. I'm going to call Liam, then I'll be right behind you."

"Where are they?" Cade asked.

"Ireland. Liam's family estate. We figured as cold and rainy as it is there, we'd be safe from that fire bitch. Plus, her boy-toy elemental can't fly."

"Will they come?" Cade helped Mara to her feet, but she shook him off and stood under her own power.

"Of course they will," Livie said. "There's nothing we wouldn't do for you."

CADE THANKED whatever deity had brought Mara to Orcas in the first place that he remembered how to drive. Once he slid behind the wheel, he knew what to do.

Mara curled up in the passenger seat and stared out the window, not saying a word for more than ten miles.

"Talk to me, honey."

Mara barely moved. "Keep the clothes," she said softly.

"What?"

"The clothes. When you go. You can take one of my suitcases. I won't need them anymore." She turned her head just enough for him to see tears glistening on her cheek.

"Goddammit, Mara. You're *not* dying. Not while I'm around." Cade slammed his hand against the steering wheel, and she flinched and curled away from him.

"No. You'll leave with your pack before I lose this fight."

"What the hell? Why are you so certain I'm going anywhere?" He gripped the steering wheel so hard, his knuckles turned white.

"Because I'm asking you to go. I don't want you to watch me die." She held up her hand when he protested, and her fingers trembled. "I'm *going* to die. Soon. This is how it starts. Every time. I had a little remission these past few days, but it won't last."

Cade ached to pull Mara into his arms, to comfort her, but at seventy miles per hour, he couldn't do more than trail a knuckle along her cheek.

"Don't," she said, choking back a sob. "It's hard enough knowing I'll never have another Thanksgiving or see Adam and Lisa's kids grow up, or swim in the ocean again. I can't let myself want something *else* I can't have."

Mara curled up in his old sweatshirt and turned away from him. "I'm really tired now. The GPS will tell you where to go."

Cade knew the second her breathing changed. In some ways, he'd already mated with her. His wolf—now allowed to exist only within his human form—had memorized the pattern of her heartbeat, her breathing, even the flutter of her eyelashes. If she *were* still dying, he was damn well going to be there at the end.

The last sight she'd see would be his face, the last sound would be his voice. She'd admitted she wanted him, and that was all he needed. But he'd give up his own life if it meant saving hers.

Ten miles from her house, her phone buzzed, and Cade flicked his gaze to the screen. *Aunt Lil.*

Mara forced her eyes open and yawned. "Was that my phone?" As soon as she saw the missed text, she was almost instantly awake, her fingers flying over the screen.

Another buzz, another response, and she groaned. "My aunt and Eleanor will be at the house when we get there. We should, um, figure out how we're going to explain you. Neighbor again?"

"No." Cade had never been more sure of anything in his life— that he could remember. "This woman, Eleanor? She knows about elementals?"

"Apparently."

"Then she'll know about werewolves."

"Cade," Mara said, an edge of exasperation to her voice, "you can't."

"Give me one good reason."

Mara sputtered for a minute, looked out the window, and ran a hand through her damp hair. "I give up. Clearly you don't listen to me."

"I listen. I *hear* you, Mara. You're scared. So am I. But that's why I won't hide who I am from your aunt and Eleanor. They're going to figure out pretty quick I'm not some random neighbor."

"Only if you tell them."

Cade pulled off the freeway, and when he had to stop for a red light, arched a brow at Mara. "You let random neighbors do this?" Cupping the back of her neck, he pulled her close and brushed his lips to hers. "The only way we're going to stay safe is to put all of our cards on the table. You're important to me. I won't hide it."

"You've known me all of two days."

"No, I've known you for two weeks. My wolf couldn't speak, but that didn't stop him—me—from learning who you are. You talked to me all the time. Those memories are coming back. I know you better than I know myself right now. Can you tell me honestly that you don't feel anything for me?"

Mara blushed. "No."

"I want to be a part of your life, honey. And not just for another few days. For a lot longer."

"You wanted to stay dead."

He shook his head. "I was wrong. I need my pack. I need to find out what happened after I disappeared. I need my memories. But I need you too. Please. Let me stay."

Mara pinched the bridge of her nose, and a single tear escaped the corner of her eye as she nodded. "Okay."

20

Cade

HE PULLED the car into Mara's driveway, and she groaned as she gestured to a red roadster parked at the corner. "Great. They're already inside. Probably wondering where the wolf is."

"Well, we should show her." Cade passed her the keys before rounding the car and helping Mara to her feet, wrapping an arm around her waist and holding her close.

"You're not going to shift...are you?" Mara asked.

"No. You've seen the last of my wolf."

Confused, she peered up at him. "Cade?" The drapes covering Mara's front window fluttered, and he caught a glimpse of white hair before the deep blue material settled back into place.

"Never mind," he said. "Come on. The longer we stay out here, the more they're going to talk in there."

"This isn't going to go well." Mara wriggled out of Cade's grip and trudged up the steps. Before she could reach for the knob, her front door flew open and Lillian stood there with her hands on her hips.

"Mara Elizabeth Taylor. What in the fresh hell are you doin' driving yourself to Bellingham? And who is this?"

"We're cold and wet, Aunt Lil. Can we do this inside?" Mara said with a sigh.

The elderly Southern woman stepped back, but watched Cade with a wary eye as they slipped through the door.

A woman in her late fifties rose from one of Mara's kitchen chairs and smiled. "Mara. I'm Eleanor. Your aunt told me about —" Her gaze snapped to Cade. "Well, that explains it."

"Ma'am?" he asked.

"Lillian wondered where Mara's wolf was. I didn't think there were any werewolf packs left in Washington."

Cade inhaled deeply. Air. Eleanor smelled like the wind. She didn't just know about elementals. She was one.

"Are you tellin' me he's a damn werewolf?" Lillian glared at the air elemental.

"Yep. A scruffy one, at that. Looks a bit more wolf than man right now. Handsome enough, though." Eleanor offered her hand.

"Cade Bowman," he said, then turned towards Lillian. "Ma'am, I'm sorry we're not meeting under better circumstances."

"Don't you *ma'am* me. You knockin' boots with my niece?"

"Oh shit," Mara muttered. "I'm going to go change. Cade, you might want to do the same." Turning on her heel, she strode towards her bedroom.

He watched her go, stunned at Lillian's directness and Mara's quick retreat.

"Well?" Lillian asked. "Mara's sick. I don't want her losing even a single day with us over some shaggy wolf who can't keep it in his pants."

"I think I should have listened to Mara." Cade rubbed the back of his neck, his unkempt hair too long. "But if it makes you feel any better, my clothes are in the guest room and I'm quite capable of keeping my pants zipped."

Eleanor stifled a laugh. "Give him a break, Lil. He's about to topple over and he's soaked to the bone. And he looked at Mara like she's his entire life."

"She is."

"Go on, then," Lillian said. "But the two of you are going to come clean in two shakes of a lamb's tail. I'm makin' coffee. You drink it?"

"Yes, ma'am. Lillian." Cade hurried into the guest room and shut the door. After draping his wet clothes on a chair, he sank onto the bed. Exhaustion pressed down on him. If he weren't so worried about Livie showing up or leaving Mara to explain his presence alone, he'd let himself sleep.

He'd just pulled on a dry pair of jeans when a quiet knock sounded at the door.

"Cade?"

"Come on in, honey." Cade reached for a sweatshirt as the door opened, but froze as Mara stepped inside the room. She wore a pair of gray fleece pants, a faded green sweatshirt at least two sizes too big for her, and thick socks.

Fear hunched her shoulders, and she looked so lost. Her gaze locked on his naked chest, and her cheeks flushed. "Sorry," Cade said as he tugged on the sweatshirt.

"I wasn't complaining." Stifling a laugh, she stared down at the floor. "Clearly the stress is getting to me. What did you tell Aunt Lil?"

"That my clothes were in here."

"She's going to give you the third degree," Mara said as she leaned against the door jamb.

"I think she'll be more interested in what Eleanor has to say about your illness. Though they *have* been gossiping about me the whole time I've been in here."

"What?"

"Weres have better hearing, sight, and smell than humans." Snaking an arm around her waist, he pulled her close, and she tipped her head up at him. "I saw those dark circles this morning," he said as he brushed his index finger along her cheek. "They're gone now."

"But my hands. The shaking's getting worse." She spread her fingers, and Cade covered them with his own.

"Your element is water, my dear. You're dehydrated. Come sit." Eleanor's voice floated into the bedroom on a breeze. Mara frowned, confused.

"Well, it's not like that's the weirdest thing that's happened today," she muttered.

"Air elementals can eavesdrop," Cade said.

For one brief moment, Mara sank against Cade and let him hold her. "Is it too early for a drink?"

Mara

"Bottom's up," Eleanor said as she set a glass of water in front of Mara.

The liquid soothed her nerves. If she could only get into the pool for a few dozen laps, she'd feel better. But with Cade at her side and Livie on the way, she wasn't going to be able to swim any time soon.

Plus, Aunt Lil didn't look like she planned on letting Mara out of her sight.

Cade's stomach growled, drawing Mara's gaze. She hadn't even noticed how haggard he looked. His eyes were practically hollow.

Mara rose and grabbed the box of cookies, a chocolate bar, and a large slice of pie and dumped the lot in front of Cade. "Eat something, shaggy man."

"Are we havin' high tea or talkin' about who the hell this werewolf is and what's makin' Mara sick?" Aunt Lil demanded.

"Cade's about to pass out. He needs to eat a lot more often than we do. Especially now." Mara glared at the two women, then sank back down.

Three cookies disappeared in under two minutes, and not a single crumb hit the table. He dug his fork into the pie, but paused before taking a bite. "Thanks, honey. I'm okay. I want to know what Eleanor has to say about your illness."

"You call all the women you know 'honey'?" Lillian asked.

"No." Cade draped his hand over Mara's. A subtle tingle ran through her body.

If only they had more time. Mara wanted to see what they could become. But for the moment, she relished the feel of his strong, rough hand gripping hers. She needed all the comfort and reassurance she could get.

Eleanor grinned from behind her coffee cup. "There are four main elements. Earth, air, fire, and water. My element is air." A cool eddy ruffled Mara's curls. "It's how I heard you talking about your symptoms earlier. You'd be surprised how often air elementals work for the government. I spent several years with the CIA in my youth."

"What...what else can you do?" Mara asked.

"I can carry sounds and scents for up to half a mile. I can also move objects." Eleanor held her hand over the chocolate bar and inhaled deeply. The candy rose from the table, flipped in midair, and landed in front of Cade. "Outdoors on a windy day, I would even lift *you* five or ten feet."

This was too much. Mara tightened her grip on Cade's hand, unsure what to say, and after a moment, Eleanor continued. "Your element is water, Mara. What happened earlier? You and your wolf were soaked. Did your element do that?"

"Y-yes. I was scared. I heard—this is going to sound crazy—but I heard music. Like this deafening roar of noise, but it was a sound I *craved*. I knew I had to get away, so I followed it."

"Get away from what?" Lillian asked. "Did that wolf hurt you?"

"No!" Mara glared at her aunt. "It was a misunderstanding. Cade didn't touch me. What caused it isn't important. All of a sudden, there was water everywhere and I couldn't feel my body anymore. And the music was gone."

"She passed out," Cade said quietly. "For maybe five, six minutes."

"When I came to, everything hurt. I couldn't even get up. And my hands started shaking again. If that's what using my element is...I don't ever want to feel like that again." Her voice cracked, and Cade shifted his chair closer so he could wrap his arm around her waist.

Eleanor shook her head. "It won't be like that every time, my dear. You'll get used to the power. Think of this like a muscle you need to train. The music you heard...that was your element resonating with your body and the world around you."

Lillian raised a thin, white brow at her friend. "How is all this related to what's killin' her?"

"You're familiar with yin and yang?" Eleanor asked. "Water's opposite is fire. The two must always be in balance with one another. Mara has fire within her. Too much, somehow. Not using her water element is letting the fire take over, and her body can't handle it."

Mara straightened in her seat. "That's why my blood doesn't carry oxygen properly? Fire consumes oxygen, right? If there's too much fire inside me, it robs my blood of what it needs?" Despite how outrageous Eleanor's claims sounded, there was a logic to them Mara couldn't deny.

Eleanor smiled, a teacher proud of her student. "Yes, dear. If you used your element every few days, it would keep the fire balanced." Her expression turned serious. "When I have to spend time in a basement or in a stale, sealed office building, I feel ill.

Earth elementals cannot fly in airplanes. It can quite literally kill them. And fire elementals do not deal well with rain."

"The one that nearly killed me didn't seem to mind being on Orcas Island for seven months," Cade muttered. "Even when the rains came. She and her earth elemental had no problems maintaining their charms on the ground or on me."

"May I?" Eleanor asked, holding out her hand. Cade let her run her fingers over his palm. "You bear some residual fire, wolf. But I can also sense the earth clinging to you. What were the charm's effects?"

Cade rubbed the back of his neck and stared down at the chocolate bar. "It stopped me from shifting. I think she explained it to me, but those memories are fuzzy. All I know is whenever I tried to shift, it was like my insides were burning up. I couldn't think. Couldn't breathe. Even after I escaped the island and was here with Mara, I couldn't shift back." He shuddered, and Mara rested her palm on his thigh until he linked fingers with hers.

"And you, Mara? How did you break the charm?" Eleanor asked.

She tightened her grip on Cade's fingers. "I think I was dying," she said quietly. Aunt Lil made a disapproving sound, but Eleanor shot her a look that shut her up. "I'd never felt as terrible as I did that night. I was holding the wolf, convinced I was going to die, and then...the whole room was terribly humid, I was on the floor, and Cade was...not a wolf anymore."

"Tell me, wolf... You're experiencing some physical weakness? Exhaustion?"

Cade nodded.

"I will teach Mara a few simple charms. Ones that won't leave you half-drowned. They'll help." With a gentle smile, Eleanor withdrew a small, leather pouch from her pocket and dumped the contents in the center of the table. Four clear glass vials. Red, blue, brown, and clear. "The four elements. These are yours now,

Mara. Keep them close while you learn. They'll help you focus. For now, both of you put a hand on the table, palm up."

Mara chewed on her lip as Eleanor placed the water and air vials in Cade's palm and the earth and fire in hers. A vague sense of nausea flared in her belly.

"Focus on the fire, Mara, and take Cade's other hand."

As soon as she touched Cade, the nausea faded. Behind the brilliant blue of his eyes, she could see his wolf. Wild strength and dominance. For a moment, she forgot the burning vial in her palm.

"Try to sense the water Cade has. Let me know when you feel it."

Mara closed her eyes and let the tingling energy flow between them. A familiar melody, the one she heard every time she used her element, started as a whisper and grew steadily louder. It flowed from Cade up her arm, through her chest, and all the way to her other palm, easing the pain from the vial of fire. "I feel something. It's...odd. But nice."

"Can you send it back to him? Use the points of contact in your palm." Eleanor pressed her own hand over the vials Mara held, and the fire burned her skin, so hot and so fast, she could almost hear the sizzle.

"Stop. It hurts," Mara whispered. Cade tightened his grip on her fingers and growled.

"You can end the pain," Eleanor said with a hint of disapproval to her tone. "Find the water around you. Use the connection between you and the wolf."

It was no use. The nausea crawled up her throat, and her body started to shake. Sweat beaded along her forehead, and pain sliced through her chest with every beat of her heart. "Can't."

"Mara!" Cade grabbed her as she slid off the chair and snatched the vials out of her hand. She slumped against his hard chest and buried her face in his neck, inhaling his scent as tears stung her eyes. "You're okay, honey. I've got you."

It took several long minutes for Mara to feel strong enough to raise her head. All the while, Cade rubbed her back.

"What...happened?" she managed when she looked up at Eleanor. Her palm bore an angry, red burn.

"I don't know." Eleanor shook her head and whispered a few words, sending a breath of cool air across the skin. "The vial is barely warm. The fire you carry is so much stronger than it should be. One of your parents must have been a fire elemental. But fire usually begets earth or more fire, not water."

Pushing up and starting to pace the kitchen, Eleanor ran a hand through her salt and pepper hair. "You are a mystery, Mara."

"As much as I hate to do it," Mara said as she extricated herself from Cade's embrace and sank back into her own chair, "maybe we should try to find my sister again." With a quick glance at Aunt Lil, she frowned. "She might know more about our parents. I think she was twelve when our mother died. I don't want to have *any* contact with Katerina. She scares the crap out of me. But—"

Cade's entire body stiffened. Shoving his chair back, he stood with a low growl. The wolf flashed in his eyes, gold and silver flecks swirling around his irises. "Katerina? Olmstead?"

Mara jerked up, forcing her knees not to buckle and bracing her hands on the table. "Yes. Cade, what's wrong? How did you even know her last name?"

Cade took two steps back, almost to the hall. "Katerina Olmstead is the fire elemental who trapped me as my wolf. Who killed my father and his *entire pack*. *She's* your fucking *sister?*"

21

Mara

HER SISTER? Katerina had done this? All of it? The lump in Mara's throat felt like it was about to choke her, and she clenched her fists at her sides, desperate to stop them from shaking. "Katerina is only my sister by blood. I don't even *know* her. The only time I met her I told her to go to hell." A few drops of water escaped her balled hands, and a high-pitched hum filled her ears.

"Mara, calm down," Eleanor said sharply. "I don't fancy a shower." A breeze ruffled Mara's hair and brought Cade's scent to wrap around her. But when she met his gaze again, his eyes were wild, and his chest heaved with each breath.

"Cade?" she asked.

"That's not...there's more." He swallowed hard. "My father killed your mother. That's why your sister is out for revenge."

His words barely registered before a knock at the door made everyone jump. Cade growled and whirled around. "Fuck. Livie."

His gaze pinged between the door and Mara, as if he couldn't decide whether to stay or go.

"I don't understand any of this." Mara took one step forward, then another, then another until she was so close, she could hear Cade's strained breathing. But he made no move to touch her.

The doorbell rang five times in a row, followed by another round of knocking.

"I need some air," Cade said roughly and brushed past Mara. The door opened and shut with a slam.

A single tear trailed down Mara's cheek, and she wiped it away before sinking down to the floor and dropping her head into her hands. "I've lost him."

Lillian made a vague sound of disapproval. "A few minutes ago, that wolf looked at you like you were his reason for living. He sure as shit ain't goin' to walk away from you. And if he does, he don't deserve you. As for yer mama—the one who birthed you—there's more to that story. Some I know, some I don't. Now get back to this table. Tell me who this Livie person is and everything you know about what your no-good sister did to your wolf."

Mara couldn't force herself to move, but she did sigh and tell her aunt and Eleanor about Cade's seven months of hell trapped as his beast, how she'd come to find him, their trip to Bellingham, and the heated—or watery—encounter with Livie.

Aunt Lillian huffed and dug around in her purse, coming away with a small, heavy-looking leather pouch. "Livie and I are goin' to have a little talk. No one messes with my niece."

"No!" Mara pushed to her feet and stopped Lillian, gently taking the older woman's shoulders and guiding her back to the table. "She didn't know who I was. She smelled my—whatever the hell it is—and she got a little upset. I'm fine. Cade made her promise not to touch me again. He's her alpha, and I don't think she's allowed to cross him."

"If she does...she's going to meet my .38." Lillian nodded at the leather case and shoved it back into her purse.

Mara managed a laugh until her aunt's words sunk in. "Wait. You have a gun?"

"I'm from Memphis, hon. They issue you one when they print your birth certificate. Now sit back down and let's get you some tea." Lillian patted Mara's shoulder and headed towards the stove.

"I need something stronger."

Lillian stopped mid-stride and reached for a bottle in the top cabinet instead. "Whiskey, then."

The drink burned its way down Mara's throat, but she did feel marginally better.

"They're going to be out there for a while," Eleanor said. "I think this is a good time to teach you how to work with your element."

Cade

Livie leaned against Mara's garage door. Though it had stopped raining, the wind ruffled her angled blond bob. "One question. Gut answer. Don't think about it," she said. "Do you believe her?"

"Yes." Cade stopped pacing and stared at Mara's front door. "She's the purest soul I've ever met. If she were working with Katerina, she could have let my wolf die. When she found me, I don't think I had more than a couple of hours left." He ran a hand through his hair, trying to remember that first, panic-filled night. "There was this friend of hers. A vet. She called him to help me. He...wanted to euthanize me and she stopped him."

Livie muttered a quiet oath, then forced out a breath. "So why are you still outside with me?"

"I don't know what to say to her." He slouched against her car. "She's my mate, Livie. She doesn't understand yet, but I'm already falling for her. It's more than just the instinct to claim her, I want to *know* her. And for her to know *me*. Part of that is hearing what happened to me. All of it. How's she going to feel knowing it was her blood who did this?" Cade turned his hands up to show Livie his scarred palms. "And what about my father killing her mother? She'll never forgive me."

Livie's lips pressed into a thin line, and she swallowed hard as she rubbed her arm. "You won't know until you talk to her."

Cade trudged back to the porch and sank onto the steps. "You're on her side now?"

Cradling her belly, Livie eased down next to him. "No. I'm not. I'm on *your* side. But I saw how you looked at her. And I know how I feel about Shawn. If you can have what we have—even with an elemental—that's what I want for you."

"I never thought I'd mate," Cade said quietly.

"I don't think anyone does until they find the one for them." Pain edged Livie's voice as she ran a hand through her hair. "You weren't there after the fire. Liam dragged my wolf out of the ruins of the building. Shawn was unconscious—smoke inhalation. And I...couldn't shift." She shuddered. "That bitch's charm kept me in wolf form for three days. By the time it wore off, the damage was done." Rubbing her arm, she let out a sigh. "Shawn stayed by my side the whole time. Holding me, talking to me, keeping me calm. I don't think I could have made it without him."

For a long time, neither of them said another word. For December, it was a dry day, but cool, and Livie played with the hem of her sweatshirt. "You don't look so good, boss-man," she murmured. "I'm worried about you."

Cade nudged her shoulder with his. "I'll be okay. I need to see everyone. Figure out how to tell Mara I won't leave her. That she's...mine. I'll be steady once I do that." His stomach growled. "And I need a whole pan of lasagna. Shit. A couple of steaks too. Maybe another pie."

Arching a brow, Livie asked, "Has Mara learned how much we eat yet?"

"I've cleaned her out the past couple of days." Cade went on to explain what he knew of Mara's illness, how little she'd eaten before she'd freed him from his wolf. "I want to cook for her. I used to cook, didn't I?"

"Yeah. At least once a week. Lasagna. Every single time. Want to try making it? I can go to the grocery store. Provided you promise to stay inside until I get back."

"Fuck. Yes, please. Get enough stuff for a couple of pans." He was already salivating, and he glanced back at Mara's front door. "Just...give me a couple of minutes first."

Livie rubbed her belly. "Well, you don't have too much longer. This one's kicking up a storm today. He's going to be strong, and I'm pretty sure he heard the word lasagna."

In all of his memories, he didn't think he'd been around any other pregnant wolves. Not that he could be sure of anything, at the moment. "Can I?" he asked.

Taking his hand, Livie laid it over her rounded belly, and a tiny kick hit his palm. Then another. Harder this time. He laughed. "Future alpha, you think?"

"That's what Shawn wants. I don't care as long as he's healthy. Or she. I feel like it's a boy, but I haven't tried to find out. Couldn't go to a human doctor in Ireland. Too risky."

Cade's brows furrowed. "Mara's a neonatal nurse. Maybe she knows someone we could trust."

"You think we'll be here long enough for that?"

Glancing up and down Mara's street, he spied a for sale sign on the house next door. Three stories. Five bedrooms, three baths, a full basement. From the looks of it, the place needed work, but it had good bones. Liam and Peter could fix it up.

A glimmer of hope ignited deep inside him. There was no way in hell he could leave his pack, but he wouldn't leave Mara either. Not if she'd have him. But they had to figure out if Katerina was still a threat before he made *any* decisions.

"Maybe. Do you think...?" He couldn't ask her if the pack would accept Mara. An alpha didn't *need* permission—one of the stupid unspoken rules they all lived by. And fuck. He didn't even know if he *was* their alpha anymore. Liam could have taken over.

"Cade?" Livie squeezed his arm. She never called him by name. "I didn't think I'd see you again. None of us did. Not really. Not after seven months. There isn't anything I won't do for you. Or her."

Cade wrapped his arms around Livie and tried to hold back the emotions that threatened to drown him until her phone buzzed with a text message.

Got a last minute flight. Cost a fucking fortune, but we'll be there tomorrow night. Liam hasn't stopped pacing since you called. Love you.

"Leave it to my mate to be worried about the cost of the tickets," Livie muttered.

"Well, he does handle all our finances."

"Yeah, but if there were ever a time to spend money, it's now. Liam, Ollie, and Peter have been working at one of the local pubs. Christine got a job in a surgery, but all she can do is answer phones. I want to come home, boss-man. I don't think I can stand another potato or stew. We couldn't run free. Not as a pack anyway. Shawn and I came back here a few times looking for you and we ran together—conceived the pup in our woods in Bellingham—but otherwise we've had to confine our wolves to Liam's castle. Three stories isn't enough. Plus, our nails did a number on his hardwood floors. He was pissed."

"I imagine so," Cade said with a genuine smile. It felt good to laugh and grin again, to feel the camaraderie he thought he'd always enjoyed with Livie.

They talked for another hour, filling in some of the gaps in Cade's memories, Livie explaining how they'd survived for so long. How Liam had the most trouble returning to Ireland, the ghosts of his past—of the elemental he'd loved years ago— haunting him.

The front door opened, and Lillian cleared her throat. "Wolf? I need a minute of your time before Eleanor and I leave."

"Is Mara okay?" The bitter taste of guilt made him frown. He shouldn't have left angry, shouldn't have assumed...anything. She'd saved his life and he'd known all along she'd been adopted.

"She's resting, and I don't want either of you to disturb her," Lillian said, ice edging her tone as she fixed Livie with a hard stare.

Cade stood, then helped Livie to her feet. "This is Lillian. Mara's aunt. Lillian, this is Livie."

Lil huffed. "How many more of you wolves are there?"

"Five more," Livie replied. "They're on their way."

"Well, y'all better not give my niece any more stress. She's had enough to deal with of late. It's why she's restin' now. You keep it down and let her sleep till she's good and ready to get up again. Usin' her element tuckered her out, and if she don't replenish her energy, she's gonna get sick again."

Cade puffed out his chest and stood up straighter. "I won't let that happen. I swear. I'll take care of her."

Livie stared between the two of them, then took a step back. "You don't need me here for this. I'm headed to the store. Boss-man, you do not leave the house. If you do anything to put yourself in danger, Liam will have my pelt."

Flinching, Cade grunted, "Okay."

Liam will have my pelt.

She wouldn't have said that unless Liam was her alpha now. Cade ran a hand through his shaggy locks to give himself a moment to grieve the loss of the role that he'd never wanted, but couldn't imagine ever giving up. Liam had done the right thing. When the rest of them got here, Cade would pledge his allegiance to his former beta. It was the only thing he could do.

"Well, come on, then." Lillian turned and headed back to the kitchen. "Sit down and stop acting like I'm about to hit you with a rolled-up newspaper," she snapped. From the living room, Eleanor chuckled.

The air in the house was thick with humidity—and Mara's

scent. It wrapped around Cade like a warm blanket, and he ached to lose himself in it.

Taking his seat across from Lillian, he watched her warily.

"What are your intentions towards my niece?"

"I care about her. She's...I think she's my mate. I want to ask her if she'll, um, date me." He wanted to do a hell of a lot more than that, but he and Mara were from two different worlds, and he couldn't make assumptions.

"What if she asks you to leave?" Lillian's bright blue eyes sharpened as she leaned forward in her chair.

"I'll go. Mara has nothing to fear from me. Ever. Walking out earlier? That was a mistake. Livie was pretty damn clear I was an idiot."

"She's not wrong." Lillian took a sip from her coffee mug and shook her head. "Though Katerina is somethin'. Mara was sick for a week after that hussy came to visit when she was a teenager. I didn't put two and two together at the time, but I should've. Might have saved some lives. I'd wager that one hasn't limited her killin' to your relations."

A long-ago memory fought its way to the surface. Something his former alpha had said to him. "Regrets are useless," Cade said. "You can lose your whole life to them."

Lillian laughed. "You really are hers, ain't ya? Mara started sayin' somethin' like that after she got sick. She spent the past nine months convinced she was dying. She'd accepted it. Hell, I think she was lookin' forward to it in a way. No more transfusions, no more fallin' asleep on the couch before the sun went down. No more havin' to put on a brave face. No more unknown."

"But she's not dying," Cade said.

Eleanor came to lean against the doorjamb. "No, she's not. But if she's going to stay that way, she has to use her element. Every day. She's got so much fire within her that it'll kill her if she's not careful. I taught her some things, simple charms really. I'm not a water elemental. I can only do so much. When you can—when things are safe—bring Mara to Cannon Beach. To the elemental community there. They can teach her everything she needs to know."

Cade nodded. Once he settled things with the pack, he could leave. A vacation, even if it was to a community of people with the same sorts of abilities as Katerina, sounded like a good idea—as long as his mate was at his side. He had to tell her soon. He owed her that much. "We'll go. I promise."

22

Mara

STRETCHING OUT UNDER THE BLANKET, Mara focused on the candle burning on her dresser. All of the other lights in the room were out, and the flame seemed to give off a low, out of tune melody that ran afoul of the light, sweet tones of her water element.

As her fingers started to tremble, she struggled to sense the water in the air. A single drop formed in her palm, and then the reassuring sounds of her element took over.

She'd done it. Stopped herself from giving in to the fire in her blood. And all she wanted to do was tell Cade. Was he still here? She'd dreamed of him. Kissing her, smoothing his hand over her hair, whispering something in her ear. She'd felt safe and cherished, and she needed that again.

A thundering fall of rain pelted her roof and windows, and the wind howled. As she pulled the blanket up higher, she realized someone had taken off her shoes. And the blanket...it had been on the back of the couch earlier.

Had the dream been real?

Her stomach rumbled, and she headed for the kitchen. Oh, God. The most amazing scents wafted towards her. Cheese, tomatoes, spices... Candles burned in the living room and a fire roared in the hearth. The discordant song from the flames echoed for a brief moment, then faded.

Cade stared out the kitchen window, his feet bare, the sleeves of his sweatshirt pushed up to his elbows.

"Hey."

He turned, and Mara tried, unsuccessfully, not to let the sight of him stir up all those familiar butterflies in her stomach.

"Hey, yourself. Feeling better?"

Mara shrugged. "Jury's still out." Leaning against the kitchen counter only a few inches away, she inhaled his scent, and Cade rested his hands on her hips, pulling her close enough for her to feel the heat rolling off his body.

"Why? What's wrong and how can I help?"

Unsure what to say, she held his gaze, and her lips curved into a small, sad smile. "It's not physical. Don't worry."

"I'm always going to worry."

Always was a long time. How could he say that? She squeezed her eyes shut and took a moment to gather her thoughts. "A month ago, I knew werewolves weren't real. The closest things to elementals were the Wiccans who run the occult shop up on Phinney Ridge. They have a wild party every Halloween. Usually someone ends up running down the main drag naked before the night's over."

Cade chuckled, and the rumbling in his chest spread through her.

"I'd made my peace with dying. I was ready. By the time you found me, I had maybe five weeks left. I was on the island to say goodbye. To everything. Not suicide," she added hurriedly when Cade's fingers tightened on her hips. "I wanted one last swim. One last night alone in my favorite hotel, one last sunset on the balcony. But then this sick animal showed up in my trunk and all of a sudden my life turned upside down. And now, not only are you—*you*, but I might not be dying at all. I could have a future. It's...a lot to process."

"What do you need?" Cade slid his hands up her back, and she rested her head on his shoulder and melted against him. He felt so good. How could she be so comfortable with him this quickly? In just a few days with the wolf, she'd started to care— deeply. And now that he was a man? Her feelings had only intensified.

"Cade," she breathed. "I need to know what you're going to do about my sister. How can you even stand to be around me when I'm related to the woman who tortured you?" Mara tightened her embrace, hoping he wouldn't make her let go.

Her heart sank as he took her by the shoulders and eased her back to look into her eyes. "Nothing. You're not her. You're kind and compassionate and...mine." His breath hitched, and he averted his gaze. "I shouldn't have walked out earlier. I was scared and stupid. I'm sorry."

He wasn't leaving her. At least...not tonight. Relief flooded her, lessening some of the tension in her neck. "I don't blame you."

A little thrill raced down her spine as he pulled her back against him. *Mine.* He'd said *mine.*

His growing arousal pressed to her belly, hinting at his unspoken desires, and when she raised her head, his lips found hers.

The kiss was anything but hesitant. He took everything. Strong hands cupped her ass and lifted her up onto the counter.

His stubble tickled her upper lip, and rough fingers slid along her sides under her sweatshirt, branding her skin with his heat. A moan vibrated in her throat, and Cade nipped the corner of her mouth.

"Mara," he managed, "I want—"

Her stomach growled, and her cheeks caught fire. Along with

the rest of her. "So do I. But I'm also really hungry, and whatever's in the oven smells amazing."

Cade lifted her off the counter, taut muscles and a dark, hungry gaze turning her insides to jelly. "Lasagna."

With more than a little difficulty, she wriggled out of his arms and popped the oven door. "How much longer?"

"It's done. I was going to wake you up soon. Sit down, and I'll take care of the rest. There's wine on the table."

Mara frowned. "Where is everyone?"

"Lillian took Eleanor back to her condo. Livie's resting. We had a snack while you were sleeping."

"A snack?"

Cade chuckled. "We shared a pan. This is the second one. Don't worry. I'm still hungry."

His rich, deep laugh warmed her down to her toes. It seemed to vibrate his whole body, crinkling his eyes and rounding his cheeks.

She wanted to hear that sound every day. See him happy every day.

"Is Livie all right?" Mara poured them each a glass of wine and sank into one of the chairs.

"She's fine. She'll patrol tonight." Cade cut two generous slices of lasagna, retrieved a salad from the fridge, and joined her.

"It's miserable outside. A pregnant woman should not be— what? Patrolling in this rain and wind?"

"She'll be in wolf form. She won't even notice. She loves the rain."

OVER DINNER, Cade told Mara what he remembered about his childhood. "My father was pack alpha, so he was always kind of scary. He loved me, but he made it pretty clear that crossing him wasn't an option."

"Was he abusive?"

"No. Intimidating. He never had to hit me because I knew instinctively that his wolf was dominant, even before I shifted for the first time."

"When was that?"

"I think I was thirteen. It happens around puberty. The first shift is terrifying. It feels like dying. Hell, it feels like dying every time, but at least after the first you know what to expect."

"Why do you do it then?"

"We have to. Until you get control of the wolf inside, there's no fighting it. But once the wolf emerges, it's an amazing feeling. At least when you're free." He smiled sadly and forced his shoulders back. "You can run farther and faster than ever before. You can smell everything. See so much more. A wolf's senses are better than a human's. Even in this form." Cade held Mara's hand to his lips. "I can still smell chlorine in your pores after what? Three days?" She nodded and he kissed the inside of her wrist and the fleshy pad of her thumb. "A bit of marinara here. And me. I can smell my scent on you."

Mara pulled her hand away and looked down at her plate. She traced a pattern in the sauce with her fork until Cade gave up his intense scrutiny of her and sat back, returning to his meal.

"Does it always hurt?"

"Yeah. You feel every bone break. The teeth are the worst. That pain shoots right through your skull." Cade shivered and rubbed his jaw.

Mara polished off the last of her salad. "What about your mother?"

"I don't really remember her. Too many holes yet. Her name was Rachel, and I know she died well before my father. But that's it. Other than some vaguely warm feelings. I know I loved her."

His last words were thick and strained, and Mara reached out and draped her hand over his. "You'll find her again. Your memories of her. I believe that."

"I hope you're right." Cade's eyes glistened in the glow from a battery-operated lantern in the center of the table.

"My mom had a heart attack when I was sixteen," Mara said quietly. "Right in front of me. One minute she was joking around, and the next she was on the floor. She was gone before the paramedics got there. Dad basically drank himself to death five years ago. He couldn't live without her."

Silence stretched between them, and Cade cleared his throat. "Mara, my father...what he did..."

"Lil told me what really happened." She reached over and linked their fingers. "After my sister came to visit, Lil wanted to find out the real story." With a snort, she shook her head. "She can't remember who she talked to in Barstow, but from how she described him? I think she talked to your father."

Cade jerked his head up and held her gaze. "My father?"

"She said you kind of look like the sheriff she met with. Lil's kind of like a divining rod," Mara said with a smile. "She can tell when people are lying. Kind of freaky. And not so much fun when you're seventeen and trying to sneak out of the house. But she believed him. My birth mother was at fault. Not your father."

Cade seemed to deflate in front of her, and when he leapt up to take his dish to the sink, Mara followed.

"Hey." She reached for him, and a spark ran up her arm. "What is it?"

"You're my—"

The bedroom door opened with a subtle click, and Cade's mouth snapped shut as Livie staggered out with a yawn. "Oh, thank God. There's still lasagna." Rounding the corner into the kitchen, she stopped short. "Shit. I interrupted something important."

"Yes." Cade glared at Livie, but Mara rolled her eyes.

"It's fine, really." Despite how very *not fine* it was, Mara wasn't willing to cross the fierce blond wolf. Not even after Cade had assured her safety. "Can I get you something to drink? I don't have much..."

"Oh, I went shopping," Livie said. "Sorry, I kinda took over your fridge. But mama's gotta eat every few hours. And boss-man looks like the walking dead." She rummaged around for a minute before coming away with a bag of carrots, a plate of lasagna, and a bottle of juice.

Mara gaped. She'd seen Cade devour two sandwiches in under five minutes, but Livie was so tiny—even with her growing belly.

After she'd finished, Livie pushed back from the table. "Okay. I'm going to shift in the bedroom and then go patrol. Someone's going to need to let me outside."

"Are you sure?" Mara asked. "It's awful out. The baby—"

"He's fine. I was running in the woods all night last night. It was awesome." She took two steps down the hall, then turned with a gleam in her eye. "Hey, you didn't get to see Cade shift, did you?"

"No."

"Want to watch?" Her gaze turned hard, almost challenging.

"Livie," Cade growled. "Don't."

"What?" Mara turned to him. "I want to know what it's like."

"She's trying to scare you. It's not a pleasant thing to watch if you don't know what to expect. Stay here." He reached for Mara's arm, but she shook her head and pulled away.

"I don't scare easily." Mara nodded at Livie. "After you."

With a quiet huff, Livie shrugged. "Come on, then."

Back in the guest room, Livie stripped, and Cade hovered in the doorway, glowering. Mara could *feel* his anger, but also, a strange sense of jealousy deep in her own belly. She didn't want Cade's eyes on the naked woman, even if Livie was mated and quite obviously pregnant.

Reddish ropes of scar tissue covered Livie's left arm and shoulder, winding down to her hip. The realization that her sister had done this hit her, and she clenched her fists, calling on a bit of her element when her fingers started to tremble.

Livie took a deep breath as she sank to her knees. It started with her skin. Darkening from pale pink to gray, fur sprouted all along her spine. Pops and cracks of bones followed, and her blond hair disappeared, replaced with a luxurious brown and gold pelt.

She released a mournful howl as her shoulders dislocated and her arms and legs transformed. Sharp, black nails extended from each finger.

Mara was mesmerized. When the large wolf sat up, panting, awe filled her. "That's...beautiful."

Livie's wolf cocked her head.

"And the baby?" She turned to Cade. "Does the baby shift too?"

"No. He's still human." Cade fixed his glare on Livie. "Mara could check on the pup, Liv."

Padding over to Mara, Livie snorted, then lay down on her side, belly exposed.

Mara knelt, resting her hand over the baby bump. A kick stretched Livie's pelt and bristled the fur. With a practiced touch, Mara stroked her fingers over Livie's belly. "He's perfect. That's a little fist right there," she said, pointing to a sudden protrusion just under the wolf's ribs. She held Livie's gaze. "Thank you. Really."

With a yip, Livie nodded and headed for the front door. Cade let her out, told her to be careful, and to scratch when she wanted to come back in.

"She doesn't like me," Mara said when Cade joined her on the couch and handed her a glass of water. "That was a challenge."

"It was."

Mara tucked her legs under her with a sad sigh. "The rest of them are going to feel the same way, aren't they?"

In the firelight, Cade's eyes glowed, the silver streaks in the deep blue depths even brighter than usual. "Mara, please. Trust me for a while. Until I have a chance to talk to all of them."

You mean until you leave.

She didn't voice her fears, only nodded. She didn't want to lose him, but she did trust him.

23

Katerina

THE GUTTERS OVERFLOWED WITH RAINWATER, souring her mood, but at least the inside of the van was warm, fueled by her element. Bella, who'd flown in from Phoenix several days prior, had her nose pressed to a crack in the window.

"Anything?" Katerina asked.

Barely breaking focus, Bella shook her head. "There's been nothin' since I lost his scent on the beach on Orcas," the air elemental said softly. After a lot of yelling—mostly by Katerina—and some quick thinking on Bella's part, using her air charms on a hotel proprietor who'd admitted there'd been a car parked at the beach the day the wolf had escaped, they'd headed to Bellingham.

He must have found his way off the island, and perhaps, he'd tried to go home. Jeremy turned the van towards the empty lot where the pack's apartment complex had been, and Katerina strained to see through the downpour.

"I'm tired," Bella said. "And there's somethin' about this place

I don't like." Her voice held a hint of an accent—had ever since she'd stepped off the plane.

"We could get a room for tonight." Jeremy parked and glanced at Katerina. "We've been driving for hours."

Gritting her teeth, Katerina tried not to get angry with the two people who meant the most to her. They were both trying to help —she knew it—but losing the wolf had nearly destroyed her. Killing him had been the sole focus of her life for so long, she didn't know what she'd do if she couldn't finish the job.

"Wait!" Bella cried as she rolled down the window and stuck her whole head outside the van. After another moment, the air elemental leapt out of the van and took off at a run towards the end of the block. She veered left and disappeared.

"Follow her," Katerina said.

They found Bella in front of Cade's old woodworking shop, her dark hair plastered to her head, makeup running down her cheeks. "He's been here. In the past twenty-four hours. And...there's something else, too."

"What?" Katerina asked.

"Water. He had a water elemental with him."

———

JEREMY CAME AROUND to the passenger side of the van and held an umbrella open to protect Katerina from the rain. Using a quick fire charm, she melted the lock on the back door, and the three elementals hurried inside.

Bella inhaled deeply, and her charms filled the room, stirring the dust that covered almost everything.

"Three of them," she said. "Two wolves, one water elemental." Kneeling next to a puddle of water, Bella touched the water, then brought her fingers to her lips. "Metallic. It's almost...like blood. There's something wrong with this elemental. Her power tastes...burnt. Have either of you heard of one of us with two elements?" Bella shivered, as if she couldn't stand the thought.

"It's impossible," Katerina replied. "One element is always dominant. No one has ever been known to be able to work with two."

Bella's disbelief was written all over her face, but she continued to explore the shop. "The female wolf spent a lot of time in this back room."

"Can you track them?" Katerina asked.

Bella nodded. "I need to get outside. It's easier there."

Wrapping an arm around Bella's shoulders, Katerina guided the woman through the front door. The air elemental was a fragile woman and hated the Pacific Northwest as much as Katerina did.

Eleven years ago, while chasing the elder Bowman's pack, Katerina had found Bella washed up on the beach in Mexico with no memory of...anything. She'd barely been able to speak.

Something about the woman had called to Katerina, and she'd abandoned her search for the old wolf—the one who'd warned Cade she was coming—and taken care of Bella. She'd even invented the woman's name.

The air elemental stopped at the empty lot that had once housed the werewolf's apartment building and cast another charm. "She was here, but she didn't stay." An eddy of air made the raindrops dance across the sidewalk, and Bella rushed across the street.

A row of townhomes stretched out along half the block, and Bella pointed to one on the end. "There."

Katerina knocked, and a light flickered on as shuffling footsteps sounded inside the house.

"Who is it?" an elderly voice called.

Bella cleared her throat. "Ma'am, my name is Christine. I used to live across the street with my brother. He disappeared almost eight months ago, and I'm trying to track him down."

Several locks clicked. The door opened a crack, and a white-haired old woman peered out over the chain. "You're with those wolves?"

Katerina gestured to Jeremy, and he shoved the door open, snapping the chain and pushing the old woman against the wall.

"What the hell?" the woman spat.

"Where's the elemental?" Katerina followed Jeremy into the house as Bella shut the door behind them.

"What elemental?" The old woman backed away slowly towards her living room, but Jeremy pushed her down onto the sofa before slapping her across the cheek. "You need a serious lesson in manners, young man."

"I need to know everything, Bella." Katerina crossed her arms, leaning against the wall across from the couch. Air elementals could weave charms so powerful, they could compel a person to tell the truth—no matter how hard the victim fought back.

"Listen to me," the woman grumbled. "I'm eighty-three years old. Buried my husband a decade ago. I've survived cancer, a heart attack, and a stroke. Not to mention the World War II. Lost my son to Vietnam and my home to the Nisqually earthquake. There is *nothing* that scares me. You want to slap me around? Burn me alive? That's right. I know who you are. These eyes might need reading glasses, but they never forget a face. I'm not telling you anything."

Katerina smiled. The old woman was no more than a hundred pounds, dressed in a fuzzy pink housecoat and slippers. White hair haloed her head and her lined face bore the distinct imprint of Jeremy's hand. Her pale blue eyes were defiant, but that wouldn't last long. "Bella, do your thing."

AN HOUR LATER, the old woman—Bella had learned her name was Maggie—huddled in the corner of the sofa, chest heaving.

Despite the strongest of her air charms, the woman hadn't divulged a thing.

"Get the hell out of my house," Maggie gasped. "Bitch."

Katerina's hands itched. The notes of her fire started deep within her as a low baritone. She grabbed Maggie's wrists. The old woman screamed as her flesh sizzled, and Bella dampened the sound.

"Tell me where they went," Katerina said, eyes blazing.

Maggie slumped in Katerina's grip, unconscious. "Dammit!"

Jeremy poked his head in from the kitchen, a triumphant smile on his thin face. "Babe. Take a look at this." He handed her a slip of paper. "This was tacked up on the fridge."

Mara Taylor - 206-555-1212

"Mara. Taylor. Goddess. That's my sister," Katerina said.

Bella reached over and lifted the note to her nose. "This was written by the water elemental."

"My *sister* is with the wolf."

24

Cade

HIS BODY TREMBLED. He couldn't move. Couldn't breathe. Pain wracked his body from his snout to his tail. Fur fell off in patches as blisters formed and broke open. He howled at the new moon, cursing it for weakening him, letting him fall victim to Katerina's charms.

Mara. Where was Mara? He couldn't see her. Flames and smoke obscured her sweet scent. He had to get to Mara.

"You're going to die, dog."

The wolf whipped his head around, searching for the elemental. No stars lit the night. All he could smell was smoke. His lupine howl turned into a throaty human scream. "No!"

"Cade!"

Gentle hands stroked his bare chest. An intoxicating scent he wanted all around him slid into his nose. His scarred fingers ached with the start of his shift, but he held on with everything he was and willed it to stop. He couldn't. If he did, he'd never come back.

Curling away from the reassuring, cool touch, he rocked back and forth in this unfamiliar bed surrounded by the scent of something wonderful and familiar he couldn't identify.

Don't shift. Can't shift.

"Cade. Breathe for me."

He choked and sputtered and tried to pull away from the hand that smoothed down his bare forearm. "Help," he croaked.

A cool body pressed to his side, and he whimpered softly.

"I'm here, I'm right here."

Mara. Mara was here. *His Mara.*

Cade grabbed her and yanked her against him, holding her like his life depended on it.

She feathered kisses from his neck to his shoulder and back up again. "Say my name, Cade. Tell me where you are."

"Mara. Mine."

"Well, okay." Mara wrapped her body around his. Her fingers slid over the light dusting of hair on his chest. "You're safe." When his breathing steadied, he could focus on her. Her eyes glistened like brilliant green stars, and her legs wrapped around his waist.

"Water." His throat was parched. The memory of the flames was so close to the surface. He didn't want her to leave the bed, but he could barely swallow, let alone speak.

"I'll be right back, shaggy man. Don't move." Mara's hand trailed down his arm, lingering on his fingers for a single breath, and then she hurried out to the kitchen.

When she returned, he stared down at his hands before taking the glass she offered. He had to make sure the shift had halted. But all he saw were his scarred fingers. Steadier now, Cade drained the glass in four swallows.

"Shaggy man?" He arched his brow. His voice wasn't steady, but he felt calmer now that he could see her face and knew he wasn't going to shift.

Mara ran her fingers through his hair. "Yeah. I like it. Don't cut it. It suits you."

Cade trailed his knuckle over her cheek. "I didn't mean to wake you."

"Well, I would hope not," she replied. "Few people *mean* to have nightmares. Especially not ones that leave them screaming and begging to die."

Cade rested his head against hers. "God, honey. I'm sorry."

A frantic scraping against the front door had Mara scrambling off the bed. Cade didn't understand. He didn't want her to go.

"Livie," Mara said.

Shit. Livie had heard him screaming. She'd break down the door if they didn't let her in.

Cade threw back the blankets, ignoring his distinct lack of clothing. Clad in only his boxers, he pushed past Mara and ran down the hall.

The female wolf bounded in and growled as soon as the door opened. She looked from Cade to Mara and back to Cade again. Stalking over to Mara, she sniffed and glared until Mara took a step back.

"It's okay, Livie." Cade knelt next to her and smoothed a hand over her gold and brown fur, then stroked her muzzle. "I'm all right."

A wet nose nudged his neck, accompanied by a thin whine. Cade wrapped his arms around Livie's torso and whispered in her ear. "I'm sorry I scared you. The fire. I thought I was back in the apartment." It wasn't the truth—not exactly—but it was close enough and Livie would understand. "Mara helped me."

Livie nodded with a soft vocalization, accepting the explanation. She pawed at the wood floor and looked towards the kitchen with a whine.

She needed to eat. To Cade's surprise, Mara was already rummaging in the fridge. She came up with a package of the bison and a container of leftover lasagna.

"Which?" she asked Livie. "Lasagna? Or the raw meat?"

Livie barked at the second option. Mara got a bowl and tore into the bison package before adding some blueberries and baby carrots. She set the bowl down on the floor, and Livie padded over and started to lap up the meal.

"What about you?" she asked Cade as she looked him up and down, her cheeks flaming with heat.

Cade rubbed his still-hollow stomach. Amazingly, he wasn't hungry. The nightmare had stolen his appetite. Even with Mara's calming touch, he was still on edge. "No."

Livie ate quickly and loudly, slurping, crunching, and lapping up every bit of bison in the bowl. She looked up at Mara, yipped in thanks, and sat at the front door until Cade let her out.

"How did you know she was hungry?" he asked.

Mara leaned against the kitchen counter with exhaustion weighing on her shoulders and pulling at the corners of her mouth. For the first time, he took in what she was wearing.

The dark blue tank silhouetted her small breasts and her tapered waist. Silky pajama pants in a paler blue with silver stars cascaded down her legs.

"You were here with me for two weeks. I speak wolf now. A little anyway." She ticked words off on her fingers. "Yes, no, hungry, thirsty, outside, please, thank you, sleep."

Mara was everything he'd ever wanted. Smart, compassionate, practical. She didn't panic. Hadn't let Livie intimidate her.

Even accepting the truth of her element—and his wolf—she'd handled with ease.

"You're amazing." He hadn't meant to say that, and Mara looked away. "I should...I'm...going to..." Turning, he fled back to Mara's guest room.

Behind the closed door, he kicked himself. That wasn't the behavior of an alpha. Hiding away from the woman who meant more to him than anyone? He was so fucking stupid, but at the same time, too scared to face her again.

Twice he rested his hand on the knob and twice he let it fall before pulling back the blankets. Shit. He didn't want to sleep in this bed alone.

A quiet knock had his heart in his throat.

"Cade? Can I come in?"

He scrambled for his jeans, tugging them over his hips. He couldn't face Mara half-naked. The door cracked open just as he picked up his sweatshirt.

"Are you okay?" she asked.

The concern in her voice melted any resistance he had. He'd worried her with his nightmares. He had to fix this. "No." The sweatshirt fell away, and he pulled her close so her cheek rested on his bare shoulder. Cool skin, soft curves against his chest, the tickle of her long hair over the hand he pressed to her back. "I need you."

Mara pulled away, sending disappointment flooding him. But instead of leaving, she laced her fingers with his and pulled him into the hall and down to her room. He hesitated at her door. "Mara."

"What? Is there some anti-werewolf force field around my bed? One that sprang up in the past two days?"

A chuffing laugh escaped his lips. "No. It's not that."

She raised a single brow in question.

"We need to talk."

"Shit, Cade. Didn't anyone ever tell you never to say that to a woman?" She dropped his hand and climbed into her bed—the one place he was desperate to be—and patted the blankets next to her. "If you want to talk, you'll do it right here."

He stared, indecision staying his steps. "If I get in bed with you, it's over for me."

"You're the master of cryptic sentences, you know that? Fine." She nodded towards the cedar chest in the corner of the room. "Go sit there and don't move. Other than your mouth. Explain yourself."

Cade sank down onto the chest. "I told you alphas don't have casual sex." At her nod, he continued. "It's been a long time for me. Before I was an alpha, back in college, I dated a little. Nothing serious. Never wanted anyone permanent in my life. I had a few one-night stands, trying to avoid who I was. This part of me that was born to lead. But I hated it." At Mara's raised brow, he cracked a wry smile. "Fine. The sex was good. I hated how I felt after. Once I moved to Bellingham and fell in with my pack, there was no one."

"How long?" Her legs shifted under the blankets. They'd felt like home wrapped around his hips earlier, and he wanted them there again. Without the barrier of her thin pants. Or his.

"Six years."

Mara's jaw popped open. Her pale pink lips formed an *o* as a mask of confusion slid over her face, and then fell away with a shake of her head. "Wow. I thought *I* was a monk. I haven't been with anyone in three years."

It was his turn to be shocked. This beautiful, intelligent, and empathetic woman should never have been alone. But she wasn't alone now. She'd never be alone again if he had anything to say about it.

"Once I found my place in the pack, it all changed for me."

"Why?"

"Because I have responsibilities. Or I did anyway." His shoulders slumped. "I don't know if I'm still the alpha. I was gone for a long time. Liam should have petitioned to take over. If he did, I won't upset the balance by challenging him. I have to do what's best for all of them."

"That still doesn't explain why you can't let me comfort you. You were begging to die." Her voice cracked. "Sleep here. With me. Nothing else needs to happen."

The tension in the room was a physical presence, heavy in the air, an electricity that prickled along Cade's bare chest, raising the fine, sandy hairs.

"I want more." At his words, she took a single stuttering

breath. "You're mine. My wolf—he knows it. Hell. *I* know it. I can't get into your bed—even be close to you—without wanting all of you. Werewolves mate for life, Mara. I'm not afraid of it. But this isn't your world, and I can't change who I am to give you what you want. If we do this, I'll be yours. For the rest of my life. Even if you reject me. I'd leave if you asked, but it would be the hardest thing I'd ever do. Which is why I have to go back to my room." He tore his gaze away from her face and got to his feet. "I'm sorry."

"Cade, wait." Mara caught him at the door.

"If you don't want me to take you right now, you'll let me go," he growled.

She didn't move and held his gaze. "I'm not afraid of you. Never of you."

"Fuck it." He swept her into his arms. "Tell me to stop and I'll walk away. But if you don't, I need you naked. Right now."

Her body melted against him. A tear shimmered in her eye. "I can't promise you anything, Cade. I want this. You. More than anything. But I'm still getting used to the fact that *I* might have a future. I can't promise it to you yet. All I can give you is right now. Today. Tomorrow. Next week. After that..."

"My eyes are open, Mara." His cock strained against the press of her body.

Cade swept her up and laid her on the bed, and she fought with his zipper, then shoved his jeans down around his thighs. His dick strained against the boxers. Fuck, he needed her.

Frantically, he tugged at her silk pants and sent them sailing across the room.

Mara's arousal surrounded them like a steamy summer rain. Heat licked at his arms wherever she touched him, igniting a need he couldn't deny.

Cade memorized every curve of her body with his eyes and his lips. "You smell like home," he said, running a hand over her hair. "I could lose myself in you."

Kneeling between her thighs, he helped her sit up and eased the tank over her head.

He took his time, drinking in the toned muscles of her stomach, the curve of her breasts, the tight, dark nipples, and the delicious hollow above her collarbone.

This...she...was everything. Cade worshiped the bud of her right breast, tasting fresh rain, cocoa butter, and hints of salt. Her back arched, offering him better access.

When he closed his teeth over the taut nub, Mara shuddered and moaned, clutching his arms to keep herself upright.

Nipping up along her collarbone, all the way to her ear, Cade bit down and sucked the sensitive lobe between his lips.

"Oh, God. Don't stop."

"If I don't stop, I can't do *this*." He moved the flat of his hand against her mound in a small circle. She gasped, and her hips jerked. "Still don't want me to stop?"

Her reply was lost to his greedy mouth on hers, the fierce flare of need spurring him on. They fell together, Cade's lean body covering Mara's and his hips and cock replacing the pressure of his hand. The thin barriers between them did little to dull his pleasure. If he didn't enter her soon, he was going to come in his boxers like a teenager. It had been too long.

She dragged her mouth away. "Cade, inside me. Now."

He growled and sat back, panting, sweat glistening on his bare chest. "Protection."

"I'm on birth control. I haven't had sex in so long, I don't have any condoms." Her cheeks turned a bright red, and her lower lip found its way under her teeth.

"Werewolves can't carry diseases," Cade said, battling the lust and desperation raging inside to force the words from his lips. "When we shift, any illnesses we have go away. We don't even get colds. But all I can offer you is my word."

"I trust you," she said as she tugged at his boxers. Her fingers were damp with her element, desperate. Short nails scraped along his hips and dug into his ass.

He ripped away her pale blue panties to find a reddish triangle of curls beckoning him. "I want to make this last. I want to see you come." Hooking his rough hands behind her knees, he slid her onto her back.

She laughed and trembled when his stubble tickled her thighs but she stopped breathing completely as he tasted her.

Spring rain. Honey. She was an oasis in the desert. He'd never had anything so sweet, so life-sustaining. Lapping at the singular spot he knew would send her over the edge, he savored the way she bucked against him. Cade drank her in, quenching the thirst that had plagued him since he'd woken up in Mara's bed.

"Cade, please."

He couldn't wait any longer. He vaulted up to his knees, grabbed her hips, and brought her to him, plunging deep. "Mara. God. I won't last."

Once. Twice. On the third thrust, he lost himself to his mate.

25

Mara

SCRAPING at her front door dragged Mara out of the best sleep she'd had in weeks. Cade's arm draped over her waist, and his shaggy locks hung over his eyes.

Their first time had been frantic, desperate, and short. Afterwards, they'd both collapsed into exhaustion. She'd stayed awake for a few minutes longer than Cade, listening to him breathe, savoring the feel of his arms around her.

He slept easily now, relaxed in a way she'd never seen. Another few scrapes, and she realized what she was hearing. Livie.

Sliding from Cade's embrace, she pulled on her robe and crept quietly to the front door. Barely 6:00 a.m., and the sun was just starting to brighten the sky. The female wolf padded inside, sniffed the air, and growled.

"What?" Mara asked.

Livie growled again, headed for the guest room, looked inside, and met Mara's gaze, daring her to follow.

Once they were both inside, Livie sat on her haunches. Her eyes changed first, glowing brown, gold, and finally blue.

Her pelt bristled, fur disappearing, her snout shrinking into a small, upturned nose. Her back broke, and a soft whine escaped her lips. When the shift finished, she lay naked and panting on the floor. Mara approached, but Livie glared and held up her hand. The feral sound that rumbled in her chest sounded a lot like her wolf.

"What did I do?" Mara asked.

"I smell him on you," Livie panted. Her limbs shook as she climbed to her feet and pulled on her maternity jeans and sweatshirt. "He claimed you."

"I don't understand."

Livie got right in Mara's face. "He. Fucked. You."

"We had sex. Yes. I don't see how that's any of your business. He's not allowed to do that?" Mara wanted to shove Livie back, but her pregnancy made that a bad idea. Even if she was a werewolf and could probably take it.

"Allowed? Sure. Has he once in all the years he's been our alpha? No. And now he's mated to an elemental."

"Hey!" Mara stepped back and tensed, preparing to defend herself.

Livie's eyes flashed with gold. "I've got one question for you. Don't lie to me."

Those glowing, wolfish eyes stared her down. Despite having a good four inches and a few years on Livie, she felt like a child under that glare. "What do you want to know?"

"What are your intentions?"

"Cade is important to me."

"No shit. That doesn't answer my question. I want to know if you're going to break his heart. Because if you leave him now, that's what'll happen. Werewolves mate for life." Livie's stomach growled.

"Come on. Let me get you something to eat." Mara turned for

the kitchen, desperate the diffuse the tension, but Livie grabbed her arm, fingers digging into her bicep through the robe.

"No," she said, her voice a low growl. "Answer me."

Mara wrenched her arm from Livie's grip and sat down on the bed. She was going to have a bruise. "Yes. I know. Cade told me. I didn't lie to him. I can't promise him a lifetime. Not yet. I don't even know I'm going to live another month. But he matters to me. I can't explain it. I shouldn't care this much about him after only a few days, but I do. I won't hurt him."

A tear rolled down her cheek, and Livie sank down next to her. "He's in love with you."

A wave of panic roiled in Mara's belly. Her palms dampened, and she rubbed them on her robe as her element pulsed against her skin, itching to escape.

Livie wrapped an arm around Mara's shoulders. Stiffly at first, then with warmth Mara didn't expect.

"I didn't mean to upset you. That was supposed to be a good thing. Don't you want a mate?"

"I'm not a werewolf. Humans don't think in those terms. That only happens in romance novels. We date, we fall in love, we get married. Y'all go right from first date to a lifetime."

"Y'all?"

Mara snorted quietly. "When I get stressed, my Southern comes out. Aunt Lil's rubbed off on me." She rolled her head around, trying to relax her neck.

"You're tired. He'll be mad at me if he finds out I kept you up. Go back to bed. I'm going to eat something. It'll be light in half an hour. I'd have stayed out there, but the pup wants his breakfast and he's pretty damn insistent about it."

Livie rose, but Mara snagged her wrist, turning the tables. "Wait. I need to ask you something." A quick shrug gave Mara the opening she wanted. "Is he still your alpha?"

"Huh?" Livie jerked in surprise. "Of course he is. Why would you ask me that?"

"Because Cade doesn't know. He thinks Liam challenged. It's eating at him."

Livie's stomach growled. "Boss-man needs to chill out." With a yawn, she cradled her belly. "I'll tell him when he wakes up. Now go. He's mated with you. He's not going to want you out of his sight for a while. And I mean that literally. He won't be able to stand it—not touching you, seeing you. Werewolves are a little...possessive."

Back in her bedroom, Mara dropped her robe on the foot of the bed and slipped under the sheets next to Cade. A quiet rumbling thunder rolled through his chest. "Mara."

"I'm here."

"Mine." His arm banded around her waist, and he nuzzled her hair, pressing his lips to her neck and biting down lightly. "Mine."

SUN STREAMED in through a crack in the drapes, but it did little to heat the room. They'd slept another hour, perhaps two, after Mara's conversation with Livie.

Cade rolled over and slid his hand down her arm until Mara winced, and he growled softly.

"Where did these bruises come from?"

Mara twisted to face him, gently flipped his palm, and stroked her fingers over the scarred flesh. "Don't be angry."

"Mara." The single word warned her it was too late for that.

She curled her fingers around his. His bright blue eyes were flecked with silver as the wolf simmered under his skin. "I let Livie in earlier. We had a little talk."

"She did this?" Cade tried to pull away, but Mara cupped the back of his neck.

"I'm fine."

She didn't see him move, didn't even know his arms were

around her until he rolled her atop his lean, hard body. He was too thin. They both were, but the strength of his embrace shocked her, as did his heavy breathing.

Mara dipped her head, brushing her lips against his cheek, along his jaw, down his neck to his shoulder.

He shivered, and Mara wriggled so she could look him in the eyes. They were both still naked, and the feel of his length under her quickened her breath. Her palms dampened as her element swam beneath her skin.

Parting her legs in a not-so-subtle invitation, Mara ground her hips against him.

"Clothes. Now," Cade managed. "Otherwise I'm going to take you again."

"And that's a bad thing?" Mara hadn't felt this desperate for a man's touch in years. With Cade, every feeling she had was dialed up to eleven. Or higher.

"Mara. Please." Cade grasped her hips firmly and slid her off his body. "Put something on."

He rolled away, threw his legs over the side of the bed, and tugged on his boxers. They couldn't hide his hard length, and his breath sawed in and out of his chest. The taut muscles of his stomach quivered, and his irises glowed with power.

Something inside him was about to snap, and while a part of her wanted him to lose control, to take her and do whatever he wanted with her, Mara sensed he'd never forgive himself if he did. Not until he'd talked to Livie.

Mara scrambled off the bed and tugged on her pajamas. She could smell him on her. In her tousled hair, on her oversensitive skin, inside of her. Cade was everywhere.

"I need to see Livie," he said, donning his jeans awkwardly, grimacing as he tried to force his cock behind the denim. His bare chest heaved with one heavy, deep breath. "And I need a couple of minutes. A little space. It's too hard. Not...taking you. Stay here. I'll bring you coffee."

With that, he strode from the room and slammed the door.

"I hope wolves aren't always this temperamental," Mara muttered. Wandering over to the window, she peered out a crack in the drapes. Clouds gathered on the horizon, dark and foreboding. It would rain soon.

Mara flexed her aching fingers. Her entire body felt like she'd run a marathon. She hadn't confessed to Cade—or to anyone else —but using her element still hurt. She felt better than she had in months, but she was exhausted, sore, and spent.

With a shrug, she climbed back into bed and pulled the covers up to her neck. Coffee would help. Until Cade returned, she'd relax.

_____

26

Cade

STARING OUT THE WINDOW, Cade clutched the edge of the kitchen counter hard enough he couldn't feel his fingers. Being away from Mara was hell. It didn't matter that she was less than thirty feet away.

Until the full moon when they'd seal their mating, he'd be irritable and insanely jealous of anyone who touched or even looked at her the wrong way.

Fuck. He didn't even know how mating would work between a wolf and a human—or elemental. Usually, newly mated wolves would shift together and run under the full moon, then couple *as* wolves. But Cade wouldn't shift again, and Mara...

"Boss-man?" Livie padded out to join him, wearing a pair of gray yoga pants and faded blue sweatshirt.

Cade saw red. For the second time in as many days, Livie had hurt his mate.

He growled and grabbed her by the arms, lifting her onto her toes, and barely avoided shaking her. Despite her pregnancy, she wasn't fragile, but fear flashed in her blue eyes. "You put your hands on Mara. You left a bruise."

Her pale cheeks flushed with color. "I'm sorry. Really. I didn't mean to. I needed to know she wasn't going to hurt you. I'm not used to touching humans. Or elementals. We don't bruise like they do. All I wanted to do was stop her from walking out on me. She's yours. I get it. I'd never hurt her."

Livie looked away, a sign of submission Cade couldn't ignore.

"You shouldn't have touched her at all." He couldn't stand the idea of another wolf hurting Mara. Not now. Not when the mating call was so strong.

A tiny whine, Livie's wolf apologizing, made him sigh, and he let her go and turned back to the kitchen window. "I can't handle being close to her. Or being apart. I feel like I'm about to come out of my skin. I shouldn't have let myself lose control and take her last night. Now I have ten days of this shit to deal with."

"I remember." Her voice dropped. "Shawn and I couldn't stand to see each other for a couple of days before the ceremony. I locked myself in Christine's apartment. She had to babysit me so I wouldn't go to him."

Cade pressed the power button on the espresso machine. A whir and hum from the machine marked the grinding of beans, and the rich scent of coffee wafted over him. "It gets better, doesn't it?"

"Yeah." She chuckled. "The first month I was with Shawn, it was terrible. I didn't want him out of my sight. Christine brushed against him by accident about a week after we mated, and I nearly lost it. But it passed." She laid her hand on Cade's arm, and he stiffened. She laughed and pulled away. "Sorry. You need to go screw her again. It'll lessen the pull. Always did it for me."

Livie snagged the first mug of espresso out of the machine and cupped it protectively in her hands. "This pup lives on caffeine. I'm going to turn on the TV. I won't hear you."

He shook his head and ran a hand through his hair. "I've

missed you." If it weren't for the mating, he would have hugged her. Instead, he withdrew a carton of almond milk from Mara's fridge and proceeded to make them both cappuccinos. A splash of vanilla syrup and a sprinkle of cinnamon dusted Mara's mug. He hoped he'd gotten it right.

When he returned to the bedroom, she was curled on her side, facing him, her eyes closed. Grinning, he knelt and held the mug under her nose.

"Honey, wake up. Coffee."

Mara stretched under the blankets as her eyes fluttered open. Cade smoothed a hand over her hair, needing to touch her to calm the storm inside of him. He'd known from the start, he realized now. From the first moment he'd seen her, from the first time he'd inhaled her delicious scent, he'd known she was his.

"I could get used to this," she said, sitting up and accepting the coffee. Bringing the mug to her lips, she took a sip, and her eyes narrowed. "What is this?"

"An almond milk cappuccino with cinnamon and vanilla. I got it right, didn't I?"

"How'd you know?" She took another sip and licked her lips, holding him mesmerized with the tiny flick of her tongue and the swell of her breasts under her tank as she moved.

"You made them a couple of times. The steamer wand was loud. My wolf didn't like it. The first time I heard it, I hid under your bed." Cade forced himself to look away as he shed his jeans, slid under the blankets, and rested his back against the headboard. "Some things I remember."

"What else?" Mara snuggled close to him, and he draped an arm around her shoulders. Everything about her was soft. Her back against his chest. Her hair brushing his arm. Her legs tangling with his.

"Sleeping on your bed. I wanted to be as close to you as I could. You made me feel better. I didn't even remember I was a man when I found you. I was too far gone. I hadn't had a coherent thought in months. That first night, all I knew was that I had to be next to you or I'd die. You saved my life." Cade flushed a deep crimson. "And you smelled good."

Mara laughed. "You like chlorine? I think it comes out of my pores these days."

"Not chlorine—though I could smell that." Cade pulled her closer and pressed his nose to her hair. "Your shampoo is coconut. Your soap, almonds. You smell like fresh rain. And coffee, of course. Every morning I could smell it on you. I remembered coffee. I knew that scent—missed it." He smiled, an intense longing prickling along his spine. "The pack owned a coffee shop in Bellingham. Best beans in town. I never much liked coffee before that. Your beans are almost as good."

"Almost?" Mara chuckled. "Well, fine. Tomorrow, you can come with me to the roaster in the University District and pick your own beans. Don't insult my coffee, shaggy man. I take that *very* seriously. Does the shop still exist? Did you see it yesterday?"

"I didn't look. I didn't remember it until now." He pinched the bridge of his nose, furrowing his brow. "Every few minutes, there's something new. It's like a dam broke. All these memories just...like a flood."

Mara slid her arm around his waist and squeezed. She'd done this. She'd fixed him. Not only had she freed him from his wolf, but accepting his feelings for her had changed something inside of him. Despite the scars and the lingering weakness in his body, he was whole now that he had his mate next to him.

"So what happens now?" she asked. "You can shift at will, right? Like Livie? Can all wolves? Will you run with your pack tonight when they get here?"

The bottom dropped out of his stomach, and the mug shook in his hand. He shrank away from her, desperate to escape, but he couldn't force himself from her bed.

"What is it?" Mara set her coffee down and eased his mug from his unsteady hand. "You're scaring me." She straddled him, framing his cheeks and forcing him to look at her. "Cade." The last word snapped out of her like an order and freed his tongue.

"You'll never see the wolf again. I can't shift. I won't. I wouldn't come back from it."

"But he's part of you. I can see him in your eyes. You can't ignore who you are. I did and it nearly killed me." Mara tried to lean forward and brush her lips to his, but he jerked his head away.

"You don't understand. You can't. It was more than the starvation, Mara. More than being burned day after day after day. I'd given up. Before I realized that she'd let the charm on the earth lapse, I was ready to die. I can't take the chance that anything—anyone—could trap me again." He grabbed her hands and held on tightly. "I used to love the wolf. Running under the moon. Shifting with my pack. I don't know if I have a pack any longer—if they're still mine—but if I do, I sure as shit won't run with them again. The wolf is dead. Or he might as well be."

Mara bit her lip. "I freed you once and I didn't even know what I was doing. Now?" She extricated one of her hands from his death grip, turned her palm up to the ceiling, and closed her eyes. The air in the room thickened, and Cade's skin prickled with energy.

Above her upturned palm, an eddy of air tumbled over itself, thickening, slowing, and finally turning into a tiny droplet of water. The drop grew, slowly, undulating and elongating until it was the size of a dime. Mara's cheeks flushed. When she opened her eyes, they were glowing.

"Shit."

"If you're trapped again—won't happen—I'll free you. You can trust me." She focused her gaze on the trembling sphere of water, pursed her lips, and sent the water into her empty coffee mug where it landed with a plop.

It didn't matter. He had to make her understand. And fuck, he needed her to hold him and tell him it would be okay if he never shifted again.

Jerking away, he stood, his chest heaving. "Seven months. Seven months of rotten meat, being burned and blistered within an inch of my life, always cold but still burning up inside. I didn't know my own name, Mara. I lost my words, my balance, everything to the wolf. I hate him. I can't ever let him free again. End of discussion."

Mara tried to reach for him, her eyes burning brightly, her lips pressed together, anger and horror playing across her face. He had to get away. At least for a few minutes. Otherwise, he'd say something he'd regret. "I need to be alone."

Mara waved her hand. "Fine. Be that way. I need more coffee anyway."

She slipped out of bed and strode out the door, slamming it behind her.

Mara

Livie glanced up from the couch where she was stretched out watching the morning news with a mug balanced on the swell of her belly.

"Pup makes a good table," she said with a grin, but the smile faded almost immediately. "What's wrong?"

"Is it that obvious?" Mara beelined for the kitchen and punched the button on the espresso machine for another cup. "You want one? Or tea?"

Livie muted the TV and joined her in the kitchen. "I can handle coffee. Wolves burn it off really fast. I was only sitting here with the news blaring so the two of you could screw. And it's pretty obvious you didn't. What'd he do?"

"What makes you think it's him?"

"He's male."

Mara couldn't stop her laugh. "That he is."

After both mugs were filled, Livie gently took Mara's elbow—careful not to bruise her again—and led her back to the sofa.

Mara had no idea how much she could—or should—tell Livie about the fight. But as she was about to speak, images of a fire filled the TV screen, and Livie sat up with a jerk.

"Oh, my God," she said as she turned the volume up.

"An early morning fire in Bellingham burned through an entire block of storefronts, including the law offices of Baker and Folsom, the First National Bank of Washington, and a children's bookstore. A second fire destroyed a row of townhomes next to Maritime Heritage Park. This was the second suspicious fire near the park this year. Back in May, the Whatcom Mariner Apartments burned to the ground, killing seven local residents."

Mara's heart started hammering in her chest. "Maggie. That's Maggie's house. Oh, shit. Katerina's in Bellingham."

Springing up, she ran for the bedroom with Livie at her heels. When she burst into the room, she found Cade sitting on the floor on the far side of the bed, staring out the window. He wore jeans but nothing else and his eyes were bloodshot and red rimmed.

"What?" he asked, barely glancing at her, but something on her face must have conveyed her horror because he jerked up and grabbed her by the shoulders. "Honey, you look like you've seen a ghost."

"There was a fire. Maggie's house burned down. The news didn't say if she'd died, but..."

Cade pulled Mara against his bare chest and wrapped his arms around her. His entire body shook, though with anger or fear she couldn't tell. "It's my fault," he whispered. "We shouldn't have gone to Bellingham."

"You don't know that," Livie replied. "This is Katerina we're talking about. For all we know she would have burned down the whole town to get to you. She clearly has no qualms about killing an innocent old woman. Your shop is gone, along with every business on that block."

"We need to leave," Cade said, tucking Mara in the crook of his arm.

"Why?" Mara asked. "She couldn't possibly know where I live. I haven't had any contact with Katerina for eleven years. I was living in Sacramento then. I'm not in the phone book. Lil's my only family, and she certainly wouldn't say anything. And if Katerina *did* know where we were, she would have found you already. The fires happened in the early hours of the morning. If I remember anything about my sister from our single encounter, it's that she doesn't have a shred of self-control."

Both werewolves stared at Mara for several tense seconds until Livie broke the silence. "She's right, boss-man. It's been like eight hours. If that bitch knew where you were, she'd already be here. I don't think we should be shouting your presence from the rooftops or anything, but as long as we stay in the house, I think we're safe here."

"I'll call Eleanor," Mara said. "Make sure Katerina can't track us somehow. I don't understand how her fire element works. Hell, I barely understand how my own element works yet. As long as Eleanor thinks we're okay, we should stay here until the rest of your pack arrives."

"And I'll let Liam know what's going on." Livie streaked out of the room, and Cade buried his face in Mara's neck.

"It would kill me if anything happened to you," he said, the subtle vibrations in his chest reassuring, even if his words weren't.

"Nothing's going to happen. I've got two werewolves protecting me."

Flinching, he released her and stalked over to the window to stare out into the street. "I told you. I won't shift."

"I wasn't asking you to," Mara replied with a tiny shake of her head. She ran her hands through her hair and tugged, hard. The pinpricks of pain along her scalp focused her thoughts and helped her get past her frustration with the man standing in front of her. "Even if you never shift again, you're still a werewolf. The sooner you get that through your head, the sooner you'll feel steady again."

A rough snarl escaped his lips. "Goddammit, Mara. Stop reminding me of who and what I am. Don't you think I know? Don't you think I wish I could shift? Fuck." Cade stormed out of the room. "I need a shower. Alone."

"Stupid alpha male bullshit." Mara belted her robe tighter and headed for the kitchen to call Eleanor. In the hall, she nearly ran right into Livie.

"What's up Cade's ass?" Livie asked. "He growled at me on his way to the bathroom. Even in wolf form he's not usually that angry."

"I don't know if I should tell you," Mara replied. "He's your alpha."

"And you're his mate. Which makes you part of the pack whether you want to be or not. We're a family. There aren't any secrets among wolves."

"But isn't it kind of like tattling on dad?" Mara asked. "I don't know any of the rules. You obey him. Right? I heard him yelling at you earlier. I'm sorry for that." She rubbed her arm and gestured towards the living room sofa.

Livie shrugged. "He was right to. I shouldn't have hurt you. And yeah, he is kind of like my father and big brother rolled into one. Which would make you my big sister. Assuming you accept the mating."

"You're...really okay with this?" Mara asked.

A serious look darkened Livie's blue eyes. "When I found him —found both of you—he was hurting. I'd never seen him so weak. It wasn't physical, though he still looks too thin. He was haunted. This morning, everything changed. He's back. He's my alpha again—the wolf I've known for years. Even if he is angry as fuck. You did that. So we're solid."

Livie ran a hand through her hair and gave a small shake of her head. "Cade's the strongest of us. Liam's next. He's our beta. I'm third. It's all based on bloodlines and how much Lycos is running through our veins. The way things work? He can take any mate he wants. But it'll be easier—for you and for him—if you ask the pack for our blessing. If anyone challenges, they'll have to fight his wolf. No one wants to do that." Livie grinned, but Mara stifled a groan.

"And what if he refused to shift?"

"Huh? Why the hell would he do that?"

Mara looked away, focusing on a tiny bird hunting for food on her frost-ravaged lawn. "Forget I said anything."

A low growl rumbled in Livie's chest. "Not a chance. Tell me why you said that."

When Mara didn't move or speak, Livie pushed herself up. "I'm getting to the bottom of this."

She strode towards the bathroom with Mara at her heels. As Livie wrenched open the bathroom door, Cade shut off the water and pulled back the shower curtain. He made no move to cover himself, and Mara couldn't tear her eyes away from his body.

"What the hell, Livie?"

"You won't shift?" The female wolf jabbed Cade in the chest and stared up at him. Water dripped from Cade's hair and he growled. Not exactly thrilled with another woman seeing *her* naked man, Mara stepped forward and handed him a towel.

"*Sorry,*" she mouthed. He spared her a single glance, made a deep, rumbling sound in his throat, and wrapped the towel around his hips.

"Answer me," Livie demanded, then thought better of her tone and lowered her voice. "Please."

The look of betrayal on Cade's face and the pain in his eyes cut Mara to her core. Memories shadowed his features, hunched his shoulders. "I can't shift. Not anymore. I won't survive it. I don't expect you to understand. Either of you." He pushed past the two women, heading for the guest room, where the door slammed firmly.

Mara leaned against the sink. "Well, that went well."

Livie's lower lip quivered. "I know that look in his eyes. It's the look Shawn gets when I forget about this—" she gestured to her left arm, hanging awkwardly at her side, "—and try to reach for something heavy. It's fear. Guilt. I spent three days as my wolf after the fire. Probably got hit with a small bit of the charm that kept Cade trapped for all those months. When I finally could shift, I could barely remember how to talk, let alone think properly."

Nodding, Mara said, "Cade...it was the same...but...worse." He was wrong about one thing, though. She did understand a little. She'd been trapped in her own body for months. Unable to see anything but death in front of her and memories behind.

Livie touched her arm. "What do we do now?"

"You're asking me? You've known him for years, haven't you?"

"Yeah, but you've been with him since he shifted back. You were with his wolf before. You saw him when he was half-dead. And you're his mate. Which means you're above me in the pack. So it's your call."

Mara rubbed the back of her neck. "Fine. We're not doing anything. Yet. I need to call Eleanor and take a shower. You look like you're about to fall over. Go tell Cade that you need to rest and kick him out of the guest room. He's probably sulking in there. I'll talk to him again after I don't smell so much like him. It's driving me insane. All I want to do is wrap my arms around him. And...do other things."

The blond wolf giggled. "Gotcha. I'm mated, remember? You don't want to hug him. You want him naked. I saw you ogling him."

Mara grimaced. "Like you never looked."

"Ew!" Livie wrinkled her nose. "That's basically my brother you're talking about. Wolves don't care about being naked. We shift in front of each other all the time. I don't even think about it. And no. I've never looked." She drew her fingers across her heart. "He's all yours, babe. I promise."

Mara shook her head as Livie trudged out of the room. She wasn't used to this level of openness with a woman she barely knew. If she stayed with Cade, she'd have to get used to a lot of things. Not the least of which were his terrible memories.

Please, let me die. You killed my family. Let me die.

The desperate words he'd uttered the previous night would never leave her. Her sister had made a strong alpha wolf beg for death. It terrified her to think that Cade's pack and her uncontrolled elemental power might be the only thing that could stop Katerina's vengeful flames. And now, with her sister no more than a hundred miles away, what could she do to protect the man she was falling in love with?

27

Mara

ELEANOR PICKED up on the first ring. "Mara? How are you feeling?"

"Like I've been run over by a truck." Sinking down onto her bed, she rubbed the back of her neck. "It won't always be like this, right?"

"No, dear. Of course not. Do you want me to come over and work with you again today?"

"No, that's not why I called. My...my sister burned down a whole block in Bellingham last night. She's looking for Cade."

"Goddess," Eleanor whispered. "Lillian was right. She's out of her mind."

Nerves twisted the ball of ice in her belly. "Can she track us?" Mara asked.

"No. Only air elementals can track scents," Eleanor said, "and only over short distances. Once you factor in the drive from Bellingham to your house? It's not possible."

Relief washed over Mara, and she let her lips curve into a hint of a smile. "You're sure?"

"Yes. Absolutely. Now, listen here. Lillian and I are going to the movies in an hour or so, and then I'm headed back to Cannon Beach tomorrow. If I don't see you before I go, you take care—and keep practicing, okay?"

"I will. Thank you."

After she hung up, Mara found Cade making an omelet in the kitchen. She tugged at the black sweater that hugged her subtle curves, and felt almost...human after dabbing on some founda-tion—despite the lack of sleep and frustration with the man at her stove. "Hey. Where's Livie?"

Cade spared her only a terse nod. "Resting."

"Eleanor says there's no way Katerina could track us. Even an air elemental couldn't do it. So we should be safe here."

His shoulders relaxed a fraction, and he flipped the omelet, sending the scents of butter, cheese, and peppers wafting over her.

"That smells good." She brushed her fingers against his arm, but he just glared at her and braced his hands against the counter.

"Sit. You need to eat."

"I need you to stop being an ass and talk to me," she replied.

"Mara," he said with a low growl of warning.

"Don't you 'Mara' me. You're not my alpha. You think I don't understand. Well, I do. At least a little." She rested her hand on his. Something in him calmed at her touch, but his shoulders were still too tense. If he didn't lighten up, he was going to snap in half.

"I know you're scared," she said quietly. "I get it. You can't show that to Livie or the rest of your pack. I get that too. But you can show it to me. I'm scared too. I don't want to lose you—to your pack, to Katerina, to anything."

Cade dropped the spatula and grabbed her, holding her in a fierce embrace that let her feel his body shaking against her.

"Don't ask me to shift," he whispered. "I'll do anything for you. Anything but that."

Why couldn't he trust her? Mara slid her fingers underneath his sweatshirt and along his skin. The various scars and burns were smooth to the touch, and though they'd healed, he still carried the memories.

So much pain. Too much. She didn't care if she ever saw the wolf again as long as the man holding her was whole.

"I won't ask again, Cade. I promise."

With those two sentences, all of the tension in his body melted away. He held her for so long, the eggs burned, but he divided them between two plates anyway.

After three bites, Mara snorted. "I'm sorry. I tried, but I can't." She retrieved the dish of leftover lasagna from the fridge and set it on the table between them.

Cade stared at her when she sunk her fork directly into the pan, then laughed. "I'm sorry, honey. I didn't think eggs could taste that bad."

As cold, alone, and afraid as he'd been just minutes ago, he was almost relaxed now. Their fingers twined around the casserole dish while they traded heated glances over the cold pasta.

Several times, he tightened his grip, taking a deep breath like he was about to say something, but only shook his head and returned to eating.

"What is it?" Mara asked. "Whatever you have to say, go ahead and say it. What do you want?"

Something dark and dangerous churned in his eyes, and his chest stuttered with each ragged breath. "I want to tear your clothes off and lay you out on this table like a banquet. I want to make love to you for hours, not take you like I did last night, like some desperate schoolboy who can't hold his load. I want you out of mind with lust for me because that's sure as shit what I'm feeling for you right now."

Mara's fork clattered to the table. "Oh. Is that all?"

Cade shrugged. "You asked."

"I did."

His rough fingers caressed the inside of her wrist, and electricity shot directly to her core, tightening her nipples under the sweater. "You're mine, Mara. And I'm yours. Body and soul. It's hard for me to even be near you right now, and harder for me not to be. All I can think of is fucking you."

The crude words gave her a thrill, but Cade hung his head. "You deserve so much better than me. Tell me to leave, and I will. You should have romance. Dating. A *normal* relationship." Releasing her, he shoved his hands under the table.

"No."

A muscle in his jaw twitched under the layer of rough stubble. "No?"

"Do I look upset?" At the shake of his head, she offered him a sad smile. "I'm thirty-one, Cade. I've spent the last eight months preparing to die and now I find out that I can control water. I don't think the word normal applies to me. I want someone who cares about me. I want someone I don't have to hide from. If you really do remember your time as the wolf, you've seen me at my worst. I was ready to die. I'd made peace with it. When I came home after Thanksgiving dinner, I wanted to give up. I was so tired of fighting. But you were here and—"

A knock at the door made them both flinch. Frowning, Mara hurried over to check the peephole. "Shit."

"What is it?" Cade was at her back in an instant, his arms wrapped protectively around her waist.

"Jen." What was she supposed to do now? Jen still thought Cade was a neighbor.

"Invite her in." Cade nuzzled Mara's neck and trailed tiny kisses and nips along her skin.

"Mara? You home?" Jen's voice was muffled through the door, and a moment later, Mara's phone chirped with a new text message.

She twisted in his arms and stared up into his steely blue eyes. "Are you insane?"

He grinned. "Maybe. But unless you're planning on telling me to leave, she's going to meet me again eventually. Might as well be on our terms."

Our terms. The fact that Cade considered there to be terms that were theirs wasn't lost on her. "Katerina."

"Isn't here. Eleanor told you she couldn't track us. Jen knew about the wolf. She's seen me with you as a man. If she was working with that bitch, I'd already be dead. I'm not worried. But I will go warn Livie so she doesn't go batshit crazy." Cade pressed his lips to Mara's forehead. "She's your best friend. If you think she can handle knowing about werewolves, if you think she'll keep my name a secret if anyone were to ask, then tell her. But at least tell her I care about you."

As soon as he disappeared into the guest room, Mara took a deep breath. "Here goes nothing."

Jen cocked a hip and glared at her. "It's Sunday. You said we'd talk on Sunday. And since you didn't bother responding to my call last night, you're going to talk to me now." Her gaze roved over Mara's face, taking in the flushed cheeks, the bright eyes, and the shine to her hair. "You look good. Really good. What happened?"

Stepping aside, Mara gestured for Jen to come in. She hovered in the doorway, glancing back and forth, scanning the hall and the living room. "Where's the wolf?"

Mara cast a quick look at the guest room door. "Gone. Sort of. You don't have to worry. He's not coming back." Jen's eyes narrowed but she stepped into the house. "Coffee?" Mara asked.

Jen nodded, her short-chopped hair settling around her narrow face. Warily, she reached out and pulled Mara into a hug. "I can take care of it if you need to sit down."

"I feel good." Mara gestured towards her living room, watched Jen go, and turned to her espresso machine.

Once she'd brewed two cups, she tried, unsuccessfully, not to drag her feet on her way to the couch. How was she supposed to do this? Explain werewolves. And how she'd managed to fall for a man in the space of just a few days. Jen wouldn't understand. Would she?

She caught sight of rumpled sheets through the crack in her bedroom door, and her thoughts returned to the previous night. Cade's mouth on hers, his hands in her hair, his quiet words of affection. He was right. Whether she could give him what he wanted—a mate—or not, he was part of her life now, and that meant her friends and family had to meet him.

If they could escape her sister and feel safe again, they'd try for a future together. Maybe she'd be able to ask his pack to accept her.

"What happened to him? The wolf," Jen asked once Mara had settled on the couch across from her. "You loved that animal. I saw it in your eyes on Thanksgiving. Did you call Fish and Wildlife?"

"No. I didn't."

"Oh shit, Mara. Did he die? Adam said he was half-dead when you found him. I'm so sorry." Jen leaned forward, reaching across the short distance to touch Mara's arm.

A tiny smile played on Mara's lips. "He didn't die."

"What? So where is he then?" Jen asked.

The guest room door opened and shut, and Cade walked calmly to Mara's side, dropped down next to her, and slid an arm around her shoulders. "The wolf healed enough to go. He's not coming back." He extended his free hand. "I don't think we've been properly introduced. I'm Cade."

"You. You're still here." Jen's voice hardened and she jabbed a finger towards Cade, refusing to shake his hand. "I knew that story was bullshit. You *were* fucking him."

"Jen! Shit." Mara's cheeks burned. "I was *not* fucking him when you came over the other day."

"But I am now," she added in her head, squirming in the warmth of Cade's embrace.

Jen's sharp blue eyes searched Mara's face, and she clucked her tongue in disapproval. "You're too sick—"

"She's not. Not anymore," Cade insisted.

Jen sputtered, and Mara held up her hand. "He's right. I think. Something happened to me, and I'm okay now. My doctor confirmed it. My numbers are normal. I feel good. I've felt good for days. Good enough to—" she looked at Cade, drawing strength from the smirk on his face and the alpha wolf staring at her from behind his eyes, "—to start uh, a relationship with Cade."

"A relationship?" Jen repeated, her gaze flicking from Cade to Mara and back to Cade again.

"Yes. Cade and I are together."

A low rumble in Cade's chest, appreciative and possessive, stirred Mara's insides, and warmth bloomed in her belly.

"Together?"

"Will you stop repeating everything I say?"

"Only when you give me something besides these half-ass answers."

"This isn't a half-ass answer. It's the truth. I wasn't with him when you came over the other day. He was here, yes, and it wasn't because he got locked out. But we're together now. There's a lot I can't explain, and I need you to trust me."

Jen glared at Cade. "What do you have to say for yourself?"

Cade straightened. "I'd never hurt her. I couldn't. If you're worried about her health, don't. I'd do anything to protect her."

Silence filled the house, stifling and oppressive. Mara could almost taste it, and the tips of her fingers prickled—her element rising to the surface. She needed her best friend to accept Cade's presence in her life as much as she needed Cade's presence in the first place.

"Where do you live?" Jen asked, her quiet voice resigned with only a hint of disapproval. "How did you meet?"

Cade

He curled his fingers around Mara's hand. Shit. Why hadn't he thought this through? Of course Jen would have questions. Ones he couldn't answer.

Cool fingers encircled his wrist and traced patterns on the back of his hand, anchoring him in the here and now. Mara looked up at him, a shy smile on her lips. "We met the last time I was on Orcas. He needed a place to stay—in Seattle. I offered."

"So you've moved in? Isn't this way too fast, Mara? You were on Orcas what? Three weeks ago? Two?"

"You've known me a long time, sweetie. You know my history. Roger. Tim. Phil. Hell, you nursed me through all those breakups—even when I was the one to initiate them. I've never found someone who felt like my other half. Until now." Mara's voice lowered. "Be happy, okay? I'm not likely to die in the next few months and I've found someone I care for who cares about me."

Jen fixed them both with a hard stare, and Mara shifted closer to Cade. He ached to drag her back to her bedroom and make love to her until they were both too spent to move. Shit. He wasn't going to be able to keep his hands off of her much longer. The mating call sang through his blood while his cock shouted its desires directly to his brain.

"Okay," Jen said.

"Okay?"

"Yes. You look happy. You look like you're healthy. I love you, Mar. You're hiding things from me, I can tell. But I'm so happy you're not dying that I don't care."

The two embraced, and Cade averted his gaze, giving them a private moment.

When Jen sniffled and wiped her nose on her sleeve, Mara released her. "When are you going to tell Adam and Lil?"

"Aunt Lil already knows. She met Cade yesterday. And she gave him the third degree. You know her. If there was something to worry about, she never would have let him stay."

Cade chuffed and ran a hand through his shaggy hair. He really needed to trim it. And shave. "I think she did more than give me the third degree. She practically threatened my life if I ever hurt you."

A smile tugged at Mara's lips. "She liked you."

Pride and relief washed over him as Mara sat on the arm of Jen's chair.

"I don't want to deal with Adam right now. I go back to the doctor tomorrow. Once I have another good blood test, then I'll tell him. Plus, he and Lisa are up at Snoqualmie for the weekend. They get so little time alone since her parents won't take the kids often. Keep my—our—secret a little longer?"

"For a while. But I'm going to the salon with Lisa next Friday. Tell him by then?" Jen took Mara's hand and squeezed.

"I will."

"What do you do, Cade?" Jen asked.

He cleared his throat and looked at Mara for help. How much did Mara trust this woman? His mate's subtle nod encouraged him.

"I had a woodworking shop up in Bellingham. Toys, art, furniture. I'd like to do that again." His hands itched to work. He missed the feel of the sawdust between his fingers, the scent of it in his hair.

Muffled voices pulled him out of his thoughts. He shook his head. Jen was asking him something.

"So are you?"

"What?"

"Are you the guy who did the installation at the Gates Foundation? Because he's dead. At least that's what the press said." Jen narrowed her eyes. "His photo was all over the papers for a week after he died. Bill Gates went to his funeral. You look kinda like him. Skinnier. Scruffier. But..."

Panic slammed into him. This woman had put his name, face, and profession together in under a minute. If she could do it, so would others.

Mara joined him on the couch, held up her hand to stop Jen from saying anything else, and cupped his cheek. "Look at me," she whispered.

He turned his gaze to his mate's reassuring emerald eyes.

"Trust her. Trust me."

Jen frowned, watching them intently. He had to make a choice. Trust his mate or run away. And he couldn't leave Mara.

"Yes. That's me."

"Why does everyone think you're dead?"

Mara answered for him. "It's a really long story. Like my recovery."

Cade sank back against the couch cushions. "Because the person who set the fire at my apartment is still after me."

"What?"

Mara's head snapped around. "Cade!" she hissed.

He stood, grabbed Mara's hand, and pulled her to her feet. "Give us a minute, please," he said to Jen, then guided Mara into her bedroom and shut the door.

"What are you doing?" Mara asked.

"Trying to get my life back."

"You wanted to stay dead yesterday."

He held her against him and dug his fingers into her ass. "Yesterday, my pack was gone. Yesterday, you thought you were still sick. We hadn't... I didn't think I could stay with you. A lot can change in a day. I'm not suggesting we go to the *Seattle Times* and announce my triumphant return to the world of the living. But tell your best friend. I'm not leaving you, Mara. It'll be easier if she knows the truth."

Mara stared at him for a long time. Too long. He could barely resist stripping her naked and taking her. Dipping his head, he nipped at her lower lip. A tiny purr of pleasure escaped her throat and her body melted in his arms. God, he wanted her.

She slammed her hands into his chest and forced a few inches of space between them. "Not now," she gasped. "Not with Jen right outside."

Cade growled in frustration and released his mate. "Soon. Very soon."

Mara shivered and grinned. "Promise?"

"Promise."

28

Cade

As he told his story—minus the part about being a werewolf—he paced Mara's living room. How his father had been involved in a woman's death long ago, how her daughter had come after him. He hid his time as a caged animal, the endless nights of pain and loneliness...

"I was trapped on Orcas for a long time. No way off the island. She took my ID, money, everything. Mara saved me."

After he'd finished his story—despite it having more holes than anything else—Jen asked for an Irish coffee.

"Is Mara in danger?" Jen whispered as soon as Mara headed for the kitchen.

"I don't know. But my family's on their way." Cade clenched his hands on his thighs. "We're tight. They won't let anything happen to Mara. This is going to sound insane, but...I'd die for Mara."

Jen stared him down, challenging the wolf inside, but Cade wouldn't look away. Mara was *his*, and he'd defend her and protect her until the end of his life.

When Mara came back and handed Jen the mug, her brows furrowed. "What are you two talking about?"

With a smile, Jen toasted no one with the drink. "Today, the role of Mara's father will be played by Jen Larsen." She turned back to Cade. "I've got a shotgun and I know how to use it." Her expression was deadly serious, but a moment later, she burst out laughing. "I don't really."

Mara stifled a giggle. "Give him a break, okay? What's been going on with you since Thanksgiving? Are you on break next week? I can't make any definite plans yet, but maybe dinner next Friday? If I can work up the courage to tell Adam about Cade by then, he could meet everyone."

Cade relaxed with Mara at his side. The three of them fell into easy conversation, chatting about the holidays, Jen's job as a grammar school teacher, Mara's hopes that she could return to work after the first of the year. Cade didn't have a lot to contribute, but he made the occasional joke, tried to get to know the petite raven-haired woman who was his mate's best friend. When his stomach rumbled, close to noon, Jen glanced down at her watch.

"I should get going. I told my mom I'd help her set up her tree today. Cade, walk me out?"

"Jen, be nice," Mara warned.

"Oh, please." The brunette rolled her eyes, but the look she shot Cade held weight.

"Give me your worst," he said when they were outside.

Jen's lips quirked into a small smile. "So where's the wolf?"

"Gone."

"You convinced her to get rid of him?" Jen asked.

A headache started throbbing behind Cade's eyes. He should have known. Everyone who knew about the wolf would need an answer. "Not exactly. He left when I showed up."

Jen leaned forward, searching Cade's eyes, curiosity in her own. "Huh."

Cade braced himself. "What?"

"I've known Mara for more than a decade. I know when she's lying to me. In fact, I know when everyone's lying to me. Some people can sing, others can dance, I can spot a liar a mile away. The wolf didn't...leave, exactly, did he? He's right here."

The wave of nausea made him clutch his stomach and stagger back against the house as he cast a quick glance towards the door.

Mara, please come out here.

"Calm down. I'm not going to tell anyone. Least of all Lil or Adam. I probably should have let you off the hook earlier, but I had to make you squirm a bit. She's important to me. So don't you hurt her."

"She's my mate."

"Huh," Jen said again. She shrugged and shook her head a little. "Well, then I believe you. You'd die for her."

"How'd you know? About the wolf."

Jen flashed Cade a bright smile. "Now that, Cade, is a story that not even Mara knows. Stick around, treat her well, and maybe one day I'll tell you."

Mara

She cleaned up from breakfast. Even loaded the dishwasher. And still, Cade was outside with Jen. What the hell was she doing?

Unable—and unwilling—to let Cade twist in the wind any longer, she threw open the front door and gaped. He sat alone on the stoop, leaning back on his hands.

"Where's Jen?"

Cade tipped his head back to look at her. "She left."

"And?" Mara shivered, though it wasn't all from the cold.

"We had a little talk. She knows where the wolf went."

"What?" Mara's heart thudded against her chest, and a few drops of water escaped her clenched fists.

"Calm down, honey. She wouldn't tell me how she knew about werewolves, but she knew."

"Oh, my God."

"I'm not sure she likes me yet, but she knows I'm not leaving you."

Something deep inside her broke, and a prickle of tears threatened to overwhelm her. The two of them could work. Together.

"Mara?" Cade's deep voice cut through her thoughts, and she flexed her fingers. They'd gone numb in the cold.

"Come inside," she said quietly.

The look Cade shot her brimmed with intense passion. His glacier-blue eyes were like an ocean during a storm, and his lips were set in a scowl. Under the Seahawks sweatshirt, his chest heaved. He sprang for her, grabbing her and tossing her over his shoulder.

Giggling and squirming, she beat her fists on his back, but she had no desire to be anywhere but held against his body. The front door slammed, locked, and she was flat on her back in bed before she could say a word.

Cade's arms caged her, and a growl shot raw need right to her core.

"You're mine, Mara. I want you. I need you."

Mara slid her hands under his sweatshirt, over the ridges of his abs, and up to his chest. He growled again, grinding his pelvis against hers. She fumbled for his belt, then ripped it off and shoved the denim down to his knees.

"I can't be gentle," he said a second before he attacked her with a savage kiss that left her breathless, her lips swollen and tingling.

"Do I..." she gasped, carding her fingers through his shaggy locks to pull him down for another kiss, "...seem fragile right now?"

"God, no."

"Then what are you waiting for?" She tugged on a fistful of his hair, forcing his head up to look at her. "Take me."

Her sweater sailed across the room.

I want you laid out like a banquet.

Cade tugged off her jeans, purring at the sight of the black lace against her pale skin. Mara let her gaze trail slowly down his body. The scars would forever be a part of him, but after just a few days, they'd faded slightly. His chest was filling out, and his cheeks were no longer hollow. His cock jutted proudly from a patch of steely curls, a bead of his essence glistening.

The scent of him calmed the storm of emotions rolling through her. She arched her back when he wrapped his arms around her, affording him the access to loosen her bra and pull it from her body.

"God. Your breasts are perfect. You're perfect." He palmed one small mound and sucked the other nipple into his mouth. Stubble tickled her sensitive skin. Mara writhed under him, aching for release. Pain stabbed her breast and shot to her core when he bit down, hard.

"Cade! More," she begged. It took everything she had to loosen her desperate grip on the bed sheets and try to push her panties down so he could fill her.

He wasn't gentle, but she didn't care. With a grunt, he buried himself deep inside her, slick heat welcoming his length. "Not without you," he growled and thrust twice. Enough to send waves of pleasure shooting through her body, curling her toes, but not enough to tip her over the edge.

A mewl of disappointment escaped her lips unbidden when he pulled out, but the emptiness she felt from the absence of his cock was soon replaced by his fingers and tongue. Two rough digits slipped inside her, and he lapped at the sensitive bundle of nerves above her entrance.

"You taste like rain," he whispered, and the vibrations of his lips brought her closer to the edge. "All I need. Forever. You."

The storm of sensations built. Lids hooded, half-blind with the feel of him against her, Mara tried not to scream.

"Go over, honey. Come for me," he commanded, biting down on her sweet spot and simultaneously thrusting three fingers deep. Her implosion seemed to suck all the air out of the room, bathing her naked skin with dew, and then shooting out in a percussive wave, droplets of water hitting the walls, the floor, and the ceiling.

She couldn't breathe, she could only feel. Helpless, she held onto him. It wasn't until he slid into her that she managed to blink and focus on him.

"Cade."

"I'm right here, honey. Right here. I'm not going anywhere." He took up a rhythm that matched the thumping of her heart. Silver flecks glowed in his blue eyes. His wolf. Taking control even though the man refused to let him loose. Deep, satisfied sounds of pleasure rolled through his chest. "Together this time," he said with a grin and swirled his hips against her.

There was tenderness now with his lips inches from hers. "You're mine," he said again, raining kisses along her jaw. "I'll protect you forever if you'll let me."

Cade nipped at her neck, biting and holding her still as the pressure built again. This time it was sweet and luscious, taking her higher until she soared off the cliff. Held in his arms, they fell back to the earth together.

TWO HOURS LATER, totally spent, loved in every way—and every position—she could imagine, Mara rolled off of Cade. "I need a shower. I think I'm dehydrated."

He grabbed her hand before she'd made it more than two steps and brought her wrist to his nose.

"Hey." Mara twisted out of his hold. "You don't need to *sniff me* every time I mention not feeling one hundred percent."

Cade growled. Not a word, but a possessive, guttural demand for her to freeze in her tracks and look at him. Nothing prepared Mara for the shock of heat flashing through her at the sound.

"I can smell how strong your element is, honey. And you can be damn sure I'm not going to let it weaken. Go. I'll get you a glass of water."

Rolling off the bed, he released her and strode from the room.

Stupid alpha male bullshit.

They were going to have a serious talk about this. Soon.

In the shower, she sighed as the water relaxed her aching muscles. Every part of her body hurt. But even with the pain and exhaustion, she felt better now than she had in months.

Each droplet of water produced its own unique vibration against her skin. Eleanor thought she'd one day be strong enough to make it rain. Could she really muster that much power?

Start with one drop.

Tipping her head up, she watched the water fall and let her element tug on her soul. Tiny vibrations hummed, resonating with her heartbeat. Mara focused on just one drop—one note—holding it in her mind and slowing its vibration. Slower. Slower. A single droplet hovered over her breast, then veered away from her body.

Then another note. Another drop. A third. A fourth. The water pooled at her feet, ran down the drain, but not a single drop touched her torso, arms, or thighs. She was doing it. She was controlling the water.

"Shit."

Cade's deep voice startled her, shattering her concentration and letting the water resume its gentle caress of her body.

Too much. Her knees buckled, and Cade caught her in his arms. "Sorry," she said. "I'm okay."

"No." He kept an arm around her waist and let the water sluice down his back, protecting her. "Save your strength in case we need it."

"I have to practice. And back off a little, okay? You're not my alpha." She extricated herself and dumped a bit of shampoo into her hands, massaging it into her scalp.

Anger—both at his tone and her own body's betrayal—thrummed through her, but she couldn't help staring at the naked man only inches away from her.

He was breathtaking. Strong shoulders, an eight-pack Olympic athletes would envy, and obliques that angled in the best way towards his cock.

Under the hot water, her cheeks flamed, and she turned around to rinse off the shampoo.

"Let me."

Mara dropped her hands. His capable fingers massaged her scalp, and she moaned, leaning against him. Cade's touch worked the knots out of her neck and shoulders. "You're too tense. I don't like it."

Suddenly, he spun her around and kissed her like she was his entire world. Her back pressed against the tile, her arms draped around his neck of their own volition, and her hips pressed urgently to his. Cade's stubble scraped over her upper lip, his teeth nipping, his tongue demanding.

She couldn't get enough of him, and she fought against the urge to slide her legs around his hips.

"Mmmm, Cade, stop." She pulled away. "You can't honestly want to go again."

"If we don't, I'm not going to be able to stand it. You don't understand. The mating—it's..."

"I need a break," Mara replied with a wince. "I think we've had more sex in two days than I had with my last boyfriend in a year. I need an hour. Maybe two. Keep it in your pants."

"I'm not wearing any."

The absurdity and obviousness of that statement pulled a bubbling laugh from her lips. She couldn't help it. His pack was on their way, he'd claimed her as his mate, and she suspected that despite his possessive nature, she might be falling in love with him.

"No, you're not. Fine. Keep it...over there." She pointed to the far corner of her small shower. Rinsing the last bit of soap from her body, she slipped out and wrapped herself in a towel.

Cade hadn't moved from where she'd ordered him. Two could play at this alpha game. "Fine. You don't have to stay *right* there. But keep a few inches between us, okay?"

"For a while. Not for long." His gaze trailed up her body while she worked a little mousse into her hair, and he groaned in frustration. "I'll be out in a couple of minutes."

Mara snagged the glass of water from the counter and smirked all the way to her closet.

Knowing that a man with Cade's body wanted her as much as she wanted him shocked and pleased her. Still, they were going to have to have a talk about his overprotective tendencies. But not right now. Now she wanted to do something normal. Something...date-ish. Dinner and a movie. They couldn't go out—not with Katerina out there somewhere close—but they could have a date night in.

29

Livie

A LITTLE AFTER SEVEN, half-starved and almost refreshed after a three-hour nap, Livie shuffled into the hallway.

A single, dim lamp illuminated the living room, and the television flickered. Superheroes battled for control of the world on screen. She couldn't remember the name of the movie, but it had come out six months prior. Another thing Cade had missed.

He sat on the couch, watching intently with Mara in his arms, her head on his shoulder, her eyes closed.

"Shhh," he whispered as he grabbed the remote and paused the movie. "She fell asleep half an hour ago."

Livie slid her hip onto the arm of the couch. "She okay?"

"Exhausted." Cade curled a lock of her hair around his finger. "She worked with her element for a bit. It's hard for her."

"Oh?" Livie had never seen an air elemental work—or any elemental, other than the fire bitch.

Cade leaned his head back, his bright blue eyes glowing in the dim light. "God, you should have seen it. She was in the shower bending the water *around* her. Standing right under the spray, bone dry."

Livie's brows shot up. "Can she fight Katerina? I mean, water cancels fire, right?"

"I don't know. Even if she can...I don't want to put her in harm's way."

Livie's rumbling stomach made Cade cringe and look down at Mara. She shifted slightly with a sigh, then settled.

"There's pizza," Cade whispered. "In the fridge. Sausage and mushroom. Pepperoni. A veggie for Christine. We got four. In case...the pack was hungry." His shoulders hunched, and he leaned down to press a kiss to Mara's forehead.

"It'll be okay, boss-man." Livie stopped herself from squeezing his shoulder. Instead she padded into the kitchen for a couple of slices of cold pepperoni while Cade went back to the movie.

Her phone buzzed in her pocket. Thank God.

Shawn: *Landed. You still with the elemental?*

With a quick glance at Cade, who was still focused on the television, Livie thumbed out a reply.

Livie: *Yes. Cade's mated with her. She's okay. Kind of cool. Don't be asses to her.*

Shawn: *Liam's not happy.*

Livie: *Liam's rarely happy.*

She could almost hear her mate chuckle.

Shawn: *You have food? We're starved.*

Livie: *Pizza. Bring beer. All Mara has is a half a bottle of wine. I think we'll need it.*

Cade

The movie credits rolled as Mara stirred and blinked up at him. He had his hand on her shoulder, the soft, silky fibers of her sweater so odd under his rough fingers.

"Sorry," she murmured with a sleepy smile. "Couldn't stay awake." With a shake of her head, she sat up and stared out into the darkness of the backyard. "I missed most of the movie."

"Yeah, but you'd seen it before." He'd missed so much. Movies, TV, books... He wanted to catch up on everything—as long as Mara was by his side.

She ran a hand through her tousled hair. "I hope Eleanor was right and using my element won't be this hard forever. I could probably sleep the rest of the night."

Wrapping her in his arms, Cade relished the satisfied hum she made as she nuzzled his neck. Even after her nap, her eyes were still bloodshot, and shadows dwelled just above her cheeks.

"You two are cute," Livie said with a chuckle. "I'd send you into the bedroom, but they'll be here in a few minutes."

Cade's entire body stiffened. He ached to see his pack again, but fear sat like a cold ball of ice in his gut. Until Mara's lips brushed his ear. "It'll be okay," she whispered. "I'm scared too, but they're your family."

He held her until the doorbell rang, and she scrambled off Cade's lap. Livie beat him to the entryway, but Cade cleared his throat. "I need to do this."

The petite wolf took Mara's arm and guided her a few feet back. With a last, lingering look at his mate, Cade turned the deadbolt. He could do this. They were still his pack, even if he was no longer their leader.

The sound of Liam's soft, Irish brogue hit his ears before the door was completely open. "Shite."

The big man stood in the doorway, hands on his hips, green eyes dark under his reddish brows. A white t-shirt strained over his chest under the brown leather jacket. "I didn't believe it. Not truly."

"Liam." Cade's voice was scratchy as he fought with his wolf, strained not to assert his dominance, to stare Liam down until his former beta showed the proper respect. But that wasn't his place any longer.

His heartbeat roared in his ears, and just as he was about to look away, to offer his submission, Liam stepped forward and folded Cade into a massive hug.

"Ya' bloody bastard. We thought ya' dead."

He couldn't breathe. Couldn't do anything but hold on to his closest friend, his brother, and stare over the man's shoulder at Shawn and Ollie, then Peter and Christine behind them. His family.

"Gonna die for real if you don't let me go so I can breathe," Cade grunted.

With a chuckle, Liam released him and stepped into the house, motioning for the rest of the pack to follow and shut the door behind them.

In his periphery, Cade caught a glimpse of his mate standing behind Livie, looking so lost, his heart ached.

"We came as soon as Livie rang," Liam said. "Ya' have to tell us everythin'. Includin' how the hell ya' came to be with that elemental." The big Irishman angled his head towards Mara, and Cade bristled.

"*That* elemental has a name." Cade held out his arm, and Mara darted to his side. He tucked her close, needing to protect her, but also show the pack how much she meant to him. "*Mara* is the one who saved my life. She nursed my wolf back to health, then she broke the fire charm on me. And she's mine. You'll treat her with respect."

"Apologies, Cade. I didn't mean to offend ya'. Or 'er. But can ya' not understand our fears?" Liam gave Mara the side eye, then lowered his head.

"I do, but I won't tolerate anyone so much as looking at her the wrong way. If you need to take your pack and go, I'll understand." Cade tightened his arm around his mate, and she smiled up at him. Why?

As Mara angled her head towards Liam, Cade turned back to his former beta. The man looked stricken.

"Shite. We're *your* pack. Did ya' think I challenged? Never. I told ya' years ago. I'm no alpha. I admit, I lost hope that we'd ever find ya', that ya' were even still alive, but we would have gone on without an alpha. We all agreed."

Cade's knees buckled, and only his hold on Mara kept him upright. "I wouldn't have blamed you," he whispered.

"I know." Liam knelt and lowered his head. The rest of the pack, save Livie, followed. "Yer my best friend, Cade. The only wolf I'll follow to the ends of the earth and back again. We came back for ya'. Yer the leader of this pack and always will be."

"For fuck's sake, get up." Cade grabbed Liam by the arm and hauled him to his feet. The two men embraced again before Cade turned back to Mara. "You knew?"

"Livie might have answered a few questions for me," she said. "I tried to tell you, but you were being a stubborn ass this morning."

A couple of his wolves stifled chuckles and snorts, but the rest looked away. With everything he was, he wanted to grab his mate and spin her around, haul her off to the bedroom and ravage her, but he forced himself to remain calm and focus on the more important matter of introducing her to his pack. "Liam, this is Mara."

His beta nodded tersely. "We owe ya' a debt for takin' care of Cade."

"Y-you're welcome." She offered Liam her hand, but Cade growled and stepped in front of her, glaring at his beta. She frowned at him. "What?"

"Weres are possessive," Livie answered for Cade. "He's not going to want any of the males touching you."

"Oh." Mara dropped her hand, and Cade relaxed.

One by one, the pack lined up behind Liam. Shit, he'd missed them. The scents, the individual sounds of their breathing, the way they each said his name—old friends, family. He'd been unprepared for the overwhelming crush of emotion seeing them brought.

One by one, they embraced him, until only Peter was left. The man's neck was covered with burn scars above his blue flannel shirt, and he moved stiffly.

"Shit, Peter. How bad?" Cade asked.

The wiry, dark-haired wolf shrugged as he loosened a couple of the buttons on his shirt to show Cade the scars winding down his torso. "I was too good looking anyway. I have some sensation. Enough to work."

With a bow of his head to Mara, Peter ducked back among the rest of the pack. He'd always been a quiet man, but scars had changed him.

Gathering in the living room, the pack scarfed cold pizza and drank the beers Shawn had brought. Cade and Mara sat together on the couch while he traced patterns on the inside of her wrist to try to calm her. Or maybe he was trying to calm himself.

Mara slid her arm around his back. "Tell them, Cade," she whispered.

He cleared his throat. "There's so much that's happened, and I know you need to hear it all, but the most important thing? Katerina's in Bellingham. Or was, anyway. She burned down my shop and killed Maggie. Mara's aunt has a friend who's an air elemental. She's convinced Katerina can't track us here, but we have to be careful. She's still hunting me. And by extension—all of you."

He hadn't told them the most important part—that Katerina was Mara's sister. The omission sat on his shoulders like a stone, but he had to find his footing first.

"Goddammit," Liam said. "We shouldn't stay. Cade, ya' have to come back to Ireland with us. I doubt we can get a flight until tomorrow morning, but if we make the arrangements now—"

Cade shook his head. "No. Mara's here, and my place is with her. We've been safe for two weeks. And now that we're all together again and know what Katerina is capable of, I think we could fight her if we had to. Mara's element is water. She's only started working charms, but my God. You should see it. She's so strong."

Mara huddled closer against Cade's side. "I wish I had your confidence in me," she whispered.

Liam's lips pressed into a thin line and he tightened his grip on his bottle of beer. "If we go back to Ireland, she won't find us. Here, there's no guarantee. She found ya' once, she could do it again. Livie told us...ya' spent all this time trapped as yer wolf?"

Cade nodded. As much as he didn't want to relive those terrible months, he needed his pack to know the truth.

By the time he'd finished, every one of them looked dazed, shocked, and horrified.

"Cade?" Mara asked, tipping her head up at him. "You have to tell them the last bit. Much as I don't want you to, they need to know."

"Not yet," he hissed at her.

"Tell us what?" Peter asked from his spot leaning against Mara's sliding glass door.

Mara worried her lip for a moment and then cleared her throat. "I was adopted when I was six months old and raised as an only child. I have a sister, though until yesterday, I hadn't given her a second thought for more than a decade. She's never been part of my life. In fact, the only time I met her, I kicked her out of my father's house in Sacramento and told her I never wanted to see her again."

Cade squeezed her hand. He had to be the one to deal the

final bit of news. And the one to protect her from whatever fallout happened after. "Katerina is Mara's sister."

"Fuck!" Liam leapt up, but Cade growled at him, the wolf pulsing under his skin. He wouldn't shift. Couldn't. But he could still assert his dominance.

"Sit back down. Now," he ordered. "She didn't know and she saved my life. No one touches Mara or even raises their voice to her. Understood?" He met each of his wolves' eyes and one by one, they all nodded. "Livie?"

The blond wolf took her mate's hand. "Mara's cool. She's on our side. I didn't much like it either when I found out, but she's not interested in helping that bitch any more than I am."

Heavy breathing, stifled growls, and Mara's heartbeat were all Cade could hear. He held her tightly, prepared to fight every single member of his pack to protect her, but desperately hoping he wouldn't have to. He was their alpha and they needed to remember that.

"Bloody hell," Liam replied with a small shake of his head. "We've been up for more than a day. This is not the time to discuss the elemental and Mara's tie to her, much as I'd like to. Ya' goin' to call a pack meeting tomorrow?"

"First thing."

"Then I've only one more question for ya' tonight. How did ya' escape?"

"Luck." Cade recounted what he could remember—though it wasn't much, still—about how the charms keeping the ground so hot had faded. "They were gone, I think. I wasn't sure, but I dug for three nights and no one came. I tested that fucking dirt every few days—whenever she'd come to feed me—and that was the first time I could stand to touch it."

"And comin' back from your wolf?" Liam asked. "Seven months with the animal in control shoulda driven ya' mad."

Cade bristled at the vague hint of accusation in Liam's tone.

"It did. Mara brought me back. She saved my wolf and then

she saved me. I can't explain it to you, Liam. When I shifted back, I couldn't speak or move at all. Mara took care of me."

Cade looked at the wolves strewn about the room. They were exhausted. Shawn rested his head in Livie's lap. Christine was already half asleep with her head resting against the wall.

Mara caressed Cade's arm. "There are air mattresses in the hall closet and I have extra blankets in my room. They need to sleep."

"You look pretty tired yourself," he replied, brushing his thumb under her right eye. "I don't like seeing these dark circles."

Liam stared at them, green eyes bloodshot, a muscle in his jaw throbbing, and his hands clenched on his thighs. "I'm going for our luggage," he said with a snarl. "I'll be right back."

"What's his problem?" Livie asked, yawning.

"He's been on edge since we lost Cade," Shawn replied. "He hated Ireland as much as the rest of us. More."

"Why?"

Every werewolf turned to Mara and stared at her. Drawn eyebrows, hard, cold eyes, and thin-lipped frowns had her shrinking into Cade's arms even further. Peter was the one who finally answered. "It's personal."

Mara looked at Cade, confused. He didn't disagree with Peter that it was Liam's story to tell, but Mara was one of them now. "Liam loved once," he said, keeping his answer vague. He'd give her the details later. Or ask Liam to do so. "She lived in Ireland. He lost her and he's never settled over it."

"Oh. I'm sorry." Her words weren't perfunctory. The emotion in them seemed to touch every wolf in the room, and they all nodded.

The door opened and shut with a slam and Mara flinched. Cade stood with Mara tucked against him, and addressed his pack. "I'll be back in a few minutes with the air mattresses and blankets. Bathroom's down the hall. We'll talk more in the morning. Livie, are you going to patrol again?"

"Yep. With that bitch so close, I'm not taking any chances and, unlike the rest of them, I slept half the day." She got up and headed for the guest room. "Shawn, come with me. I want a couple of minutes with you before I go."

Cade led Mara into her bedroom and shut the door. "I'm sorry for their behavior."

"I can't blame them. Not really. If I were in their shoes, I wouldn't trust me either. Should I go to Lil's for the night? I could give you time with them."

The idea of being without her, even for a few hours, gave him a throbbing headache. "No. You're staying here," he said, bringing her to the bed and pulling her down next to him. "I need you, Mara. The mating is driving me fucking insane. I want to tear your clothes off. Taste you. Hear you say my name when I bury myself inside of you."

A throaty laugh escaped her lips, and the scent of her arousal wafted over him. "Well, then get going. Blankets are in the closet. Deliver them, and maybe I'll find something you can rip off me."

Cade raced over to the closet and found a stack of blankets and sheets for his pack. As he left the room, Mara pulled off her sweater to reveal a black lace bra. He nearly turned around right then, but forced himself to keep moving. She'd be there when he came back and he'd have her in every way she let him.

30

Mara

SHE FELL asleep before Cade returned, but rolled over when her bedroom door clicked shut.

"What time is it?"

"Eleven." His voice held the strain of the late hour—and of dealing with his pack—and she threw back the blankets, revealing the small silk slip that barely covered anything. She'd bought the chemise on a whim and had never been brave enough to wear it.

With his eyes glowing brightly, he stalked towards her, the storm within the blue orbs one only she could quiet.

"Mine," he groaned, running his hands up her thighs, over the green silk, and resting them at her waist.

Time stopped as he kissed her, and his entire body vibrated with need.

Parting her lips, she let him in and reached for his arms, but Cade growled and pinned her wrists to the bed. "No. You. Don't. Move."

"Cade."

The alpha wolf flared in his eyes, and she let him take control, guiding her arms up over her head so she could curl her fingers around the brushed iron bars of her headboard. "Hold on."

Her belly quivered. She'd never been so turned on in her entire life. Cade stroked down her arms, cupped her breasts, and pinched her nipples. Her lids lowered, fluttering in time with the tremors that shook her entire body.

"Kiss me," she begged, meeting his gaze. "I love how you kiss me."

With a wicked grin, Cade stretched his body over hers. He planted a gentle kiss to her parted lips and pulled away. "You love that?"

"Tease."

He laughed, deep and throaty, and leaned in again. This time, the pressure was insistent, firm, hard. But he pulled away too soon. "That?"

"A little better. But come on, shaggy man. Put your back into it." She held his gaze, seeing the gleam in his eyes.

"Oh, I'll put *everything* into it," he said. Hands threaded through her hair, lifting her mouth to his. The crushing pressure of his lips, the all-consuming hunger as his tongue played with hers, the sharp nip of his teeth, and the needy, guttural rumble in his chest were everything. Life sustaining.

As was his scent. She could lose herself in it. Cade's erection pressed against her, and she ground her hips as best she could under his weight.

Teeth scraped along her lower lip, sending sparks shooting through her. "That?"

"Yes," she panted. "God, Cade. How can I need you *this* much?"

"We're mating, honey. You're not a wolf, but whatever part of you isn't human...it recognizes our connection."

Too many words. Why was he still talking?

Mara strained to reach him, a low whine accompanying the slight movement. "Please," she whispered.

Cade took mercy on her and brought her hands to his neck. She grasped fistfuls of his hair, tightening her grip until he growled, "Mine."

Roughly, he pushed up the thin chemise to find her naked and ready for him.

Mara pulled his sweatshirt over his head and marveled at his corded muscles, his strong chest. She ran her hands over the distinct ridges of his eight-pack, down to his navel and the trail of sandy hair that disappeared into his jeans.

When he shed his pants, his cock was ready for her. The scent of him hit her, and she inhaled deeply, wondering what he'd do if she let her own desires take over.

"What?" He rolled, pulling her on top of him. The room was warm, but the air coaxed gooseflesh from her bare arms.

"Hush, shaggy man. Now it's time for you to hold still." Mara wriggled out of his grip and lowered herself between his thighs. He called her name as she brought her lips to brush against him, swirling her tongue around the head of his cock. "Shhh." Her breath whispered over the sensitive skin and he groaned, jerking his hips slightly.

"Marrrr..."

Licking her lips, she took him slowly and firmly into her mouth. He was hard, hot, and needy. Blood pounded through the thick vein on the underside of his length, and she traced it with her tongue. She'd only done this twice before and wasn't exactly sure what she was doing, but she knew she wanted nothing more than the taste of him filling her.

Something raw and primal drove her on. Her lips tired, her jaw ached, but the discomfort barely registered. Cade's spasms and quiet growls encouraged her. "Can't hang on," he muttered. She reached up and cupped his balls, rolling them slightly and scraping her fingernails along the delicate skin.

A hoarse cry escaped his lips, and he jerked as his seed filled her. She fought not to gag, swallowed, and savored the intimacy growing between them.

Gently, she drew her lips off him, wriggled up, and rested her head on his hip. His fingers brushed her hair back from her face as he panted weakly, his stomach muscles trembling.

"Come here," he said quietly.

Mara blinked hard to clear the haze that had settled over her. She was spent, sated, and he'd barely touched her. When she didn't move, he grasped her under the arms and tugged her up so her head tucked against his shoulder.

"Better."

Lines had deepened around his eyes and his lips. As he stroked her shoulder, she noted bruises along his knuckles. He'd had to hit someone. His eyes were closed, and his breathing slowed. A sheen of sweat covered his skin, lending a deep maleness to his scent that comforted her. Forcing herself up, she grabbed the sheet and blanket and drew them over their intertwined bodies.

"No," he protested, but the word escaped slurred. "Want you."

"I know. But you're exhausted. What took you so long?"

"Ollie and I got into it. He wanted the pack to leave. And he wanted me to go with them. I had to remind him that if he wanted to stay in my pack, he was going to listen to me." Cade rolled slightly and pulled her closer. "He owes you an apology in the morning."

"Get some sleep, stud."

Hours later, Mara woke with a headache and Cade's body draped over hers. The scent of them—their coupling—filled the room. Cade's pure male strength, a hint of the woods he'd been such a part of before his capture, fresh rain, and a note of coconut. Mara inhaled deeply and licked her lips. She needed water. Her element was weak. She recognized the signs now.

Water would help, would hydrate her enough to pull more from the air to balance herself.

Cade groaned quietly as she shifted his warm weight off of her. "Shhh, shaggy man. I'll be right back."

"Marrrrra," he growled, then settled when she pressed a kiss to his full lips. Her fingers trailed over his hair, savoring the silky locks.

"Sleep," she whispered. "I won't be long."

Cade's sweatshirt was crumpled on the floor, and Mara tugged it over her head. It smelled like him. She snuggled within the warmth and crept quietly out into the hall. Several distinct pitches of snores rumbled from her living room. She ran a bit of water from the sink and filled a glass, staring out into her starlit backyard while she sipped.

A growl raised the hairs on the back of her neck, drowning her in fear as she turned.

Standing a few feet away, easily four-and-a-half-feet tall, with black and reddish fur and glowing green eyes, was a wolf that could only be Liam.

Glistening teeth bared, nails clicking against the hardwood floor, he took one step forward. Then another. A deep vocalization she didn't understand came from his throat and moments later, the entire pack—save for Livie, Shawn, and Cade—stood behind him.

"Liam?" she squeaked. "You're scaring me." Liam growled again.

"How did you find him?" Ollie asked. A bruise darkened his right eye. Though he had at least twenty years on her, he was also a big man, and his hands were clenched at his sides. "Some of us don't trust you, elemental. Cade loves you, but we don't. Why should we believe you won't hurt him?"

"Because I won't," she said. "I care about him."

Christine slipped between Peter and Ollie. She touched Liam's neck, and the wolf sat down on his haunches. "Mara, we're concerned about your sister and whether we'll be safe here. We lost Cade once. We won't lose him again. We want him to leave with us. To come back to Ireland where we know he'll be safe."

A stab of fear lanced her heart. If Cade went back to Ireland, she'd lose him. "Cade's your alpha and he said he wanted to stay here."

"Cade's blinded by his feelings for you," Peter said. "Your sister nearly killed all of us." He yanked open the collar of his shirt to expose a neck of red scar tissue.

Liam growled again and advanced. Mara pressed her back against the counter, shaking with fear. The wolf sniffed her legs, her torso, and his vocalizations grew louder. When he bared his teeth and snapped at her, Mara screamed.

"Get the hell away from her!" Cade roared, flying towards Mara. He wrapped her in his arms, still naked, and the heat of his body seeped through the sweatshirt. "Shift back. Now."

Liam shrank away, sat down, and howled in pain. Popping, cracking, and groaning followed. Dark, silky red hair sprouted from his now-rounded head. He was a massive man, corded muscles lining his arms, his thighs, and his calves. Mara looked away from his groin after getting way more of an eyeful than she bargained for, and buried her face in Cade's neck, forcing deep breaths through parted lips.

Cade's voice vibrated through his body. "Would you like to explain why you were threatening my mate? Or would you prefer to leave?"

"I heard something," Liam offered, shrugging his shoulders. "I thought it was outside, and I shifted so I could see better. Mara surprised me. I overreacted. Blame the moon."

"And you think that's a good enough explanation? I told you earlier. She's mine and *no one* frightens her. What about the rest of you? What the hell were you doing?"

"We had questions," Christine said.

"Questions you had to ask her without me. In the middle of

the night. With Liam snarling at her. Pack meeting. Now. We're not waiting until morning. Mara, honey, look at me." Cade took her by the upper arms, his bright blue eyes holding hers. "Apparently they've forgotten what it means to have an alpha these past months. You can be damn sure I'm going to remind them. Painfully if necessary. Can you give me an hour? I need to do this alone."

"Don't shut me out," Mara whispered.

Cade led her back into her bedroom, sparing his pack one last lingering glare as he went. He tugged on his jeans. "I'm not shutting you out. Give me an hour to kick their asses and then we're *all* going to talk. They'll air any grievances to your face, with me at your side, and if anyone so much as raises their voice to you, they're gone."

"They're your family. You'd really choose me over them?" She sank heavily onto her bed, overwhelmed at the thought.

"You're my mate. There isn't any choice for me." Cade knelt in front of her and cupped her cheeks. His lips brushed hers and she couldn't help herself. She slid her arms around his neck and pulled him closer. Whatever happened with his pack, she cared for him and wanted him to stay with her.

Reluctantly, she drew back. "Go."

Cade

He stalked out into the living room to find Liam, dressed again, sitting on the floor with his head in his hands. Peter and Ollie had taken their seats in the two occasional chairs and Shawn and Christine were on the couch.

"Livie's patrolling," Shawn said. "Do you want her here too?"

"No. She's accepted Mara. My problem is with the rest of you.

What the hell were you doing?" He glared at each of them in turn, his gaze lingering on Liam the longest.

"We had questions," his beta said.

"Then you should have come to me. Instead of waiting six fucking hours, you attacked my mate in her kitchen. In wolf form. You were touching her. I could kick you out of the pack for that alone."

Liam lumbered to his feet. "I don't mean to challenge ya', Cade. But ya' have to admit, this all sounds a mite convenient. The sister of the elemental who nearly killed ya' is the one to save yer life? What if she was waitin' until your pack was all in one place to strike?"

Cade's fist shot out and connected with Liam's jaw. The big werewolf stumbled back and landed on his ass. "That's for disrespecting Mara. *This* is for disrespecting me." He reached down and grabbed Liam by the front of his t-shirt, hauling him up and belting him again, this time in the gut.

Liam doubled over with an audible groan.

"If you want more, I'll give it to you. But it's your choice. What'll it be?"

"I'm sorry," Liam grunted. "I was wrong to attack yer intended."

"My mate."

"She's not yer mate until the full moon," Liam said, throwing up his hands when Cade advanced on him again.

"You're walking a thin line. What's this really about?" Cade shoved his hands into his pockets so he wouldn't be tempted to punch his beta again. Liam was rarely the most agreeable man, but this wasn't like him. Not at all.

The big wolf ran a hand through his tousled hair. "Ya' came back from seven months with the wolf in control. No one does that. Livie was trapped for three days after the fire. When she shifted, she couldn't speak for almost twenty-four hours. And yet here you are, not four days later, walkin', talkin', and punchin'. I want to know how."

"What you're really saying is that you don't believe I *could* come back. Fine." He took a chair from the dining room table and turned it around, straddling it and crossing his arms over the back. "I'll tell you what I remember. And when I'm done, each and every one of you is going to go to Mara and beg her forgiveness or leave this pack forever. Your choice."

Mara

She pulled on a pair of gray fleece pants and sat on the bed, hugging herself tightly. Cade's sweatshirt was warm and comforting, and she wanted to lose herself in his scent.

If only she could sleep. Angry sounds floated in from the living room, including the sound of a fist hitting flesh and a guttural growl.

On edge, she got up and started pacing. A flutter of movement outside had her pulling back the drapes to see Livie, mid-patrol. The little blond wolf caught Mara's gaze and cocked her head.

Would Livie help her? Mara pointed towards the front door, and Livie nodded.

Cracking the door, she listened. Cade was recounting his memories of his time as a wolf, and she slipped on her shoes and tiptoed down the hall. Peter caught her eyes and glared at her, but no one else said word until Cade heard her flip the lock.

"Mara?"

"I'm going to talk to Livie. Don't worry about me."

His eyes said so much, though he only nodded.

I want you. Be careful. I'm sorry.

It was a cool, damp night with dew glistening on the car

windshields, shining like diamonds in the glow of the streetlights.

Livie sat on the porch in human form, wrapped in the blanket that Mara had left there the night before. Her bare toes were pale pink, her cheeks flushed, and her blond hair tousled. She brushed it away and fixed Mara with a hard stare.

"Spill."

"Cade said he'd choose me over them." The words came spilling out, faster than she could think. She told Livie everything that had happened in her kitchen. "How can he possibly choose me over his family? He's known me three weeks."

"He's mated to you." Livie shrugged. "Or will be after the full moon. It's how we are. I love Cade. I'd die for every single wolf in the pack. But if I had to choose between any of them and Shawn...between *all of them* and Shawn, I'd pick Shawn every time. It isn't anything we can control."

"What's going to happen in there?"

"Cade will read them the riot act, and they'll have to either apologize or leave. Or challenge. But that's not likely."

"Challenge?"

"Think of it like a coup. It's rare, but if your alpha goes insane or gets really sick, it can happen. It's more likely that Peter or Ollie will get in his face and say something to piss him off. It's too close to the new moon. They're both bitten, not born. They have less control of their emotions this time of the month than the rest of us. Don't worry. We run hot—in more ways than one. Even if boss-man does have to throw a punch or two, everything will be forgiven by morning."

As if Livie's words were prophetic, Cade's deep baritone carried in through the closed door. "Goddammit Ollie, I don't give a fuck!"

Mara flinched. "Shit. I can't stand this. I need to get out of here." She tried to get up, but Livie grabbed her wrist and held her down.

"Mara, wait. If you want to leave, I'll go with you. But you'll tell Cade first. Katerina is out there somewhere, and you can't go running off alone."

"Fine. I want to go to Aunt Lil's. You can go with me, but once I get there, come back and take care of Cade. My aunt lives in a fifty-year-old brick building with a secure entrance. Nothing's getting to me there."

"Okay. I don't like this, but I get it. Can't say I wouldn't do the same thing." Livie groaned as she pushed to her feet. "Pup's kicking like crazy. I can't tell if he *likes* it when I shift or hates it."

The two women slipped back inside, and Mara cleared her throat. "Cade? Can I talk to you for a minute?"

He turned, and the pain and stress etched on his face came close to changing her mind. The rest of his wolves sat meekly, staring down at the ground.

"What is it, honey?"

"I'm going to Lil's for the night."

"No," he growled. He sprung up and pulled her against him. "Don't leave. I'll send them away. Hell, *I'll* leave. This is your house. And I...I'm falling in love with you. It's not the mating. It's more. You're strong, smart, funny, and so fucking beautiful. Don't leave me."

"I'm not leaving you," she said, cupping his cheeks. "I'm falling for you too. But there's too much stress here. I can't think. All I want to do is lose myself in you. One night. Find the rest of yourself. Find peace with them." She laid her hand against his heart, and he pressed into her palm.

What she felt was strong enough to be love. If only she could think, she might know for sure.

"I can tell, you know," she said. "I can see the man you once were. He's back. Or he's close. But you need them. They're your family, and I won't take you away from them or let you choose me over them."

"It's too dangerous," he insisted. "Katerina."

"Eleanor's there. Aunt Lil has a gun. She knows how to use it." Mara forced a smile. "One night. That's it. I'll have my phone. You'll be able to reach me."

Livie stepped forward. "Boss-man? Let Mara get her phone and whatever she needs for tonight. I want to talk to you for a minute."

Mara retrieved her purse, keys, and phone from her room. For a split second, she thought maybe she should take off Cade's sweatshirt, but she couldn't. She needed his scent surrounding her.

When she returned to her living room, Cade stood with his hands in his pockets.

"I don't like this," he said. "But Livie will keep you safe. Will you call me when you get there?"

Mara melted at the concern in his voice. "Yes. I will. I left Lil's number on my nightstand." She looked over at the blond were-wolf she thought she'd soon consider a friend. Maybe even a sister.

"I'll protect her, boss-man. On my life."

Cade nodded. "You'd better."

31

Mara

THE LAST THING she wanted to do was leave Cade, but being in the house with his pack was just too much.

"Don't do anything stupid," she whispered with her lips against Cade's ear. "Like following me. Stay with your family and figure all this shit out. I'll be back in the morning. I promise."

He kissed her like she was water and he was in the middle of the desert, half-dead.

One night. Not even. Eight hours, tops.

So why did she feel so unsettled?

"My spare house keys are on the hook by the door. Lock up after us."

Cade's expression sliced right through her heart, but she linked her arm with Livie's and hurried out to the wolf's rental car. "West on Eightieth," she said once they belted in. Despite her words, Cade stood in the doorway, watching them, fear etched on his face.

"He'll be okay," Livie said with a pat to Mara's shoulder. "And he'll put an end to this stupid posturing shit Liam and Ollie have going on. Ollie's suspicious by nature. He used to be a sheriff. But Liam…" She started the car and eased away from the curb. "Liam's had a hard time since the fire."

After another two blocks, Mara pointed. "Turn left here. Lillian's condo is at the very end of this cul-de-sac."

"Really?" Livie's brows shot up. "If it were warmer, we could have walked."

"It's my condo, really. I bought it when I moved to Seattle. But a few years later, my dad died and left me a small inheritance, and the real estate market was at its lowest. I kept the condo as an investment. Then Aunt Lil moved in when I got sick."

Livie parked and turned in her seat. "You were right, you know. What you did. Leaving."

"It doesn't feel right now." Mara rubbed the back of her neck. The headache hadn't fully left her. She should have had more water. "Why does Liam hate me? Besides my relationship to Katerina."

"Oh babe, he doesn't. He doesn't trust you, but he doesn't hate you."

"Then what is it?" Mara shivered.

Livie angled her head towards the condo complex and they both got out of her rental. "He fell in love once. He doesn't talk about it, but she was an air elemental. He would have mated with her."

"What happened? I mean…am I allowed to ask? I don't want to overstep." Digging in her purse, she fished out the keys for the complex's outer door.

"She died."

Mara froze, then turned back to Livie. "Oh, God. I'm—"

Something moved in her periphery, and a sense of intense…*wrongness* overtook her. In a heartbeat, she shoved Livie in the chest. Hard.

The petite wolf flew back, landing in a small bush just as fire arced through Mara's limbs, forcing her to the ground.

Rolling, she called on her element. The humid, nighttime air made it easier, as did the light mist falling steadily.

Her hands tingled, and the subtle vibrations of the droplets surrounding her formed a frantic symphony inside her head. One note at a time, she searched for them, drawing as much of her element within her as she could to fight the heat overwhelming her.

Livie's pained howl pierced the night air. Bones popped and cracked. Mara crawled towards her, scanning the parking lot for her sister.

That's what she'd seen, she realized. Katerina, her hands glowing with fire, seconds before the blast.

"Go," Mara hissed. "Run."

Livie's growl was easy to understand. *"No."*

"Mara Taylor." Katerina's gleeful voice grated along Mara's spine. "And a bitch. We could smell you at the dog's shop. All three of you. Now...where's Bowman? Upstairs?"

Livie snarled and leapt in front of Mara.

"I nearly killed you once, bitch. I can do it again," Katerina spat. She stepped out from behind a van, her fingers glowing red hot. A tall, gangly young man stood at her back with his hand on her shoulder, a slight, blond woman behind him, mist swirling around her.

"Livie, get back," Mara said sharply. "You know Liam was right when he took Cade back to Ireland. Go now."

The wolf made an inquisitive sound, then almost immediately growled her refusal.

Mara glared at Katerina, but kept her hands down at her sides, trying to appear non-threatening. "The wolf left. His pack came for him, and they all went to Ireland. Livie's leaving in the morning. The only person upstairs is my eighty-five year old aunt."

"I've kept tabs on you, *sister dear*. Bella smelled you and the dog together. And...*water*? How the hell did you end up with water as your element?"

Shit. She knows.

"I wasn't sure if you still lived here, but property records don't lie. So I decided to keep watch for a day." Her sister didn't lower her hands or take her eyes off either of them as she advanced.

Mara sidestepped Livie and forced a laugh. "Unless you're going to burn down an entire building—again—you're never getting inside."

Flinging the keys towards the street, she called forth a stream of water, sending them into the sewer grate where they clattered, clanked, and dinged their way down the pipe.

Katerina's eyes blazed, and she sent a wave of white-hot flames directly for Livie.

"No!" Throwing herself in front of the wolf, Mara prayed she had enough left in her for one last charm. A wall of water surrounded Livie and carried her twenty feet to the edge of the parking lot, where she landed with a yelp and dove into the underbrush.

The fire hit Mara in the chest, filling her ears with a sound so foreign, she didn't realize it was her own screaming until she ran out of air. But she couldn't draw in another breath. A heavy weight pressed down on her chest, and she writhed on the now-dry pavement.

"Where's the she-wolf?" Katerina shouted.

Another female voice answered. "I can't sense her. That water obliterated any trace of her."

"I've got tracks," a man called. "But they disappear when they hit the street."

Mara's vision darkened, and the entire world started to slow. Katerina's angry face hovered over her. "She's about to pass out, Bella. Release the charm."

Air flooded Mara's lungs, sweet, rich, and life sustaining. She wheezed, too weak to escape or call on any more of her element, too weak to even move as Katerina dropped to a knee next to her and pressed her hand to Mara's chest.

A low chant escaped her blood-red lips. "I call upon the earth's fiery core. Flow through me and settle in this body. Bind to her and let no water pass."

In a single blink of her hollow, scratchy eyes, Mara's lips cracked, her tongue turned to sandpaper, and every breath sent daggers stabbing her torso. Her element was...*gone*. Taken in an instant.

"Why?" she croaked.

Before Katerina could answer, the young man thrust Mara's wallet at her. "Babe, she was telling the truth. She's got a different address on her driver's license."

Her sister flicked a brief glance to the small square of plastic. "Shit. Bella? Any sign of the wolf?"

Air swirled all around Mara, cooling her feverish skin and letting her take a single, easier breath. But it didn't last. Not even the mist prickling against her cheeks helped.

"No," Bella said softly. "Only on her. I told you earlier. The wolf isn't here."

"Take her, Jeremy. We're going to pay a little visit to my sister's house." Katerina leaned closer and whispered in Mara's ear. "Don't worry, dear. That charm won't kill you. It'll hurt. More than a bit. Stop you from using your element, but I'll release it once I've killed the dog. You'll be fine. Maybe you'll even come to forgive me."

Never.

She wouldn't waste her breath on a reply. Her sister wouldn't listen. She just prayed Livie could get there in time.

Jeremy hauled her over his shoulder, and Mara tried to wriggle free, but she was too weak, too dehydrated. As she landed on the floor of the van, she prayed.

Please, Cade. Run.

Cade

Until Mara called, he wouldn't settle. Why hadn't he thought to ask how far away Lillian lived?

"She needs this. And she loves you. Trust me. And tell Liam to get his head out of his ass," Livie had said before she'd left with Mara.

The front door shuddered, and a mournful howl pierced the night air. As Cade threw the door open, Livie bounded in, skidded to a halt, and shifted back into human form, drenched from head to toe.

"Mara," she gasped. "Katerina was there... Mara saved...my life. She has...an air elemental. We have to get out of here. Now!"

"Where's Mara?" Cade grabbed her shoulders and pinned her with a feral stare. "Why didn't you protect her?"

"I tried. God, Cade. I tried. There were three of them. Fire, earth, and air. They thought you were at Lil's. Mara used to live there. And they could be here any minute."

"If she got away, she'd come back here," Cade said. He couldn't leave Mara's home. Not if there was a chance...

"And what if she didn't?" Liam's voice was rough, and the edge to it set Cade off. "That bitch bested all of us, and ya' said it yerself. Mara's new to her power."

For the second time in as many hours, Cade slammed his fist into Liam's square jaw. "I've had enough of your shit, Liam. She's my fucking mate and I love her. I'm not abandoning her."

Getting to his knees, Liam growled, "Cade—"

The alpha wolf prickled under his skin, but Liam held up a hand. "I'm not suggestin' we abandon her. But stayin' here? It's suicide." Blood trickled from Liam's split lip. "If she's alive, she might still have her phone. We need to leave. Hide somewhere. Then we'll ring her. And her aunt. We'll find her."

Cade scrubbed his hands over his face as fear chilled his bones. He'd never told Mara that he loved her. If his pack—and his failure to lead—had delivered her right into Katerina's clutches, he'd never forgive himself.

"Get yer clothes or shift," Liam snapped. "The rest of ya', shift. I'll get the bag. We leave in five."

The wolves held their breaths, waiting. Liam might have gotten used to giving orders in the seven months Cade had been gone, but he wasn't in charge now.

As angry as Cade was at Liam's tone, he knew his beta was right. "You heard him," he said quietly. Turning to Liam, he straightened his shoulders. "You've stepped over the line one too many times tonight. But we'll discuss that later. After we find her."

He tossed a sweatshirt over his head and nearly fell over trying to get his shoes on. His thoughts raced, a jumbled mess of images. Mara dead. Mara in pain. Katerina torturing her as she had tortured his wolf.

Liam's bulk filled the doorway, and the light caught the bottle of whiskey in his hand. "We have to go. Now."

"You're drinking?"

The beta wolf swallowed a growl. "Maskin' our scent. For fuck's sake, Cade, focus."

Blindly, he followed Liam out into the backyard. The pack—all in wolf form—waited by the fence.

"Over," Cade ordered, and one by one, the wolves backed up, took off at a run, and leapt over the wooden fence. Liam shook the bottle around the edges of the yard, then gestured for Cade to go over.

More whiskey painted the wood once the two of them were on the other side. "Such a waste," Liam muttered with a glance at the label.

A high pitched yip from a few hundred yards away signaled

Livie's call. Cade and Liam turned together and sniffed the air, then took off at a run towards the sound.

The rest of the wolves waited at the edge of a greenbelt, and they all ran until they found a main road, then shrank out of sight of any passing cars. Liam pulled out his mobile and shoved it at Cade. "Ring her."

The call went to voicemail. Next, he tried Lillian.

"Wolf?" Lillian's Southern twang was heavier than when they'd met. "They took her. That skinny black-haired bitch and her two young'uns shot my niece full of fire and hauled her off in a van. Now what in the damn hell are you gonna do about it?"

His ass hit the ground, and he dropped his head between his knees. "We got out. Mara saved Livie's life, and she got back in time. But we don't know where they are. Can Eleanor track them?"

"She's tryin'. Eleanor?" Lillian's voice faded a bit. "Get yer ass out here. Did you find them yet?"

"They headed towards Mara's house. Where's the wolf?"

"On the phone."

"Well? Give me the damn thing."

If the situation hadn't been so dire, Cade would have chuckled at the two older women bickering.

"Wolf?"

"Goddammit, I have a name," Cade spat. "Try using it once in a while."

"Cade," Eleanor said, "calm down."

"Don't fucking tell me to calm down. My mate is in the hands of the woman who tortured me for seven horrible, endless months. You *know* Mara won't survive that fire charm. So help me find her!"

Liam grabbed his arm. "Keep yer voice down, Cade. We can't draw attention to ourselves."

Extending his middle finger at his beta, he shook off the man's hold and turned away.

"Where are you?" Eleanor asked.

"A couple of miles from Mara's house. At the edge of a green-belt. North 105th Street."

"I'm coming to you. I'm in Lil's car. Stay hidden." The line went dead.

32

Mara

HER ARMS HUNG down Jeremy's back as he carried her, slung over his shoulder, up her front walk.

"Caaa..." she slurred. Her mouth wasn't working right, and she couldn't hold a thought in her head for more than a second or two.

Please...

Katerina would kill Cade if he and the pack were still here.

She moaned again, and Jeremy slapped her ass. "Quiet!"

Mara heard her door knob rattle. Keys. They didn't have her keys.

"Bella, do your thing," her sister ordered.

A wisp of air ghosted across Mara's cheek, and the tumblers clicked.

Panic soured her stomach as Jeremy carried her inside.

"He was here," Bella said. "But he's not now. They masked their scent. That was damn good whiskey they used."

Katerina's footsteps echoed on the hardwood floors. "Take my sister back to the van. I want to look around."

As terrified as she was, Cade's escape gave her a small spark of hope. That meant Livie was alive too. All of them.

Her head hit the floor of the van with a thud, and her thoughts fogged even more. Face down, her face pressed into the dirty black carpet with Jeremy holding her wrists tightly at the small of her back, hopelessness took hold.

Every symptom of her illness had come back with a vengeance, along with Eleanor's words.

You have too much fire in your blood. Letting it build up will kill you.

"Here," Katerina said sharply. "Secure her."

A soft whisper of one of her scarves bound her wrists tightly, and then Jeremy flipped her over and propped her up against the wall of the van.

Her sister knelt in front of her as Bella shut the back door and the interior light came on.

"I'm sorry about this, Mara. I am. I don't want to hurt you. If you tell me where the wolf is, I'll lift the charm and let you go as soon as I've dealt with him."

A burning hand cupped her cheek, and Mara tried to jerk away, but she lacked the strength.

"Don't. Know. Please...siiick." She had to make her sister understand.

"Don't be a drama queen." Katerina snorted. "I'd never seriously hurt you, sister. The charm will keep you weak and compliant. That's all. I love you, Mara."

"Nu-huh." Mara shook her head slightly. "Dying. Wa...ter."

With a fake smile, Katerina rubbed Mara's arm, sending even more heat through her body. "No water for you, sister dear. Not unless you tell me where the wolf is."

Mara tried to lick her lips, working her mouth to generate any moisture she could. "My blood," she gasped. "Too...much fire. Doctors...told me. Dying."

Katerina grabbed her chin and dug her fingers in, hard. "I

didn't expect my sister to be such a little wimp. Just tell me where he is, and I'll take the fire away."

"Fuck. You."

There was no fake kindness in Katerina's eyes now. They turned hard and cold, then narrowed into slits. "I will find him. And when I do. I'll make you watch him die." Whipping her head towards Jeremy, she thrust another scarf at the boy. "Gag her. We're going back to the hotel before we do anything else."

Jeremy tied the silk tightly around Mara's head, then shoved her onto her side before the van rumbled to life. Bella climbed in next to her and tucked a few tendrils of her dark hair behind her ear.

Haunted blue eyes looked Mara up and down, and Bella inhaled deeply. Something in her gaze churned and softened slightly, and she brushed a cool hand across Mara's cheek.

"Help me." Mara tried with everything she had left to get Bella to understand how close to death she was, but she couldn't speak, couldn't move...

The engine added even more heat to Mara's weakened and feverish body. She closed her eyes and tried to sense the direction they were going, but it was no use.

And then Mara's cell phone rang.

"What the hell?" Jeremy asked as Katerina squealed.

"It's the wolf!" Turning in her seat, she pawed through Mara's bag. The phone fell silent as she pulled it out, but she grinned. "We have his number now. When we're back at the hotel, we'll call."

Cade

He paced, hidden behind the thick trees in the darkness. Liam sat with his back against a log, watching him. "Save yer strength. We'll know somethin' soon enough."

The words held little comfort, and Cade didn't believe them. Mara was gone, taken by the woman who'd tortured him, killed his father's entire pack, and nearly burned every member of his family alive.

Pulling out Liam's phone again, he ran his finger over the screen, desperate to call Mara again. Even if all he got out of the call was hearing her voicemail greeting.

Not far away, a car door opened, and a voice whispered on a soft current of air. "It's Eleanor. Stay put."

The air elemental seemed to materialize out of the darkness moments later. "I went to Mara's. Katerina had been there. Along with air and earth."

"And Mara?" Cade had to ball his hands into fists to keep from grabbing and shaking the older woman.

Eleanor's eyes darkened. "Yes. Mara too. She has little time. I sensed a fire charm, and it will kill her quickly if we cannot find her and break it."

His knees gave out, but Liam caught him before he hit the ground. "Get it together, mate."

"Why do you even care?" Cade's voice broke, and he wrenched his arm free. "She wouldn't have left if it weren't for you and your goddamn lack of control. All of you." His eyes flashed with his wolf, and the animal prickled along his skin. "You don't want to touch me, Liam. I'm half tempted to kick you out of the pack right now."

Liam flinched as if Cade had hit him again. "I know. I fucked up. When this is over, when ya' have her back, I'll leave if ya' want me to. But for now, let me help. Please."

Cade didn't answer his beta, but instead turned to Eleanor.

"How do we find her?"

The air elemental shook her head. "I don't know that we can. They have a car."

His fingers trembled when he withdrew the phone again. "Ollie? Do you have any contacts at the Sheriff's department down here?"

The older werewolf frowned. "Maybe. They all think I'm dead, though. But I'll make some calls."

Staring down at the phone of his hand, Cade sighed. "And I'll make one of my own."

"Dog. I had a feeling you'd call."

Hearing the voice of the woman who'd tortured him for seven months was so much worse than Cade had imagined. He staggered over to a tree and braced himself against the rough trunk.

"Is she alive?"

"Of course she is. I don't want to hurt my sister. Not as long as you're willing to do what I say," Katerina replied.

"Put her on."

Katerina clucked her tongue. "Manners."

With a growl, he added, "Please."

After some quiet shuffling, a tiny moan carried over the line. "Say hello, sister."

"Cade?" Mara's voice was so quiet, so weak and scratchy, if he'd been human, he wouldn't have heard it.

"Oh God. Mara. I'm sorry. So sorry. I promise—"

Mara's sob cut him off. "Don't come," she whispered. "I won't...live."

"I am *not* abandoning you. Hold on. Fight. Please. For me. For *us*."

A strangled moan was followed by a dull thud and a rustle of fabric, and Katerina came back on the line.

"Satisfied?"

The tightness in Cade's chest threatened to strangle him. "What did you do to her?"

"A simple fire charm. It won't seriously harm her, but it'll keep her uncomfortable and powerless. Now—"

The wolf pulsing just below the surface let go with a growl, cutting Katerina off. "She's dying, you fucking bitch. Can't you see it? You're killing her. Right this second. She has too much fire in her blood, and she was almost dead a week ago. Even you can't be so heartless that you'd want your own sister dead."

"Of course not. But I want her to see *your* death, and I'm not above a little pain to make that happen." There was another thud, and Mara sobbed weakly. "You will come to a location of my choosing at dawn. My sister will watch me end you, and then I'll release the charm on her."

"She won't live that long," Cade said. "Tell me where you are. I'll meet you right now."

"Not a chance. I know you have your dogs with you. I need some time to make sure they won't be a problem. You'll follow my instructions or you'll never see Mara again. She might enjoy a little trip to Arizona. Live out her days in the desert."

"That's torture!" Cade hated Katerina with everything he was. "How can you be so cruel?"

"Oh, maybe because I grew up *without a mother*. Now shut up. I'll call you at seven and tell you where to go. If your pack of mongrels comes anywhere near me, I won't hesitate to kill them all."

The call disconnected, and Cade barely resisted the urge to throw the phone at Liam's head. But it was his only connection to his mate. "Four hours," he said.

"She may have four hours." Eleanor ran a hand through her short white hair. "If she fights."

"She'll fight." Mara wasn't one to give up. No. Not the woman who'd saved his wolf. Who'd come back from nearly dying herself.

Surveying his wolves, now all back in human form, he swallowed hard. "I'm to come alone."

"Like hell," Liam spat.

"She's got air." Cade shook his head. "She'll smell you. Katerina doesn't believe Mara's sick, and if she knows you're with me, she'll increase the intensity of the charm, and Mara won't survive it." He let the rough bark dig into his shoulders, using the pain to help him focus. "I'm doing this alone. I can die. As long as Mara lives."

Eleanor huffed. "Men. Always short-sighted."

"Excuse me?"

"We can counteract her air. I'm quite old, Cade. I know more than my share of tricks."

He teetered on the edge of control. Mara's scent clinging to him was his only shred of sanity left. His family. His mate. His own life. Of all of them, he valued his life the least.

There was no question in his mind. He'd die. But his family could help make sure Mara lived.

Clearing his throat, he hoped his voice wouldn't fail him. "What can we do?"

33

Mara

THE TINY MOTEL bathtub pressed in on her, trapping the heat relentlessly building in her body.

Mara couldn't remember much of the van ride or the outside of the hotel, but she could hear the constant hum of traffic.

The porcelain had been cool when Jeremy had shoved her in here, blessedly so, but that relief had only lasted minutes. As soon as they'd left her alone, she'd kicked at the faucet, but Katerina had heard her and, with a quick charm, melted the spout and the handle until both were unusable.

The door opened, and Bella ducked into the room. She had a single ice cube cupped in her hand, and ran it over Mara's feverish cheeks for a moment. But then footsteps approached, and Bella dropped the cube, using a quick charm to melt it away.

"She looks worse, Katerina. Are ya' sure she'll last until dawn?" The air elemental's voice carried a hint of an accent, but Mara couldn't place it. Not as muddled as her thoughts had become.

"She'll last." Katerina jerked her head out the door. "Leave her. We need to go over the plan again."

Alone again, Mara's thoughts turned to Cade. They needed more time. Time for her to tell him she loved him. Time to tell him she wanted to be his mate—whatever that entailed.

But they'd never have that again.

She was dying. She'd never felt like this before. It was worse than the night she'd freed him. Even if Katerina removed the gag, she didn't think she could speak. Her lips were cracked, and she tasted blood. She let her eyes close and prayed she wouldn't have to open them again. The insides of her lids might as well have been sandpaper.

Hours passed, and her skin now felt like she had the world's worst sunburn. "You do *not* look well," Katerina said.

When had she come into the room? Hot fingers touched Mara's face and peeled back her eyelid. But her sister's face was nothing but a blur.

As the gag was yanked down, Mara's lips started bleeding again. "Aaaaa....errrrr," she begged.

Water.

Katerina went to the sink and held a glass under the faucet, and the welcome sound of water reached Mara's ears. But only for a split second. She wanted to cry when Katerina knelt down again. Only two tablespoons. At the most. The disappointed whimper that escaped Mara's throat had Katerina chuckling.

"I'm not stupid, sister." The scant bit of water dribbled over Mara's lips and tongue but she was so dehydrated, she couldn't swallow.

"More. Please," she managed. "Dying."

"This will all be over in two hours," Katerina said and stroked a hand over Mara's hair. "When we get to the park, you'll sit quietly. If you try to run—not that I think you could manage it—I will torture your dog for weeks before I kill him, and I'll take you back to Arizona with me and let you languish in the sauna behind my home until you can't remember your own name."

"You're...a monster."

Katerina sighed, and her voice took on a longing tone. "I miss Phoenix. I hate this fucking city. I promise you, Mara. If you help me, I will make his death quick. He'll barely feel a thing."

Those searing fingers stroked Mara's cheek, but she was in so much pain that the vaguely comforting gesture threatened to shatter her.

Dry sobs wracked her body, and she leaned into the touch.

Why had she left? Why hadn't she put aside her fear of Liam and the pack and stayed?

"Shhh, baby girl. It'll all be okay. The dog will die, our mother will be avenged, and we can heal. You see that now, don't you? We can heal together. When it's done, you'll be free. Won't you help me?"

Mara glared up at her sister, the kind words and gentle touches not fooling her for a second. "Go. To. Hell."

———

The next time the door opened, Jeremy stalked over to the tub, yanked her up, and threw her over his shoulder.

She hit the floor of the van, bounced, and then everything went dark for a while. Barely conscious, she was only dimly aware of the vibrations of the engine, the turns, and the bumps as they went over...something. Railroad tracks, maybe?

When they stopped, Katerina slapped her cheek twice. "Wake up."

Mara blinked at her, desperately trying to focus, and she thought she saw her cell phone in Katerina's hand.

"Dog, listen to me. Gas Works Park. Come alone, and come now. If you don't show up in the next twenty minutes, I'm gone. With Mara."

A moment later, Katerina pressed the phone to Mara's cheek. "Say something, sister. But be careful."

"Don't...come," she whispered.

"Has she hurt you? Besides the charm?" Cade's voice was like a balm to her soul, but in twenty minutes, he'd be dead.

"No." She couldn't tell him about Jeremy slapping her, about the hours spent bound on her side in the tub, her cracked and split lips. About the absolute certainty she was going to die.

"I'm on my way, honey. All I want is to see you one more time. Hold on—"

Katerina pulled the phone away, and Mara strained for one more word, one last moment... "No..." she moaned, and Katerina slapped a hand over her mouth.

"There's a large metal structure in the center of the park. We'll be on the west tower. Because I really do love my sister, I'll even let you say goodbye before I turn you to ash. But if I see or smell a single member of your pack, then Mara comes to Phoenix with me."

Katerina jabbed the screen to end the call, and Mara's heart cracked into a million pieces.

GAS WORKS PARK WAS A LARGE, lush expanse with rolling hills and tall metal structures that had once been part of a gasification plant that had closed in the late fifties.

The scent of Lake Union refreshed Mara slightly, and she found she had enough strength to lift her head, though she couldn't see much thrown over Jeremy's shoulder.

A scorched ring of earth circled a chain-link fence around a collection of rusted, tall metal towers, and Jeremy carried her up three stories to the very top of the structure.

"I hate this," Jeremy whined. "I'm not strong enough up here."

"You're not staying," Katerina said. "You're going to be down on the ground. I don't need you to touch me. Your amulet can send me your power as long as we're close. Set her down."

Mara crumpled to the floor on one of the catwalks. They hadn't gagged her again, thank God, but her hands were numb from being bound for so long. Even the slightest movement brought pain shooting through her entire body.

From this height, she watched Jeremy and Bella take up positions between the burnt circle and the old fence. Katerina stood over Mara, arms extended, palms glowing.

"I call upon the fire deep in the earth," she chanted. Flames licked at her fingers, bloomed in her hands, and raced up her arms. She flung the fire towards the ground, and the charred strip lit up.

The fire was at least ten feet tall. Nothing could get through. The heat rose, battering Mara's body further.

The air turned dry and thin, but the lake was only a couple hundred feet away. Its dull hum whispered to her, like a quiet siren song welcoming her home.

Let go. Stop fighting.

It would be so easy. To just slip away. But she needed to see Cade one more time.

"Mara!"

Forcing her eyes open, she saw him running across the grass. "No," she whispered. He skidded to a halt a few feet from the flames.

"I'm here, bitch. Let me see Mara!"

Katerina flicked her hand, and the flames parted. Cade leapt through the opening, and the ring of fire closed behind him.

"Stop one level below us, or I'll cook you where you stand."

Mara shuddered as Cade bound up the metal stairs. One flight. Two. She caught his scent over the smoke and tried not to whimper.

"Mara? Honey? Look at me."

She couldn't remember closing her eyes, but apparently she

had, because she had to force them open again. He looked terrible. Dark circles braced his sunken and bloodshot steely blue orbs. Tousled hair stuck up in all directions.

"Say something," he begged.

"Why?" She couldn't manage more than a single word. Why had he come? Why had he risked his life for her? She couldn't do anything to save him.

"I love you."

Mara couldn't shed a single tear for the words she'd so longed to hear. Dry heaves wracked her body, but nothing came up.

"Please," Cade said, staring at Katerina. "I'm dead. I know it. Let me hold her. Give me this one thing." Dropping to his knees, he bowed his head in submission.

"Bella? Any sign of his pack?" Katerina called.

The air elemental's quiet voice floated upwards. "Only him."

Shit. He came alone. He's going to die. I'm going to die.

"Very well," Katerina said. "One minute, and you go back down the stairs."

And then she was in Cade's arms. He cradled her against his chest. "She's burning up. Can't you see how sick she is? Take the charm off. Please."

"Forty seconds."

He nuzzled her neck, kissed her cracked and bloody lips. "I'm sorry I didn't protect you. Everyone's sorry. They wanted to come. I had to blow past them so they wouldn't follow me. When you get free, they'll find you."

"They're not...you," she whispered. "I want. Don't leave me."

His fingers threaded through her hair, and his lips brushed her ear. "Never."

The single word sent hope flooding through her, as did his fingers working the knots in the scarf around her wrists.

"Hold on for another few minutes. Please, honey."

"Enough," Katerina spat. "Put her down and walk away. Get on your knees."

Cade framed her cheeks and his ice blue eyes held hers. "I love you, Mara. Always and forever. You're my air. My oxygen. And you'll survive this." As he set her down facing the far end of the park, movement caught her eye. A flash of red. Another of brown.

The pack *was* here. They'd come. Air. Oxygen. Eleanor. She was helping them.

"I'm ready," he said, shuffling slowly back to the steps. He'd just descended the first one when shouts echoed from below.

"Wolves!" Bella called.

Katerina cursed, sending a blast of fire directly at Cade's chest. He sidestepped it easily, and the flames landed harmlessly on the catwalk. Metal popped and creaked under the intense heat, then licked along the railing and the grating under his Keds.

The stench of melting rubber made Mara choke and cough, and as she rolled onto her back to see Katerina, the anger on her sister's face terrified her.

Another blast of flame landed closer to its mark, and Cade leapt back towards the stairs, landing with a thud and a shrill screech of metal.

The catwalk shuddered, throwing them all off balance. Cade grabbed for the railing, but the tube of metal was red hot. With a strangled scream, he missed the top step and started to fall.

It happened so fast. Yet the seconds stretched out over an eternity. His legs buckled, and he landed on his ass, then tumbled down the stairs, a sickening crack piercing the morning air.

Katerina hurled another three blasts towards the ground. Wolves howled, running back and forth, and the earth shook.

Mara pulled her arms free, clawing along the metal grating until she was at the top of the stairs. At the bottom, Cade lay still, his spine obviously broken.

"Cade! No!"

Pain pinched his features, but he opened his eyes to meet her gaze, and an odd peace settled over him. Below her, Liam—the largest wolf, his red fur almost luminous in the early morning light, tackled Jeremy, and for a moment, the earth stopped shaking. But then Katerina screamed, and the ring of flames exploded out with a loud *whoosh*, charring Liam's tail. He howled and retreated, letting Jeremy stagger to his feet once more.

As the metal structure started to shake, Mara got to her knees, took a deep breath, and tried to stand. One of her sister's charms hurtled towards her, wrapping itself around her legs and setting her pants on fire. Her foot slid out from under her, and she hit the top step on her ass, letting gravity carry her, one painful thud at a time, until she was only inches from Cade.

"Can't feel my legs," he panted as she cupped his cheeks.

"Shift." She brought her lips to his and kissed him for all she was worth, then whispered against his mouth, "Please."

"I can't."

Behind her, Katerina's boots slapped against the stairs.

"You have to."

A strong hand wrapped around Mara's hair and hauled her to her feet. Staring down at Cade, Katerina sneered. "I'm taking her with me to Phoenix. Locking her in a sauna until she forgets all about you."

Cade growled and tried to reach for Katerina, but he couldn't lift his torso, and the woman kicked his hand away. On the ground, another wolf, this one darker with gray around his muzzle headed for Jeremy, and a blast of frigid air so strong it reached all the way up the structure sent the earth elemental to his knees.

Mara clawed at her sister's hands, and when Katerina's fingers loosened, she fell, sucking in a cool breath and letting it strengthen her. But too soon, a flaming hot hand pressed to Mara's temple, and her thoughts fogged, her body burning from the inside out.

"Say goodbye," Katerina said.

A seizure ripped through Mara's body, and the sharp grating cut her arm. This was the end. For her and Cade.

An odd peace settled over her, and when Katerina stood, Mara turned her head to stare at Cade. He'd be the last person she saw, and that...would have to be enough.

His eyes were glowing. Silver flashed in the deep blue, and his whole body vibrated with anger. His lips curled into a snarl.

"Cade," she whispered. "I..."

"No!" His scream turned into a deep growl. Fabric ripped, and Katerina took a step back.

Mara gaped as his bones shattered, his whole face changed shape, and fur sprouted over his skin. His shift only took seconds, and a massive gray wolf—her wolf—stood over his shredded clothing. His fangs glistened, the menacing growl deepening as he leapt for Katerina. His paws caught her in the chest, and they both went flying back half a dozen feet before crashing into the catwalk.

Cade snarled as flames licked at his paws, but he dipped his head and clamped his jaws around Katerina's arm. Bone snapped. Katerina bucked against his hold, her scream full of rage and pain.

"You filthy mongrel. You'll both pay for that."

A blast of fire sent Cade's wolf crashing through the burning railing and falling to the catwalk below.

"Hide," Mara whimpered. "Please! Run!"

Flames gathered in Katerina's palms. When they shot across the gap, Cade sprinted to the other side of the massive water tower.

Water. She needed water. If she could just pull even a hint of it from the air, she could fight. On her stomach, barely able to move, she stared over the edge of the catwalk. Three wolves circled Jeremy, and though rocks pelted them from all directions, none of them seemed to care.

Liam—it could only be Liam—sprang, and a mound of dirt and grass rose up like a wave and rolled him away. But a second later, a smaller, brown wolf raced in from behind Jeremy and sank her teeth into Jeremy's gut.

"Jeremy!" Katerina screamed. "You fucking dogs. I'm going to kill every last one of you!"

Cade growled from a few feet away, and Katerina advanced, keeping Mara between them. His pelt was burned in patches, and blood oozed from his shoulder. One ear was scorched, but he stared her down with the intensity of seven months of pure hatred.

"I call upon the fire of my mother, the fire of the earth, of my Goddess. Die!"

A massive ball of fire gathered between Katerina's outstretched hands, and she sent it hurtling for Cade.

No. Not this time. Not her mate. With her last burst of strength, Mara sprang up, right in the path of the flames. Katerina screamed, the sun at her back painting her with a golden halo. For a second, she almost looked like an angel.

The fire turned Mara's shirt to ash in an instant. When the flames hit her skin, she expected pain, but felt nothing. Only a great void. A nothingness she didn't expect.

She let herself burn as she took one step, then another, and another towards Katerina. The comforting tones of her element mixed with a deep, baritone hum. It was everywhere. All around her. Under and above her. *In* her.

"No more," she said as she wrapped her arms around her sister, finding a peace she didn't know she possessed as she held her sister still.

The flames concentrated between Mara's breasts, finding their home in Katerina's amulet. The fire elemental's scream barely registered as the red crystal heated, turned pure white, and sizzled between them.

"Mara...please," Katerina begged.

Her sister's eyes turned glassy. Pupils dilated. Blood vessels burst. Mara tried to let go, but she couldn't. The fire bound them together until Katerina took her final breath, and her spirit escaped in a puff of smoke before her body turned to ash at Mara's feet.

A dull roar filled her ears, and darkness stole her sight. She could die now. Cade wrapped his arms around her and her scorched cheek rested against his chest, the last thing she'd ever feel.

She'd done it. Her mate was safe.

34

Cade

HIS MATE'S skin glowed white hot, and he pleaded with her to wake up, to answer him, to even open her eyes, but she lay still in his arms.

"Cade!" Eleanor's voice floated up from the ground. Six naked werewolves stared up at him from outside the fence. The air elemental had masked the pack's scent, wrapping them in the smells of the lake and the grass, and hidden their footfalls long enough for them to sneak close to the circle of fire.

"Get her down here."

He sprinted down the two flights of stairs with her cradled to his chest. Mara was preternaturally still and he wasn't sure she was even breathing. Listening, he caught the faint, slow beat of her heart. A quarter-sized burn in the middle of her chest steamed.

When he reached his pack, Eleanor peeled back one of Mara's eyelids, then pointed to the lake. "Get her into the water. Now."

Cade raced down the hill and splashed into the icy depths.

His fingertips and toes prickled from the cold, but he didn't care. Nothing mattered but Mara.

"Come back to me, honey. Please. Don't leave me. Not now. Not when we're finally free."

"She sacrificed herself to save ya'," Liam said.

"I know."

Eleanor rifled through her bag, coming up with a bottle of water. "Get her to drink something," she urged.

"She's unconscious," Cade snapped. He supported Mara's body with one arm and stroked her hair with his free hand. It fanned out in the water like a halo of crimson. She was so beautiful, even with blood and ash streaking her face.

"Try anyway," Christine said.

Liam splashed into the water next to him. "Here." He broke the seal and pressed the bottle into Cade's hand.

A bit of the cool liquid dribbled down Mara's chin. "Drink, honey. Please." Another thin trickle washed over her tongue. No response.

"Mara," Cade said sharply. "Listen to me. You are not going to die. You are going to drink and you're going to open your eyes and say my name. Now, dammit."

Her tongue slipped over her lips, and she swallowed. He gave her a bit more. Her head turned, seeking out the bottle as a tiny wheeze escaped her lungs.

"That's it, Mara. Come on. Open those beautiful eyes for me," Cade murmured.

"Cade."

With that single word, his entire world righted. He only had a glimpse of dull green irises before she closed her eyes again, but it was enough. She was alive.

ELEANOR, Christine, and Peter stayed behind to clean up the mess —including Jeremy's body, but the rest of them piled into Eleanor's car and sped back to Mara's house.

Cade couldn't let her go, whispering to her, stroking her hair, trying to get her to drink even another few sips.

"Get her into the tub," Christine ordered when they were safely back inside. "Cool water. I'm going to make her some dandelion tea. It should absorb some of the extra heat."

He didn't question Christine. She'd been the pack's healer for three years, and in all that time, she'd never steered him wrong. Mara was pale, bruises covering her body, with patches of blistered skin at her temple. Her wrists were raw, but the scar between her breasts was the worst. The skin was black, oozing blood, and still occasionally smoking.

Sinking into the cool water with her, he held her close and prayed.

Christine came in a few minutes later and rummaged through the medicine cabinet, hummed, and called out, "I need aloe, mint, comfrey, and sage. Oh, and some shea butter. Don't forget the humidifier!"

Someone—Peter by the mumbled reply—agreed, and the front door opened and shut. "Here," Christine said as she set a lightly steaming cup on the edge of the tub. "Get her to drink this. All of it. Even if it takes an hour. I don't care how badly you prune, you don't take her out of the water until I come back with the poultice for her burns."

"Mara? Tea." Cade brought the cup to her lips, but she didn't move. "Drink this. Now."

The command in his voice must have registered on some level, and she swallowed the first sip.

"Good, honey. Good. You're going to be all right. I promise."

FOR EIGHTEEN HOURS, Mara's fever raged. Cade never left her side, dabbing her forehead with a cool cloth and gently massaging the poultice into her wounds.

His wolves came and went, bringing him food, more tea and broth for Mara, and once, setting two bags of new clothes for him by Mara's closet.

He mostly ignored them, grunting his thanks, but completely focused on his mate.

Lillian showed up and sat with him for an hour. "She's a fighter, that one is," she said. "Eleanor told me what she did. Thinks she's some sort of miracle. I told her I reckon she's right. Don't know what sort, other than the kind that you want on your side."

"I can't lose her," Cade said, breaking his silence.

The old woman chuckled. "Darlin', that child ain't never given up. Not even when she was dyin'. Oh, she'd accepted it—her illness. Her death. But she never gave up. I don't reckon she's gonna start now." She got to her feet with a groan. "These old bones need their bed."

Paper thin lips pressed to Cade's forehead. "You gonna give up on her?"

"No. Never."

"Then tell her that." Lillian leaned over and kissed Mara's forehead too before shuffling out of the room.

WHEN MIDNIGHT CAME AND WENT, Cade stripped off his clothes and slid into bed with his mate. The fever had broken and now she shivered uncontrollably.

He started to talk, telling her stories of his childhood, of shifting, of running with his pack. He kept going all night. Livie brought him cup after cup of coffee, food he barely touched, and more broth for Mara.

By morning, she still hadn't woken, but he heard his pack moving around the house. He didn't know what they were doing and he didn't care. Darkness fell again with no change.

"Cade?" Liam knocked on the bedroom door and poked his head in.

"Go away," Cade said sharply. He sat by Mara's bedside, her cool hand held in his.

Liam cleared his throat. "No, Cade. I need ya'."

"Mara needs me." He'd brought her back to the bath a few hours ago, warm this time, scented with almond oil. The burns were healing. Her color was better. But he wouldn't settle until she woke up and spoke to him.

"Ya' can't do her any good by killin' yourself. I'm not askin' ya' to leave her for long. Come to the kitchen. I need to ask ya' something."

"Ask here." Cade brushed his knuckles against Mara's cheek.

"The house next door is for sale."

Cade whipped his head around. He'd forgotten.

Liam held up a sheet of paper. "I called the realtor. If we—if ya' get an offer in before midweek, she's sure it'll be accepted—even at twenty thousand below askin'. The seller's desperate."

He rose and met Liam at the door. "I can't. What if she doesn't want me?"

"She sacrificed herself for ya'. For all of us. If that's not love, I don't know what is. And they can't keep sleepin' on her living room floor forever. I'm makin' plans to leave, but the rest of them..."

Cade grabbed Liam's arm. Despite Liam's actions, despite his mistakes, the man was his brother. And his best friend. "Don't go."

"You said..."

"I know what I said. I was angry. Can you blame me?" Sorrow and regret hollowed his voice, and he stared into Liam's green eyes. "I can't lose anyone else. You risked your life for her. That carries weight."

Liam enveloped Cade in a bear hug. "I'm so sorry, Cade. It's my fault she's hurt."

"It's Katerina's fault. I can't say if Mara will forgive you for what you did, scaring her like that, and it's her choice. Will be if she wakes up—" His voice cracked and he ran a hand through his shaggy hair. "If she can't accept your apology, you'll step down as beta. I won't disrespect her. Just don't leave."

With a nod, Liam released him. "She'll come back to ya'. Let me make an offer. It's big enough for all of us. I walked through with Peter a few hours ago. We can do the restoration ourselves. Ya' could get back to woodworkin'. And Seattle...it's a good place to be. We can all find work here. A fresh start."

"Liam?"

The quiet word sent both Cade and Liam whirling towards the bed.

"The previous owners were assholes. Picked all of my roses. You owe me a rose garden. A big one." Mara's eyes were blood-shot, but she focused on Cade and the corners of her lips curved slightly.

"One rose garden. Or two. Or ten," Liam said as he backed out of the room and closed the door.

Cade was at Mara's side in another breath.

"H-h-hey," she whispered through chattering teeth. "C-cold."

Cade shed his clothing and slid under the covers with the woman he loved. She shivered in his arms, trying to burrow into his chest, and he turned on the electric blanket. "This is familiar."

Her weak laugh righted everything that ailed his heart. Whoops and triumphant cheers from the other side of the door piqued Mara's interest, and she lifted her head. "They're all here?"

"Yep. Every single one of them has tried to edge their way in here to see you the past two days. You impressed them, honey.

What you did. Choosing me over your family. Over your own life."

"She wasn't my family. You're my family. Them too."

He kissed the top of her head, tightening his arms around her. "Do you mean that?"

"Yes." Mara pressed her lips to his neck. "Tired. Don't leave."

"Never." Cade smoothed a hand over her hair, relishing the feel of his mate's silk-clad body against his. She was ice cold, but her shivers were lessening, and her scent was returning to normal. Spring rain, almonds, and shea butter. In a day, maybe two, she'd be whole, and perhaps he'd be able to relax. Until then, he'd keep her close. For now, they'd both sleep.

Mara

She woke in the middle of the night. Cade held her against his warm, hard body, but he was fast sleep.

"Cade?" He didn't stir. Mara had heard every word he'd uttered keeping vigil at her bedside. His pleas, his prayers. His stories. She'd tried to fight her way back to him, to make a sound, to reassure him that she was still here, but her sister's charm had made that impossible.

So she'd done what she knew she had to. Listened to Cade's voice to keep her firmly anchored in this world and tried to heal, drawing upon the sweet, resonating tones of the water in the air to replenish her.

Slowly, she shifted out of his arms. Her knees buckled when she tried to stand, but she braced herself against the wall and took slow, deep breaths until she was halfway steady.

After she pulled on her robe, she shuffled out into the hallway to a chorus of light snores. Liam, Peter, and Ollie stretched out on air mattresses. Christine had the couch. She assumed Livie and Shawn were in the guest room.

Once she reached the kitchen, she had to hold onto the counter for a couple of minutes until the room stopped spinning, then got a glass of water.

"Mara?" Liam stood a few feet away, wearing a pair of pajama pants and nothing else. "Are ya' well?"

"Enough." The glass shook in her hand, but she managed to down a third of it without spilling.

"I'm gettin' Cade. Yer too sick to be up."

"You'll do no such thing. I'm not running a marathon. I needed a glass of water. Cade's exhausted, and I'm going right back to bed in a minute." She glared at Liam, and he met her gaze, then almost immediately looked down.

He wasn't challenging her. Not like...whenever it had been. Two days ago? Three? She didn't know anymore.

"Is...is everyone okay?" she asked.

"Livie's mad we didn't let her fight much. Everyone else is fine."

She nodded. "Okay. Good."

"Wait." Liam didn't touch her or even move an inch, but Mara's heart pounded and her palms dampened. "Can ya' forgive me?" He dropped to one knee and rested his hand over his heart. A single tear glistened on his cheek.

"If I'd stayed, my sister might have hurt Aunt Lil. Or, she would have snuck up on us in the middle of the night and set the house on fire. And..." Mara took an unsteady step forward and touched Liam's elbow for a second, urging him to his feet. "Livie told me you'd loved an elemental once. That...she died."

Absolute agony blanketed Liam's face. "Yeah. Caitlin. My Caitlin." His voice trembled, as if he hadn't said her name aloud in a long time. "She was air. My beauty." He drew in a deep breath, as if he were reliving his time with her and bottling it up all in one moment. "She smelled like fig blossoms, ya know. Fig blossoms and the sea."

A memory tickled Mara's mind. She'd smelled fig blossoms recently. Where had it been? Nerves fluttered in her belly, and she leaned heavily against the counter.

Liam carded his fingers through his hair and yanked on it, grimacing. "I let my own pain cloud my judgement. It was wrong, and I'm sorry."

"I forgive you."

The relief that washed over him changed his whole appearance. "Thank you, Mara. I don't deserve it. There's one other thing I want to ask. If ya' let me."

Exhaustion pressed down on her, but she couldn't refuse him. "Go ahead."

"Will ya' claim him?"

A smile tugged at her lips. She'd found her answer up on that catwalk. Cade had made her a promise the moment he'd shifted. He'd do anything for her.

As her sister's fire had spread through her limbs, she'd made her own vow. This werewolf was hers, and she'd fight for his life with everything she was.

She slipped back behind her bedroom door with a single whispered word.

"Yes."

EPILOGUE

Mara

"MORNING, HONEY." A warm hand caressed her cheek, and the scent of coffee, tinged with almond milk, surrounded her.

"You're spoiling me," she murmured as she opened her eyes.

"I'll bring you coffee every morning for the rest of my life." The mattress dipped, and Mara drank in the sight of her werewolf. As she skimmed her fingers along his defined abs, a possessive growl rumbled low in his throat. Over the two weeks since they'd battled her sister, she'd come to know that sound well. It was Cade's personal mating call.

Just outside their bedroom, the sounds of cooking and laughter filled her home. The pack had already moved in to the house next door—working out a cash offer that let them take possession almost immediately—but their kitchen was currently in the throes of a massive remodel, courtesy of Liam and Peter, and so they were all spending Christmas Day together, here.

"How do you feel?" he asked as he slid closer and took her hand. With a roll of her eyes, she let him sniff her wrist. "Strong. Like fresh rain."

"Maybe it's over?" Mara took a sip of the cappuccino and almost moaned. For days after she'd finally come back from fighting her sister's element, she'd been weak and unsteady, barely able to get out of bed without Cade's help. But after the full moon, all that had changed.

Whether because the mating was now complete or simply due to the passage of time, she was finally on the mend. A part of Katerina would always be with her. Quite literally. The burn between her breasts had healed, but a piece of the red amulet had almost melted into her, and despite Christine's efforts, nothing had been able to remove it.

"Hey," Cade said as he stroked a knuckle along her jaw. "Where'd you go?"

With a hard blink, Mara tried to banish the sadness from her eyes. What was done couldn't be undone, and though she hated that she'd had to kill her sister, she'd made the right choice. It had either been Katerina or Cade, and she would always pick the man she loved.

"Sorry. I was having a moment with my cappuccino." She chuckled, but Cade wasn't buying it. Luckily, a knock at the door interrupted them.

"Come on in," Mara called.

Livie stuck her head in. "Breakfast? Presents?"

"Can't even wait an hour? Are you *six*?" Cade asked.

"No." Livie grinned. "But I'm the only one who knows what Mara got all of you."

The pillow sailing across the room almost clipped the female wolf's hand, but she shrieked with laughter and slammed the door.

"I'm sorry, honey," Cade said as he tugged on a brand new black sweatshirt and swapped his pajama pants for jeans. "They won't always be this overwhelming. I'll tell them to back off a little."

"Don't." Mara ran a hand through her hair and savored the

sounds of the pack floating through the air. "I like having them here. I didn't think I would, but...they're family."

Cade scooped her into his arms and kissed her so thoroughly, she was panting by the time he was finished.

"I love you, Mara."

"I know. Now put me down. We have presents to open." Mara caught the quick flash of disappointment in his eyes, and she reached for him, but he was already out the door.

Despite their mating, despite how close they'd become over the weeks Cade had cared for her, Mara hadn't said those three words. She didn't even know why. She felt them. Every moment of every day. More than she ever expected she could.

But every time she wanted to tell him, something got in the way until it felt like this huge chasm between them.

As soon as Mara pulled on a flannel shirt and fleece pants, she padded out the door and was immediately surrounded by the whole pack.

Livie took her arm and waddled with her over to the couch. "They won't let me do *anything*," she muttered.

"They're right about that. That baby's going to be here any day now. You need to rest."

"Like you're much better of a patient," the pregnant wolf said.

Mara rolled her eyes with a laugh. "I know. But it's Christmas. We can all relax at least a little."

OPENING PRESENTS TOOK HOURS. But finally, they were down to the gifts Cade and Mara had for one another. She set a large red box in his lap. "Merry Christmas, shaggy man."

Cade inhaled deeply and grinned as he drew a buttery leather jacket out of the box. "This is gorgeous, honey." He ran his hands over the leather until he came to a bulge in one of the pockets. "What's this?"

A teardrop-shaped piece of glass spilled into his hand with blue swirls tangling inside, moving as if they were almost alive.

Mara swallowed hard. "I told you I hear music? When I use my element?"

"Yeah."

"There's an artist down in Fremont who turns sound waves into art. You pick the melody you want, and he runs the frequency through sand while he shoots it with a massive jolt of electricity. It's one of a kind." Mara skimmed a finger over the curve of the glass. "This...is me."

Cade grabbed her in a hug so fierce, she wasn't sure she could breathe. "I love it," he said, his voice a hoarse whisper. "It's perfect."

Cade

Liam passed him a small, green box tied with silver ribbon. His stomach churned as he handed it to his mate. It was driving him mad—not hearing those three words he'd said to her every single day since she'd saved his life.

Was she even ready for what he was about to give her? What...what if she said no?

Mara loosened the ribbon with a nervous smile curving her lips. Inside, she found the burled wooden box he'd made right before he'd been taken.

"Cade, this is beautiful," Mara breathed.

His shoulders hunched forward and he stared down at his hands as she lifted the lid and gasped.

"Wh-what...?" Her hand shook as she held up his mother's ring—a silver band with an emerald tucked in the center of the metal whorls.

The pack knew his intentions, and not a single one of them

said a word or even moved as Cade dropped down to one knee. But when he looked into Mara's eyes, his heart shattered. She was crying.

Jerking up, he shoved his hands into his pockets. "I'm…I'm sorry. I shouldn't have…this soon, I just—"

She rose and arched a brow, even as her tears trailed down her cheeks. "Do you want this back?"

"What?"

"You heard me, shaggy man. Do you want this back?" Mara enunciated each word as she held the ring out to him. "Because if you intended it like I think you did, you're doing a piss poor job of proposing."

He sputtered, unable to form a reply that would be even halfway coherent.

"I love you." Mara breathed a long sigh, and her lower lip trembled. "I know I haven't said it. I don't know why. I was sick, and you were so worried. And then it was like this *thing* that kept getting bigger and bigger and I didn't know how."

She snagged his new jacket off the couch. "There's a note in the pocket."

"For the man I love," Cade said quietly. "But…you were crying. You're not a crier."

Shut up, idiot. She said she loved you. Why aren't you holding her? Or proposing?

"No, I'm not. But this is a special occasion. Or…I thought it was."

Cade dropped down to his knee again and took Mara's hand. "I love you. We're mated. Nothing can shatter that bond. But making things official just feels…right. I want to be your husband, Mara. I want you to be my wife. I don't care where or when. I just want the world to know how I feel about you. Will you marry me?"

"Yes." She grinned, and a fresh round of tears spilled over her lashes as Cade slipped the ring on her finger. "But Livie's going to make us wait a month or two, you know. She already has a dress."

Cade shot the petite blond werewolf a look. "You told her."

Mara cupped his cheek and forced him to look at her. "She's not the best with secrets. Don't be mad at her."

There wasn't much of anything Cade cared about in that moment except the woman in his arms. His mate. Soon to be his wife. For the first time in a very long time, he and his wolf were at peace.

THANK you for reading *A Shift in the Water*. Cade and Mara found their happy-ever-after, but the action and romance continues with *A Shift in the Air*.

You'll learn how Liam lost his Caitlin. And what happens when she walks back into his life with no memory of who she is or where she's been for the past eleven years.

Then continue the story with *A Shift in the Earth* and *A Shift in Fire*. Yes...that's right. **You can binge the COMPLETE Elemental Shifter series now!**

The end of the world hangs in the balance. Don't miss a minute of the action, the adventure, or the romance!

Love,

Patricia

ABOUT THE AUTHOR

I've always made up stories. Sometimes I even acted them out. I probably shouldn't admit that my childhood best friend and I used to run around the backyard pretending to fly in our Invisible Jet and rescue Steve Trevor. Oops.

Now that I'm too old to spin around in circles with felt magic bracelets on my wrists, I put "pen to paper" instead. Figuratively, at least. Fingers to keyboard is more accurate.

Outside of my writing, I'm a professional editor, a software geek, a singer (in the shower only), and a runner. I love red wine, scotch (neat, please), and cider. Seattle is my home, and I share an old house with my husband and cats.

I'm on my fourth—fifth?—rewatching of the modern *Doctor Who*, and I think one particular quote from that show sums up my entire life.

"We're all stories, in the end. Make it a good one, eh?" — *The Eleventh Doctor, Doctor Who*

I hope your story is brilliant.

You can reach me all over the web...
patriciadeddy.com
patricia@patriciadeddy.com

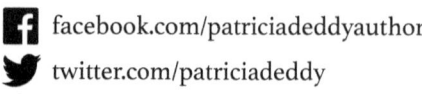

facebook.com/patriciadeddyauthor

twitter.com/patriciadeddy

instagram.com/patriciadeddy

bookbub.com/profile/patricia-d-eddy

ALSO BY PATRICIA D. EDDY

Away From Keyboard

Dive into a steamy mix of geekery and military prowess with the men and women of Hidden Agenda and Second Sight.

Breaking His Code

In Her Sights

On His Six

Second Sight

By Lethal Force

Fighting For Valor

Finding Their Forevers (a holiday short story)

Call Sign: Redemption

Braving His Past

Gone Rogue (an Away From Keyboard spinoff series)

Rogue Protector

Rogue Officer

Dark PNR

These novellas will take you into the darker side of the paranormal with vampires, witches, angels, demons, and more.

Forever Kept

Immortal Hunter

Wicked Omens

Storm of Sin

By the Fates

Check out the COMPLETE By the Fates series if you love dark and steamy tales of witches, devils, and an epic battle between good and evil.

By the Fates, Freed

Destined: A By the Fates Story

By the Fates, Fought

By the Fates, Fulfilled

In Blood

If you love hot Italian vampires and and a human who can hold her own against beings far stronger, then the In Blood series is for you.

Secrets in Blood

Revelations in Blood

Holidays and Heroes

Beauty isn't only skin deep and not all scars heal. Come swoon over sexy vets and the men and women who love them.

Mistletoe and Mochas

Love and Libations

Restrained

Do you like to be tied up? Or read about characters who do? Enjoy a fresh COMPLETE BDSM series that will leave you begging for more.

In His Silks

Christmas Silks

All Tied Up For New Year's

In His Collar